HOLDING OUT FOR A HERO

Victoria Van Tiem is an artist, gallery owner and a former creative director, with a background in marketing and brand development. Just like Libby in *Holding Out for a Hero*, she is obsessed with the 1980s.

Also by Victoria Van Tiem

Love Like the Movies

Holding Out for a Hero

VICTORIA VAN TIEM

PAN BOOKS

First published 2016 by Pan Books
an imprint of Pan Macmillan
20 New Wharf Road, London N1 9RR
Associated companies throughout the world
www.panmacmillan.com

ISBN 978-1-4472-6974-8

3 5 7 9 8 6 4 2

A CIP catalogue record for this book is available from the British Library.

Typeset by Ellipsis Digital Limited, Glasgow
Printed and bound by CPI Group (UK) Ltd, Croydon, CR0 4YY

Visit **www.panmacmillan.com** to read more about all our books
and to buy them. You will also find features, author interviews and
news of any author events, and you can sign up for e-newsletters
so that you're always first to hear about our new releases.

Close My Eyes Forever
Ozzy Osbourne and Lita Ford, 1989

For my forever Eighties friend,
Joe (Lynch) Grassi,
1970–2014

ACKNOWLEDGEMENTS

'Thank you' hardly conveys my vast gratitude to so many, but nonetheless . . .

Thank you to the *entire* Pan Macmillan team, especially Victoria Hughes-Williams (your enthusiasm and spot-on editorial eye have meant the world), Caroline Hogg, and Ami Smithson in the Pan Mac art department.

A special thanks to Jenny Bent of The Bent Agency for nurturing Libby's potential early on; and a million thank-yous to Lorella Belli, my lovely agent at the Lorella Belli Literary Agency, for all your hard work, resounding encouragement and no-nonsense business savvy. You are a brilliant agent and overall class act.

Love and many, many thanks to my insanely talented writing buddies. Amy McKinley – you honestly 'saved Libby' more than a few times with your resolute belief in her story, making you my hero as well as hers. Kaci Presnell – my reader since the absolute beginning, and my truest friend ever since. Emily Albright – what would I do without your eyes? Genius crit partner – lovely girl.

John Kang and J.C. Nelson, I'm so grateful to have the two of you in my corner as both crit partners and friends. Thanks for all the writerly chats. And thanks for the zillion beta reads, Kris Kisska!

A heartfelt thanks to my *amazing* readers, especially to those that reach out through email, Facebook, Twitter and Instagram, leaving such wonderful reviews and kind, thoughtful words. Your messages and posts mean the absolute world!

And finally, an extra-special thanks to my family – Marvin, Kirklen and Garrett – for encouraging, believing, and being quiet (sometimes). You are each my favourite, and I love you madly. xo

Prologue

My birthday hangs over my head like a noose.

I'd rather just skip it and take the day off. I'm like Cameron in *Ferris Bueller*: overwhelmed, wound up and seriously pessimistic about the whole idea. Ollie, my best friend's older brother, and I used to debate this movie non-stop when we were teenagers. He swore the entire day was a delusion created by the very sick and depressed Cameron.

'It's a crazy theory that's been floating around, but I stand behind it,' he'd say with absolute certainty. Oliver liked nothing better than to argue.

I liked nothing better than to wind him up. 'Sure, he was miserable and the timeline of events impossible, but it doesn't prove Ferris was a figment of Cameron's imagination. Was everyone fake? And *why* would he do that?'

I could hear him pacing, and imagined him at the other end of the line, wide-eyed and gesturing. I loved it when he got that way. I loved everything about him.

'They're real, Libby, just not in the context of Cameron's fantasy. He created Ferris, or at least that version of him, because he had to. He needed a hero.'

Right now, I need a hero. Seriously: where's my white knight upon a fiery steed? He doesn't need to be strong, fast, or fresh from the fight, he just needs to be larger than life and capable of saving mine. It's a mess. But there's no way I could've predicted the position I find myself in right now.

No one could.

CHAPTER 1

The Breakfast Club

Two weeks earlier

I'm more or less successful, and more than likely screwed. No wonder I don't have an appetite.

'Libby, you gonna eat that?' Dora asks, leaning, unbalanced, to stab my untouched pancake with her fork. Normally she's slender and leggy even though she's short, which completely baffles me. It's like her top half had one idea and the bottom another. But pregnant? She's a Weeble, she wobbles, and she needs to sit back down. It's that bad.

Dora gives a closed-mouth smile while chewing, then eyeballs my side of turkey sausage. *Whatever*, it's not like I want that either. I shove the plate over.

Huddled round the table are Dora, Dean, myself and Finn. Aside from Dean, we basically grew up together. Well, and Ollie, Dora's older brother – but on Saturdays it's just the four of us. Shermer's on East Broadway has become something of a breakfast ritual, and it's always an event. Our once-a-weeks, fuelled by New York's finest short-stacks, usually involve news – and not just any random bits of gossip, but something fantastical and life-changing. Today, unfortunately, is no exception.

'So, Libby, where should we have your big birthday event?' Dora asks after an oversized swallow. Her round cheeks flush pink with excitement. It could also be the hormones.

Leaning back in my chair, I adjust my stack of plastic bangle bracelets and eye her with suspicion. I know they've already planned it. 'Birthdays in general aren't my thing, as you very well know, and turning thirty-three isn't even a milestone you celebrate, so why bother? Besides, we're still two weeks out and have more important things to focus on.' I give a nod to Dean beside her. 'Like the baby and your wedding.'

Dean smiles and lifts Dora's hand to show off the custom sparkly ring that has finally arrived. It's a channel-set diamond halo, and it's simply stunning – if you're into that sort of thing.

Finn eyes the bauble with indifference. After all, they didn't go with *his* fabulous recommendation. Personally, I'd like to recommend an iron to Finn. I mean, my God, his shirt looks like he balled it up and shoved it in a drawer straight from the dryer. And his blonde hair, normally gelled back in a perfect pompadour, is seriously bedraggled. My guess? Mr Social hasn't slept yet. Usually he's a fashion-forward New York attorney, but this morning he looks as if he needs one.

Dora narrows her eyes, ignoring his grump. 'And what should our theme be?'

'For the baby shower or the wedding?' I ask, taking a sip of my sparkling water, knowing she means my party. The one I'm not planning on having. The one I know she is.

Dora's on round two of the matrimony cycle, and I haven't even had a go at one. I actually dream of lying on dates, wishing I could say that I'm badly divorced – somehow that seems better than explaining the alternative. *Never* married. People just don't understand my absolute lack of interest. My fictitious ex is called Rupert. He was a bear of a man, but devilishly handsome. I couldn't resist his charms until . . . the story changes from there, depending on how much I've had to drink.

'Forget the wedding,' Dora says, then quickly backtracks apologetically to Dean, who was only half paying attention. 'For now. Plenty of time for us, right?' She scootches close, pushes her dark bobbed hair out of the way and gives him a chaste kiss on the cheek, leaving a faint red lip print.

'The theme should be rebirth and renewal,' says Finn, dramatically. He's a bit of an instigator, only happy when stirring things up.

Dora steals a bacon strip from Dean's plate, nods to Finn, takes a bite then points the remaining bit at me. 'And it needs to bubble with fun.'

'I don't bubble, Dora.' Unless I've been outdoors too long: then my fair and freckly completion reacts violently and blisters in the sun.

'Right. And you're hardly fun,' Finn says with a head-bob. 'But you absolutely must embrace this turning point, Libbs.'

My stomach is what turns. Something's up. They're all looking at one another and nodding. I take another sip, too fast; the fizz climbs up my nose.

'OK, the thing is . . .' Dora's hand reaches for mine. She pats it. 'I'm not sure how to start, actually.' With a staggered breath, she gives it a firm squeeze. 'We just . . . Well, Libbs, we understand, of course, but every year around your birthday –'

'You're antisocial and glum,' Finn grumbles.

'And it's not getting better,' Dora continues, speaking fast but methodically, almost as if she'd rehearsed. 'In fact, over time it's gotten worse. And after chatting with you the other day about your lack of love life, we've been talking amongst ourselves, and, well . . .'

My eyebrows hike. I'm poised on high alert. Everyone's leaned in and is giving nudges for her to continue.

'Oh, for pity's sake.' Finn growls in frustration, plops down his fork and straightens. 'The thing is, Libbs, we love you madly, but we think you're stuck.'

'The neon clothes –'

'The super-big hair –'

'No wonder you're single.'

I'm hit from all sides. Everyone is talking at once. I lean back, arms crossed, not sure what to say.

'Consider this . . .' Dora looks around again, and then all together they chime, 'An Eighties intervention.'

I blink. 'A *what*?'

Dora snorts. 'An Eighties intervention.'

'We simply cannot –'

'*Will* not –'

'Must not –'

'Allow you to enter another year while stuck in the Eighties.

Things *have* to change.' Dora points at me with a chubby finger. 'You said so yourself.'

'And it's for your own good, really,' Dean adds.

'And ours, 'cause I really can't take any more of the Madonna's-early-years look.'

'Shut up, Finn.' I smack him. 'And look at you. What's sprouted from your jaw? Seriously, someone could hide in that thing.' He's sporting a full-on beard, not even remotely scruff-like or sexy.

'It's a men's movement, a modern trend, so obviously you wouldn't understand.' Finn narrows his eyes and scratches at it.

'You guys do understand I own a vintage retail store, right? We sell clothes, music and collectables from the Eighties, so I'm not *stuck* in that decade. I profit from it.' I huff a fast breath when no one says anything, adjusting my bangles again. 'It's for work. It's what I do.'

'It's what you've always done,' Dora says, arching her brows. 'You worked at Pretty in Pink when we were in high school.'

'And I bought it, and grew the business right after,' I say in my own defence.

'That's true,' Finn says, and receives an irritated look from Dora. He receives a grateful one from me, although it's short-lived. 'But this?' He reaches to my Rick-Astley-red hair and picks at a curl. The entire side lifts in tandem. 'I'd say Aqua Net, but I don't think they even make it any more.'

'They absolutely do, and I'm never gonna give it up,' I say, a tad cheeky.

'Well, it's gotta go or they'll run away screaming,' Finn says, missing my clever wordplay. 'The *Pretty Woman* big-hair thing is done, sweetie. Even Julia has her locks straightened.'

I look to Dean, but he only wrinkles his nose, shoves a monster bite of omelette in his mouth and bobs his head in agreement. *Really?*

Wait . . . '*Who* will run away screaming?' I smooth down the stray lock just as Dora reaches to pull up another. I swat her hand away. 'And who cares what Julia Roberts does? It's easier this way. Plus, she has stylists.'

'And so will you,' Dean laughs, mouth still half-full. 'I kind of like the curls. Maybe just soften the crunch a bit?'

'Eh, no.' Finn's shaking his head. 'She needs a complete make-over.'

'A *life* makeover,' Dora adds. 'That's what you said, Libbs, your own words, "I need a life makeover", so no more dating the same type of guy.'

Yeah, I said that, but . . . My brows push down. 'I haven't even been dating.'

'Which is the problem. But trust us – when you do, he's always the same type.' Dora hands Dean a much-needed napkin.

'Completely unavailable, just off a divorce, or only recently separated. In other words . . .' Finn waves his fork as a baton. 'A poor, tortured soul.'

'I'm the one being tortured, you guys,' I huff.

'Here's the thing. Based on what we know and what *you* said, we've made a pact,' Dora says, halting the roast. 'We're going to break you from your Eighties rut and drag you into the twenty-first century—'

'Kicking and screaming?' I give a closed-mouth smirk, not sure if I should be amused or irritated. I might be both. Lifting my glass, I chug down the rest of my drink. I may need a real one.

'One, that was a *private* conversation, Dora, and two, aren't we supposed to be planning your wedding today?'

'Oh, plenty of time for that.' Dora and Dean nod to one another, decidedly. 'But your birthday? That's in two weeks, and this year the gloom and doom stops. Mark my word, Libbs, there *will* be a party.'

'And you need a *viable* date,' says Finn, nodding, to which they all agree.

Dora's in Dora mode now; there's no stopping her. 'First, five dates of *our* choosing, all completely different types, all open and available for a real relationship. And hopefully you'll be open and give one a real chance. That way he can escort you to your party.'

'The party I don't want?' I say to remind them.

'The party you're *having*,' Dora mutters back.

My head shakes fervently. 'Forget it, Dora, OK? Last time you fixed me up, the guy was a Trekkie. A *Trekkie*,' I say again, demonstrating Spock's lame hand sign.

'How do you even do that?' asks Dean, trying to form the V with his fingers.

I can think of a better sign to show him. All of them. I'm officially peeved.

Dora lifts her chin, determined. 'Fine, then bring Jasper. He adores you. And I *know* you like him.'

'Which is exactly why she won't go out with him,' Finn adds. 'He's available, likes her, and it could actually lead to something.'

'No, that's not why,' I say, defensively. Jasper maybe has a small crush, but yeah, there's no way. 'He's younger than me, works for me and likes Green Day. Really, does there need to be more?'

Dora pops her brows high, looking smug.

I lower mine, exasperated.

'Look, you have to say it in a way Libbs will appreciate. *Eighties-speak*.' Finn smiles mischievously and leans over the table, zeroing in. 'It should be said in the simplest terms and most convenient definitions, right, Libbs?'

'I don't get it,' Dean says with a shrug, looking around for hints.

'Ah, but she does, and that's the problem.' Finn's smile widens. 'So, dear girl, you will break from the tragically unavailable and date –'

'A brain,' Dora says, as if on cue.

'An athlete,' Finn says.

Dean looks around. 'Oh, me? Yes, OK: a basket case.'

'And a princess,' Finn says, with a finger raised. 'Or at least a metro-type guy – unless . . .?'

'No.' I narrow my eyes, shaking my head. '*Noooo . . .*'

'Don't forget the criminal,' Dean says.

'Oh, and we're in charge of the makeover.' Dora waves a hand to indicate herself and Finn.

'Who, you and the unofficial fourth member of ZZ Top?' I smirk, pushing my teased hair from my exaggerated shoulders. Even if Finn usually is the 'Sharp Dressed Man', I don't need his advice; and maybe I did mention wanting a new look to Dora, but I don't need a *complete* makeover, do I? I really can't believe they're doing this to me. Who gave them the right to pass judgement? 'Yeah, not gonna happen,' I say with conviction.

'Looky here, Libby London . . .' Dora chomps a bite, but that doesn't stop her. 'I'm not doing this for me. I'm doing this for you.

We *all* are. We love you, and it's about bloody well time you were happy.'

'I *was* happy, until about twenty minutes ago,' I say under my breath, then look to my so-called friends: slightly eccentric, but socially superior Finn; easy-going Dean, and finally the evil mastermind, hormonally charged Dora.

She pouts her lips and shakes folded hands over the table. 'Please, please, *please* . . .'

God. She'll just keep pestering and making me feel guilty until I cave. My massively padded shoulders collapse with a guttural sigh. '*Fine*. God, fine.' Agreeing to it and following through are two different things. I just want this conversation to stop.

'Goody!' Dora claps, then stands, excusing herself to the ladies' room. I half expect her to raise her arm and make the iconic fist pump as she struts away, like Judd Nelson did in *The Breakfast Club*.

♫

I wake, frazzled, and at once realize I'm crying. *Damn it.* Not again. Stupid nightmares. I'm all fizzy and agitated. Once up, I stumble to the kitchen for water and ibuprofen, the tears in constant flow. Opening the cupboard, I find the extra-strength and take two, wishing they were something stronger and could knock me out, but knowing they aren't and won't.

My mind spins an endless loop. Pretty in Pink, my vintage thrift shop, is in the perfect Lower East Side location, and in New York City that's no small feat. I'm being forced to move. My stomach coils at the thought. I mean, how am I ever going to find affordable space? How is this even happening? How is it my fault

Crafty Cath's, the hobby shop I sublease from, went bankrupt? It's not. But unfortunately my lease was with them, not the actual commercial property owners, and they want me out.

I don't want to move my store. I also don't want to do Dora's *Breakfast-Club*-Eighties-intervention date-and-makeover thing, and I certainly don't want a pointless birthday party. Why does everything have to change?

With a pillow across my lap and a box of tissues by my side, I sit and stare at my opened unicorn Trapper Keeper notebook. I've written two lines.

Dear Dr Papadopoulos,
   I accepted your challenge to write an essay of who I think I am, but . . .

That's all I have. *Why'd he even ask me to do this?* Other than this afternoon, I hadn't seen him in almost six months; I didn't need to. But with the stupid legal notice about the store, my birthday stalking me, and today's intervention thing, I found myself back at his office.

It used to be, I'd wake and start sobbing for no reason at least three times a week. I couldn't stop. Nothing happened to upset me – everything was fine. There wasn't any explanation or trigger, but it happened on and off for years. *Years.*

Finally, fed up and exhausted, I sought help.

The space was small, cramped and dusty, but Dr Papadopoulos was kind. He was also short, hairy and Greek.

'You can call me Dr P., if you like,' he offered with a small smile at that first meeting. 'So how can I help you, Libby?'

'If I'm honest, I was hoping for some knock-out pills? Major issues with sleep,' I said, thinking this would be an easy thing. Write me a prescription, and I'll be on my way. The family doc at the walk-in healthcare clinic had prescribed some, but they weren't doing the trick: I'd wake again in a few hours, still crying and now groggy and disoriented too. I needed the hard stuff, the kind that could Quiet Riot, because I didn't want to feel the noise.

Wasn't going to happen. Dr Papadopoulos was a psychologist, not a psychiatrist. Apparently there's a difference, and only one can write a prescription.

'I guess I've made a mistake,' I said, and stood, ready to go.

'There's never a mistake in asking for help.' He shrugged, then scratched under his jaw. For a professional, he was a bit dishevelled and schlumpy. His rounded shoulders were covered by an old fuzzy cardigan with missing buttons. Its bright asymmetrical pattern was garish and distracting. 'Why do you think you struggle with sleep?'

Sitting back down, I glanced up. 'Oh, ah . . . mostly the sobbing gets in the way, probably just stress. So a good shut-eye pill will fix that little issue, I'm sure.'

He smiled. 'It doesn't exactly work that way.'

'So how does it work?'

'We talk.' He shrugged. 'We figure out why you're not sleeping. Why you wake in tears. What you're holding onto.'

'And then?'

'We work it through until you're ready to let it go.'

'Pretty sure some good sleepy-time meds would do the trick.' I smiled again, intentionally trying to keep things light.

Dr P.'s eyes narrowed, seeing through my bullshit, but he didn't call me on it. Not then.

I'm not sure why I went back to see him today.

Reaching for a tissue, I dab my eyes, then blow my nose. 'So stupid,' I mutter, angry at myself. I say this over and over, because I don't know what else to do. I'm under water again. This is what happens. The darkness creeps up, wraps itself round my ankles and pulls me under, an inch at a time.

My chest hurts, my throat's tight and I can't breathe even though I gasp with every sob. Everything floods me. The 'so stupid' becomes 'I'm stupid,' and it's repeated again and again.

Ugh, I hate this. I cry harder as the small things build to the larger, and like an anchor, they weigh me down. That's how depression works. It drowns its victims slowly, immobilizing them until they stop fighting and give in.

My eyes once again fall to the notebook, the one sentence that's incomplete. *Who am I?* This is when the voice I can never silence pipes up: I didn't go to college, I've never owned a house, never married, and have no children. *Things I don't even want*, but things most people have accomplished by now. All I have is Pretty in Pink, my store, and it's enough – but now I may lose that. I crumble the legal notice and toss it across the room. I don't want anything to change. It's so ill-timed, so unfair . . .

So stupid.

CHAPTER 2

'Pretty in Pink'
Psychedelic Furs, 1981

More like pretty panicked

The weather mirrors my mottled mood. It's been raining all night, creating a typical Manhattan mix of cool, dank air and drizzle that seeps into the joints and makes my knee flare. It also makes walking the six blocks from my apartment miserable, so I've opted for a cab.

'Right there,' I say to the driver, pointing to my corner shop through the fogged windshield. The Pretty in Pink sign illuminates in bright neon, just like the original shop in the movie. It's not the most beautiful of storefronts, at least not in the conventional sense. The outside brick could use some touching up, the awning needs repair and the building itself shows its age. But Pretty in Pink is just like me: it's a little dated, somewhat offbeat, and stubbornly stands alone.

'Thanks.' I jump out and slosh across the one-way street, unable to avoid the puddles. By the time I'm under the weathered canopy, my feet are soaked. The door's unlocked and the alarm doesn't beep, so I know Jasper, my manager, is already here setting up for the day. From habit and for safety, I twist the deadbolt behind me before dragging my feet across the doormat to rid them of excess water. Making my way to the back office, I flip the alternative rock station back to the preset Eighties.

'You're here early,' Jas says from the small kitchenette where he's fixing a coffee. Jasper's look is more Nineties surfer grunge than pop-star Eighties, and he resembles Keith Urban a bit. Although with the rolled-sleeve flannel, concert T-shirt and shaggy blonde hair jutting out from under a grey slouchy hat, he has a Kurt Cobain vibe. At first glance, you'd think he was in his late teens instead of twenty-nine.

'Yeah, just wanted to clean up some.' I swipe the duster from the cleaning pail and eye his cap more carefully. 'You can't wear the merchandise, Jas.'

'I bought it.' He motions towards the front register. 'But what I don't buy is you here, cleaning, on a Sunday morning. What gives?' He takes a sip, turns and leans against the counter.

'Nothing *gives*,' I mumble as I move towards the front.

'A good bonk usually helps,' he calls out.

When I turn with an exasperated eye-roll, he smiles crookedly with his upper lip pulled high on one side. It's more a cute snarl than a Rebel Yell.

Five years ago, when I first hired him, I thought he was a struggling musician in between gigs, figured he needed to pay some bills. Hoped it wasn't debt due to other issues, like gambling or addiction. With the earrings, tats and unkempt hair, I had to wonder. Plus, why would a grown man want a crap job at a vintage store? I even worried he'd just been sprung from the clink.

'I'll expect you to show up on time, every time, no exceptions,' I'd said when I gave him the position.

'Of course. Not a problem.'

'And the drawer has to balance, every day before you leave. We've had some trouble in the past and I have a no-mistake rule now.' I was trying to be so tough and formidable, not sure if he was the best choice to run the store unsupervised during the day. Teens were a pain in the ass, but a grown man who looked like one could be a pain in the pocketbook.

But Jasper showed every day, and worked hard. He did what needed to be done without being told and had great promotional ideas to move hard-to-sell items. In fact, I gave him a raise within the first month and promoted him to manager not long after. Over time, we've become great friends. *Friends*. Of course, both he and Dora think it should be more. In our little Pretty in Pink ensemble, Jas is my Duckman.

'How's the website coming?' I yell over my shoulder and the music. He's also my IT guy, in charge of our online presence. I don't really understand all of it, but I get the need to be current even if the majority of our products aren't.

'I have about half the inventory loaded.' Jasper ambles to the front door and flips the sign to *Open*, then moves to the register so we can start the day. 'I'll jump back in this afternoon when Robbie shows up.' He shuts the cash drawer, and again regards me. 'So, really – you good?'

I haven't told Jas the situation we're in with the store. I haven't said a word to anyone. I can't seem to bring myself to do it. This is where the hero needs to come in.

'Libbs? I asked if you were OK, you've been—'

Before I can answer, the front door rattles with a *knock-knock-knock*. Since I relocked, Jas didn't know to unlock. I turn, still wrapped in my hopeful fantasy, but instead of the streetwise Hercules fresh from the fight, it's level-headed Dean with a bag of fresh bagels. What's *he* doing here? And I hope he remembered schmear.

The door's base is jammed. It always sticks in the frame when the temperature shifts, so I throttle it open with a small kick. The *Open* sign smacks the glass from the force. 'This is a surprise.'

Dean shrugs, offers me the bag and starts browsing about. 'Yeah, well, I was in the neighbourhood.'

'You're never in the neighbourhood,' I say, already suspicious, glancing between him and Jas, but then temporarily distracted by the baked goods. Oh, yes, cinnamon raisin and schmear.

'Gonna do a trash run,' Jas says with a half-smile before disappearing.

The trash was taken out last night. I slather up a half-slice, take a bite and focus again on Dean. Something's definitely up. *Again*.

He leans over the display case, pressing palms against the glass. 'Oh, *no way*.'

'That's worth about a hundred dollars,' I say with a fast swallow, motioning to the Mr T. action figure still in its original packaging.

'I pity the fool who pays that,' he says with a small smile, then turns his attention to the items on top. 'I cannot believe you sell water ring toss.'

'I tried to get Duncan to play, but he was bored in less than thirty seconds.' Duncan is Dora's son from her short first marriage. He's just turned five and stays with her ex mostly, since he's remarried and settled. Maybe that will change when Dean and Dora are hitched? I hope so. I'm not done reprogramming him. He thinks Wham is a cleaning product.

Dean turns to flip through the poster carousel, obviously stalling. 'Yeah, well, if it doesn't have wifi, forget it. Lost cause, I'm afraid.'

I'm the one lost. 'So what's up, what are ya doing here?'

Dean freezes, as if deciding how to start, or if he should, or maybe if he should run.

'Spill it.' Wiping my mouth, I take a step forward and peer at him anxiously.

'OK.' He takes a step back, hands raised in surrender. 'Just don't shoot the messenger. Dora's arranged a full-on salon day and the first date is scheduled for tonight. Just wanted to warn you her and Finn were scheming.'

'Tonight?' My head drops to my hands. 'Nooooo . . .' It comes out as an exasperated whine.

Dean's brows are held high, his eyes filled with mirth. 'Oh yes, I'm afraid so. Expect them to pop over soon and ambush you.'

'I said I was *thinking* about a new look. That doesn't mean I really *wanted* one.' I can't believe Dora and Finn are really doing this. OK, yes, I can – but still. 'Does she know you're here?'

'Oh, heck no.' He shakes his head, then laughs. 'She thinks I'm in the bathroom.'

That's so like Dean. Under his laid-back guise of ease, there's a lot going on in there. He's the calm to Dora's storm, and the soothing yin to her ding-a-ling yang. 'Y'know . . . it's not like I'm walking around in neon-blue eyeshadow, netted gloves and leopard pants.' At least not today.

'Yeah, well . . .' He laughs and reaches in his pocket to grab the ringing phone. Glancing at the screen, his expression falls. 'Uh-oh, busted,' he says, motioning to the phone while walking to the door. 'Hello, lovely . . . no, no, I'm sure I said bye.' He nods, pops the semi-stuck door and steps outside into the drizzle. With a smile and wave, he's gone.

So is the air from my lungs. Some hero. All he brought was more bad news. At least he left the bagels.

I swipe another, then the duster, and begin frantically swooshing bins and clothing racks. Angry puffs rise into the air. This whole makeover blind-date thing is stupid. I'm not stuck in the Eighties, I'm stuck on Ollie. He's some kind of wonderful, which is *some kind of crap* because that's some kind of *over*.

My friends want me to date the *Breakfast Club* types? We *are* the Breakfast Club. We've always been. And funnily enough, I first saw the movie with Ollie when I was maybe twelve.

I remember this like it was yesterday.

I'd stayed for dinner, like I often did, and Ollie and his dad were arguing, as they often did. Oliver seemed charged up by the debate, spurred on by his father's aggravation.

After dinner I was invited to stay the night, so I heard most of their exchange from Dora's room. It was a shrine to all things rad and awesome. The walls were a bright yellow and papered with torn photos from *Teen* and *Tiger Beat*.

Dora had all the best Eighties retro, including designer jeans: Jordache, Gloria Vanderbilt, even a pair of teen-worship-worthy Guess. That was our thing: it set us apart from the Nineties drones, and enabled us to embrace our first year of junior high with major fashion confidence. 'I'm gonna grab a soda, you want one?' I asked Dora, halfway to the door.

'Naw, I'm good.' She was busy arranging puffy stickers on her closet door to frame a Luke Perry pinup, completely in her zone. He was shirtless, so it was completely understandable.

The only light in the kitchen came from the clock on the stove. I hadn't realized it was so late. I opened the fridge, swiped a can, then heard laughter. Ollie? He had the best laugh. It comforted, like grilled cheese cut diagonally and warm tomato soup.

The TV flickered from the family room, making weird shadows in the hall, so I peeked in. His long dark hair screamed rebel, and dressed in sweats and lazily sprawled over the sofa, he looked like a rock star. When he regarded me with a sideways glance, I about dropped the drink. 'Um, want one?'

'Ah . . .' His blue eyes narrowed, but then he shrugged. 'Yeah, sure.'

I gave him mine, like the kid from the famous Super Bowl commercial. Only it wasn't a Coke, and Ollie wasn't the footballer Mean Joe Green. I didn't leave, either. Instead I stood, mesmerized by the screen.

'You ever see *The Breakfast Club*?' He popped the tab, creating fizz and drawing my attention.

'Of course.' I'd only seen the trailer and caught bits and pieces.

'You can watch, I don't care.' Ollie sat up, offering some of the sectional couch to me. 'This movie completely shows the truth.

See that guy?' He pointed to the principal. His suit looked more Seventies than Eighties, with the exaggerated point of the collar. 'Major dickweed. Represents every adult who thinks they have the right to control you and everybody else.'

'Like your dad?' The words were out before I thought them through.

Ollie turned to me, surprised. 'Yeah, exactly.' He flipped the hair from his eyes just so it could settle back in the same place, and smiled slightly before turning again to the screen.

My stomach fluttered. He smiled. Kind of. In silence we watched Judd Nelson and Molly Ringwald spar, Emilio Estevez confess and Anthony Michael Hall stick a pen up his nose while asking the most profound question imaginable. Who am I?

I cut a glance to Oliver, only to catch him looking back. I panicked. 'So, who are you? Bender?' I wrung my hands, needing the movement. 'You're definitely not the jock.' Ollie didn't play sports, at least not any more. His father rode him hard about quitting football, saying he had so much potential.

Ollie shifted so he faced me, his upper lip curled back somewhat over his teeth. I should've kept my trap shut. I just knew he was going to tell me to get lost. This was cringeworthy.

'Why, you like the jock?' Ollie smiled. It was naughty and mischievous, and made my cheeks flush warm.

My forehead bunched. 'As if.' I didn't know what else to say.

'Exactly.' Maybe he didn't either.

Again we sat in silence until I couldn't stand it.

'So who do you think Dora is?' What I really wanted to know was who he thought I was, but I chickened out. I wasn't sure what to do with my face, so I stared straight ahead, holding my breath and waiting for his answer.

'Ah . . . the spoiled princess. Yeah, Dora's just like Claire, pampered and bratty.'

I whipped my head in his direction. 'But I have the red hair, not Dora.' It came out whiney, but if Ollie was Bender and Bender liked Claire, I wanted to be Claire. Even Molly Ringwald, who initially was offered the part of Allison, wanted to be her.

His eyes slid over me, top to bottom, analysing the careful ensemble Dora and I were experimenting with for next week: paint-splattered T-shirt, jeans with button-fastened suspenders, and a slathering of feathered jewellery which I didn't really like. 'The earrings were Dora's idea. They don't really go, but—'

'She convinced you otherwise. Why do you listen to her? She's a total poser.'

My face crumpled. 'You think we're posers?'

'She is.' Maybe I still looked crushed, and that's why he continued, 'Look, all I'm saying is the Eighties thing doesn't work on her, but on you . . .' He shrugged. 'You kinda pull it off. So don't let her change you, OK?'

My heart thrummed inside my chest. He thinks my Eighties style's cool? He doesn't want me to change? I couldn't help but smile, and it was a big, oversized, dopey one. 'OK.'

'Although I still think you're more like—'

The smile dropped. 'Don't even say the Basket Case. She's crazy and has severe dandruff.'

His gaze glided over my wild waves of hair, as if to consider. 'Well, you don't have dandruff, but—'

'Shut up.' I tossed a pillow his way, and he quickly sent it back.

23

Suddenly I was aware of how close we sat, the exact deep blue of his eyes, and even the small scratch on his jaw. I sat quietly, dazed, my thoughts a jumbled mess. He liked my retro look. Ollie, cool 'everyone has a crush on Ollie', liked my look. He'd finally noticed me . . . Now what? Confused butterflies fluttered inside.

Whatever I was feeling, I liked it. It also freaked me out. We were technically two and a half years apart in age, but because of our birthdays, only two years apart in school. So yeah, he was a ninth grader and he liked me. Well – my style. If I had to pinpoint the exact moment the Eighties became my signature thing, that was it. X marks the spot.

I still don't think I'm the Basket Case, but I've always liked Ally Sheedy's character. At least until they did the makeover.

The front door rattles. It's Dora and Finn.

Oh God, *the makeover.*

CHAPTER 3

'Who's That Girl'
Madonna, 1987

Seriously, who *is* that?

'I don't see why Dean had to warn you,' Dora says, then puckers in her compact mirror to apply cinnamon plumping gloss. Light catches the reflective surface and a flash bounces to my eyes, causing me to squint.

'I'm still here, aren't I?' We're at Fringe, Dora's fancy-schmancy super-expensive salon on Park Avenue. Clip-n-Snip's would've done just fine, if you ask me – not that anyone did. The only reason I'm playing along with this whole makeover-dating-Eighties-intervention thing is because Jas was standing right there when they showed up. When I refused to participate, Dora spiked her brows and unloaded a bomb of embarrassment, telling Jasper everything. So I was on the spot: accept him as my date, or happily accept theirs.

I mean, *God*.

Finn flips through a magazine, commenting on how ghastly

everyone is dressed. It doesn't matter whether we respond: he gabbles his commentary regardless, as if he's on a panel with the Fashion Police. 'Oh dear Lord, no ... just no,' he says with a scowl, holding up the page for my review.

Yeah; I have no idea who that is. I sniff, then rub at my nose from the stench permeating the place. They're burning lemongrass incense to cover the pungent ammonia smell, and it isn't working.

Dora closes her compact with a loud snap. She eyes my outfit. 'You know we're going shopping after, right?'

I stink-eye her and frown. We're not kids any more. I stopped listening to her expert clothing advice a long time ago. Plus, I'm dressed fine. The sweatshirt's comfy. It's big, hangs loose off one shoulder and has that broken-in soft feel from being washed a zillion times.

Finn's more himself today, dressed all in grey except for the muted yellow of his man-scarf, and Dora looks like a waitress in black pants and crisp white tunic shirt. It makes me itch just looking at it. Guess there's a drab dress code and I missed the memo, because my Eddie Grant *Electric Avenue* blue fights with the monochrome theme. Even the salon is papered in rigid black and white patterns and stripes.

'So, this poor guy you're setting me up with? Who is he, what does he do?' They've told me nothing except he's picking me up for a light dinner at seven, and he's Dora's choice. That's why she gets to coordinate my outfit.

Apparently the Eighties intervention has rules.

'Theodore Spalding,' Dora says, as if the name should mean something. It doesn't.

'He's the brain – an *anesthesiologist*.' Finn says. 'Think Anthony Michael Hall from *Weird Science*.' His eyes pop like I should be impressed.

I'm not. 'In that movie, Anthony Michael Hall was a teen geek who couldn't get a date. And an anesthesiologist puts brains to sleep, so it doesn't mean your guy is one.' I pop my eyes back, waiting for this logic to sink in.

'Well, he's brilliant. He's a friend of Dean's,' Dora says with arched brows.

'And Dean's brilliant?' I ask, making Finn snicker.

Dora casually assesses her nails. 'Well, they play racquetball together.'

'Well then, that explains – *wait* . . .' I sit up. 'If he's Dean's friend, who's Dean setting me up with?' Dean doesn't have a ton of friends besides us. This is something to worry about.

Dora wrinkles her nose. 'I don't know, but I called him first, so Theo's my pick . . .' She's staring at me – or rather, my hair. 'Have you considered going blonde?'

'Or maybe deepen the red so it's not so bright and *angry*?' Finn asks, leaning around me to see Dora. 'I swear, it's like Annie Lennox from Eurythmics, only it's not sweet, and not a dream.'

'Careful, you're walking on broken glass.' I smirk, thinking I'm clever. Sitting between them is maddening. 'How about we just shave it? Remember Sinead O'Connor? She was lovely bald.'

'Your head's the wrong shape.'

My eyes pinch. 'Really, Finn?'

He gives me one of his famous withering looks. I swear he reminds me of a chicken: rounded eyes, and a straight protruding beak he sticks in everyone's business. He does have great plumage, though. Silky locks the colour of tawny creamed corn.

'Yeah, I don't think I should go blonde,' I add, thinking back to the earlier suggestion.

'You said, word for word,' Dora says, lifting her hands to make air quotes. '*I need a new look, something fab and fresh.*'

'First, I didn't say fab. I don't say *fab*. And I meant maybe a trim or something, that's all, nothing drastic.'

'Well, what about lowlights? That's not drastic,' Dora says, touching my hair. 'That could really bring out your features.' Finn nods, and they're off.

I let my head fall so it clunks against the window behind me, and tune out their jabbering. I'm starting to have serious second thoughts. I'm also not sure what a lowlight is. Black lights, I understand.

Don't let Dora change you, Ollie had said, and I haven't. I'm still exactly the same. Even when Dora adopted the popular sloppy grunge style, I held onto my Eighties retro vibe. The entire decade was fun and peppy with movies like *Can't Buy Me Love*, *The Lost Boys* and *Dirty Dancing*. Malls became Tiffany and Debbie Gibson's concert venues, and damn it, parents just didn't understand. But really, how could they?

They were so *old*.

But then Y2K rolled in and although the world didn't end, mine may as well have. Ollie was gone. Everything after that was a mess. I missed him terribly. We'd been going out solid for almost his entire senior year. In teen years, that's beyond forever.

I call it my 'End of the Innocence' phase. Don Henley sang, 'Let me take a long last look before we say goodbye.' I didn't want what was good to end, so I never really said goodbye. To anything, really. As the song says, that was my best defence. Maybe my only one.

'Dora?' A young woman in her early twenties, dressed in the required black tapered pants and white blouse, approaches. Her make-up is smoky and layered thick. Her straight hair is tied back tight. She looks like one of those girls from the Robert Palmer videos – the bored ones who play guitar – only she's smiling. Still bored.

They air-kiss before she turns to Finn with the same forced almost-smile. 'And are we waiting on Libby?'

Finn shakes his head and points to me. I stand.

The woman's face drops.

At her station I'm directed to take a seat, so she can have a 'look-see'. She fumbles with the clasp of my banana clip, so I reach up and unsnap the top and yank it out. I watch her confusion in the mirror, Finn's impatience, and Dora's embarrassment. They're so serious. *It's hair*, and really, aside from a much-needed trim –

'It's a tad dry.' Finn flicks my teased tresses.

'And the colour's somewhat brassy,' Dora adds, almost apologetically.

'Oh, and she needs a pluck – no, a –'

'A wax,' they finish together, both nodding, wide-eyed.

'What are we waxing?' I ask, mentally checking off body parts. Eyebrows? Lips? Nothing else is visible. Do they even do *that* here? What have they promised this date?

The stylist spins the chair so I'm facing the occupied station across from me. I hold back a laugh and the urge to sing Styx's 'Mr Roboto'. The woman's entire head is covered in tin foil packets.

'Yes, now, what about going short?'

My head snaps up at the stylist's words. 'You can only cut an inch,' I say, setting a firm boundary while giving Dora my frostiest death glare. I'll be a good sport – after all, I did tell Dora I *wanted* a change – but I never said I wanted it all hacked off. That's something else entirely.

Finn speaks softly. 'Maybe just start with a shampoo, and see what you have to work with?'

♫

I've been washed, snipped, darkened and blown-out, all with Dora and Finn gabbing commentary from the side. I'm now under the care of Shauna, a make-up artist, while the poor un-named stylist sneaks a ciggie outside. She looks a bit frazzled. Her tight 'do has undone and the perfectly applied mask of make-up is splotchy from perspiration. She's gone from 'Simply Irresistible' to simply irritated.

A chime sounds, and Dora checks her phone. 'Oh, it's a text from Dean,' she says. 'He wants to know how it's going. I should take some photos.'

'Tell him—'

'Stay still,' Shauna says in a tone reserved for four-year-olds, nearly jabbing a liner pencil into my eye.

Dora shoves her phone in front of my face. *Snap-flash.*

Shauna jerks my head back. 'OK, almost . . . just need . . .' She feathers a huge brush of powder across my nose. 'Done.'

Another *snap-flash*, this time from Finn's.

Dora's phone chimes again and she squeaks with laughter.

'Dean asked me who's in the picture. He doesn't even recognize you!'

'OK, that's it.' I'm up, turning and – *whoa*, who *is* that girl? I step closer to the mirror, turning my chin left and then right, a bit confused. 'Why do I look like—'

'It's great, isn't it?' Dora's literally bouncing. 'I love it! Don't you love it?'

We're the Wonder Twins. Do we fist-bump and declare our powers to *activate*? Maybe we already did. *Shape of . . . Dora.* I'm seriously styled just like her: same make-up, same cut, only longer. I move so that I'm inches from the glass.

My super-long frizzy curls are now just past my bra strap and smoothed to a barely-there wave. The firecracker red is now a tame auburn with copper highlights. And my face? You can't even see my freckles under all this gunk. *Seriously weird.*

'Oh, Dean says you look divine.' Dora shoves her phone at me so I can read the text.

'He says I look like you.'

'Exactly, and he thinks I'm divine.' She smiles, flipping a hand through her dark bobbed hair. Dora turns to the stylist. 'I was thinking you could pull it to the side, wrap it in a loose bun, so she has a more studious look. What do you think, Libbs? That's not too much, right?'

I'm not sure how to answer; I'm still in shock.

Finn and my clone discuss options with anyone who'll listen. I'm not one of them.

'She has a date with an *anesthesiologist*,' Dora adds, 'and we're now running a bit behind. We still need to get her styled.'

I glance up. *Oh God.*

Apparently my Dora makeover took too long, so shopping was out. I'm now dressed in Dora's clothes. Not clothes *like* hers – not even clothes from her apartment, since we're at mine – but Dora's maternity clothes from *today*. Her black slacks, although heavily gathered and belted, and the itchy, re-ironed and freshened white tunic blouse.

There is one amusing thing that almost makes it worth it: if I'm in her clothes, guess what she's wearing? And she hates it. *Hates it*. She keeps pulling up the dropped shoulder.

I shove it over to expose her ridiculously frilly bra strap. 'See? It should just hang down.'

Dora huffs, 'It should be burned,' and gathers the excess material in her hand, clasping it near her neck.

Snap-flash. Finn has his phone in camera mode again. Why he doesn't turn off the fake shutter sound is beyond me. He pushes a hand through his flaxen hair, changes the direction of the phone, squints and . . . *snap-flash*. That one was a selfie.

'Your apartment's kind of dated, you know that?' Finn says, looking round and nosing through my movie collection. 'Even your DVDs are old.' He starts reading them off, his nose turned up. '*St Elmo's Fire, The Breakfast Club, Pretty in Pink* . . . all Eighties, and all Molly Ringwald. *Bleah*.'

'She's seen those all a million times,' Dora says, without looking up from her phone.

'You should redecorate,' Finn says, already moving on before I can defend my collection.

'Don't even think about it. My apartment's great.' I lucked out and nabbed a corner unit in Peter Cooper Village Community, better known as Stuytown. Located only six blocks from Pretty in Pink, it's perfect, all 750 square feet of it. And it's not layered with memorabilia like the shop, but it does have an Eighties charm, which means you have a few options: chintz, farmhouse, southwestern, mauve pastels, or bold. I chose the last.

The small sectional is colour-blocked, the tiles' geometric patterns and the coffee tables are oversized Rubik's Cubes collectable limited editions. I had them specially ordered. If you remove the glass top trays, they even work, how cool is that? Not that I could ever solve it. I was one of *those* people that peeled the stickers off and re-stuck them.

Snap-flash.

'Finn, stop it!' I duck from view. 'What in the world do you need so many photos for anyway?'

'Instagram. Twitter.' Finn shrugs. 'We've started a hashtag: #80sIntervention. People have started posting their own horrible Eighties pics and voting. It's going viral.' *Snap-flash.*

'I'm gonna go viral, if you don't stop it.' I swipe for his phone but miss. 'I need a drink,' I say to myself, and start searching for the wine bottle I've all but drained. This is the first time I've really felt nervous. My hands are starting to tingle. What if this guy's hideous? Or has a lazy eye? Then where do I look?

'What time is it?' Finn asks, looking to the wall clock then rolling his eyes. 'That thing's still not working, Libbs.'

'That thing' is an actual converted 45 record featuring The Smiths' single 'That Joke Isn't Funny Anymore'. I think it's hilarious. I found it online and couldn't resist.

Finn looks at his phone to check the time instead. 'Dora, you did give him the right address and tell him promptly at seven, right? 'Cause it's almost time.'

'Yeah, Dean just texted, saying he rang him and he'll be here any minute.' Dora props her swollen feet up on my end table and sighs, looking at them. 'I used to have ankles,' she says, more to herself than to us, but then holds one up for group scrutiny. 'Are they really so bad?'

Finn wisely ignores Dora and approaches me in the kitchen with his empty glass, wanting a taste.

I give him a little, then drain the rest straight from the bottle. I don't need a glass; I need a hefty dose of liquid nerve. 'Are we *all* going out with the brain guy? Seriously, why are you guys still here? I can handle this.' They're making me crazy. I set down the bottle, push up my sleeves and scratch violently at my forearms. *What is Dora's shirt made of?*

'Don't talk about music or politics. You know how you can get.' Finn's playing with his phone while pacing.

'Wait.' His words jolt me. 'How I *get*?' I push at my sleeves again, then glance at the smirking Kit-Cat clock in the kitchen, the one that works. Less than ten minutes.

'You get really opinionated, so don't talk about anything, you know, too controversial,' says Dora. She takes a small drink of her water with lemon. 'Just let Theodore steer the conversation, and be agreeable.'

My newly shaped brows furrow. 'Well, I don't agree with that.'

'Well, he's *really* shy, so I told him . . .' Dora looks at Finn, then glances back at me.

'What?' My arms cross. *Shit*, I didn't even consider what they told these guys about me. Desperate spinster, never married, has multiple cats, easy? Yeah, nothing's easy about me.

Snap-flash.

'*Stop it*, Finn.' My heart starts pounding, heavy in my chest. I unfold and scratch my arms again. 'Did you say I was shy, too? Because I'm not shy. I'm not sure how to even play shy.' Do I bat my lashes, smile and look away? Oh God, do I have to giggle? I look at the clock again. It's five to seven. 'You'd better not have said I'm shy, Dora. I mean it.'

'Well, no, I didn't say you were shy *exactly* . . .' She flips the heavy bangs from her eyes, then intertwines her fingers over her baby bump. 'I said you were . . .'

'What? Quiet? *Demure*?'

'Mute.'

'*What*?' Choking on the word, I look to Finn. 'Did she say *mute*?' I shake my head to rattle the meaning. My head swivels back in Dora's direction. 'I'm mute, as in I *do not speak*. Not a word?'

She nods. 'Mm-hmm.'

I blink. She blinks. She's serious?

'Are you off your hormonal rocker?' I'm talking quite loudly for someone who can't speak. 'So, what, you told him I'm, like, missing my tongue? 'Cause that's attractive.'

'No, I said you might have . . .' Her shoulders hike, her lips pull up, she's bracing herself.

'Have *what*?'

'A brain infection.'

'Hah!' Finn whoops a laugh, then snorts.

'I have a *brain infection*?' I spin towards Finn. 'Did you know? Are you part of this?'

'No, *no*.' Finn's shaking his head, but laughing harder. Another snort. 'Oh my God . . . *oh*, shit. Dora, what in the *world*?'

'OK . . .' I refocus, trying to stay calm, speaking slowly and enunciating every syllable. Maybe I don't understand. 'Dora.'

Her eyes widen.

'You told Theodore I have a *brain* infection?'

Dora nods, with a nose-wrinkle. Finn's now bent over, a hand covering his eyes, shaking his head. He may be laughing.

Snort.

Yup, he's laughing.

I take another step, my lips curling into a dangerous smile. 'So, like, something's wrong with my mind, is *that* what you told him?'

'No. *Noooo* . . .' She shakes her head adamantly back and forth. 'I would never, ever imply it to mean *that*. I only meant, well, because he studies the brain, that maybe you've somehow con-tracted a rare virus that impairs speech . . .' She chin-nods with a hopeful expression, as if her explanation actually makes sense.

It doesn't. My face folds as I try to work it all out. 'So, I've some-how contracted a rare *brain cold* that's caused me to lose the ability to speak? Is that it?'

She nods again.

'*This* is how you score me a date?'

She flinches. 'Technically it's not *exactly* a date per se, it's . . .'

My stomach dips. I look over to Finn, then back again, afraid to ask. I do anyway. 'It's what, Dora?'

'A consult.' She sits up, speaking fast. 'But don't get mad, I can explain—'

Snort-thud. Finn disappears behind the breakfast bar in hysterics. My mouth hangs open as I stand frozen in disbelief. Dora shields herself behind a throw pillow. Her eyes have rounded, the pupils a mere pinprick.

I don't even know what else to say, except . . . 'I'm not going.' I'm unbuttoning the shirt, heading for my bedroom to change into my own clothes, which are perfectly fine.

Dora waddles after me. 'Libbs, Libby, Libby, Libby . . . he's super-shy, never dates, is maybe a little too focused on work, so I just thought—'

'He could *cure* me? Forget it.' I spin, jabbing a finger near her face. 'First, he can't *cure* a brain infection. He's an *anesthesiologist.*' Movement from the corner of my eye grabs my attention, I glance over and . . . 'Really, Finn?'

His hands are clasped round his phone, balanced on the counter. It's shaking from laughter. He's still on the floor. *He's recording this?* I charge at him. That phone's going—

The doorbell rings. *Shit.* 'He's here.' I step left, then right, and then smack into Dora's bump. 'Tell him I'm not going!'

Knock-knock-knock.

Finn has my handbag, and shoves it at my chest; Dora's right beside him. They're pushing me towards the door, whispering commands.

'Remember, you're breaking from your rut.'

'He's just like Anthony Michael Hall.'

'You need a date for your party.'

'Wait.' I stop and turn. This is ridiculous, insane. I'm a *mute*? I have a *brain infection*? Dora's a nut-job, a nutter, she's completely lost it. 'No way. I can't do this.'

Knock-knock-knock.

'You *have* to. *Please.*' Dora says, flustered, on the verge of major hormonal tears. 'Look, I didn't mean for it to go this far or to sound so bad, I promise. I'm *so* so sorry. It started just that you were shy and then, well, he's always working . . . But you're fantastic and brilliant and he'll *really* like you, Libbs. I just know it.'

'He *can't* like me,' I say in whisper-shout, an inch from her face. 'I don't have a *tongue.*'

CHAPTER 4
The Brain

We're at Katz's Delicatessen, the iconic *When Harry Met Sally* cafe on East Houston. That's how tourists know the place, and you can always spot them. They hover round the infamous table and lean across the bar to admire the framed celebrity photos that fill the wall. But we New Yorkers know what the deli's really renowned for: legendary, mile-high pastrami on rye.

I could eat here every day. Many people do. Of course, then my backside would expand substantially, and I'm pretty sure it's already bigger than Theodore's, which I have a problem with. Finn was right: he does resemble Anthony Michael Hall in the Eighties, and just like him, Theo's a tad on the thin side. This makes my normal size feel hippo-sized. I don't need any new reasons to be at war with my body.

Right now, I'm at war with my mouth. It's an epic battle to not say anything since, you know, I'm mute and all. The napkin in my lap is rolled into a strange wand from my constant hand-wringing. Maybe it's magical, and with one swift *abracadabra*, I could make myself disappear . . . or him, or *all of them*.

He brought friends.

Dr Theodore invited Dr Weaver – a neurologist, which actually makes sense for a brain-infection consult. He also invited a trans-lator woman. Since I can't talk, he figured I signed. There's only one sign I can think of, and I'm pretty sure it doesn't require an interpretation.

We'll call bringing an entourage Strike Two. The first being, he thinks I'm a mute with a brain infection and only here for a consult.

I planned on telling them right away that Dora made a mis-take, and it was all a strange and unfortunate misunderstanding because obviously I do have a tongue and can talk; but they've been bombarding me with questions, and I'm hungry. Katz's takes thirty days to cure its meats, and oh my God, yum. *This* is what Meg Ryan was really going on about in the movie, trust me.

'Stiff neck, headaches?' Theodore asks too loudly. He's been doing that all along. For a Brain, he's kind of daft; not only can I talk, I can hear just fine.

I take another bite, and shake my head.

'What about night sweats?' Dr Weaver asks. He's roughly in his sixties with white-peppered hair, and has already downed two chili dogs and is working on a third. He also talks with his mouth full. They should've brought a dentist. I think his crown's chipped. Before I can answer, he leans in and adds, 'Have you noticed any severe mood swings?'

If they don't knock it off, they'll witness one. Are they quizzing for menopause or a brain infection? I head-shake no and swallow, then quickly take another delicious bite. Dora and Finn's words are niggling at me. Am I really *that* opinionated and gobby? And is that such a bad thing? I just know what I like – which isn't this shirt. I push up the starchy sleeves and scratch, noticing my poor forearms are a bright red from the constant rubbing. And so is the shirt sleeve, since I just smudged ketchup from my steak fries on it.

'What about fevers, Libby?'

Taking a drink of water, I watch translator-woman wiggle her fingers, then shake my head as if I understood. So far, aside from being awkward, this is a piece of cake; which I may actually order. Katz has a double-layer chocolate one that is pure sin and bliss. I deserve at least that much after this whacked mime performance.

'Can you explain your symptoms, Libby? Maybe that will help.' Both doctors turn to Miss Busy Hands, then back to me.

My insides go wibbly. That's not a yes-or-no question. They expect me to *sign*? I look down thoughtfully at my fingers and consider my choices: spontaneous jazz hands, paper-rock-scissors, or an enthusiastic *rock on*. This is when I notice my shirt's still half-way unbuttoned, revealing my 'Vogue' cone bra. *Gah.*

This is humiliating. It's like a *Revenge of the Nerds* reunion. They're the nerds, and I'm planning my revenge on Dora. I clear my throat and start to explain. 'Er . . . right, I'm afraid there's been a horrible cock-up. I've only a touch of the laryngitis, you see, but horses for courses, I suppose, eh?' No clue why I have a strange accent. Yeah, I'm not really sure what happened there.

Taking a drink of water, I watch all three exchange worried glances.

'Are you sure you don't feel warm?' Dr Weaver asks, then looks to Theodore and lowers his voice. 'Fevers most definitely cause delusions.'

'I'm *not* delusional! Dora's deranged, OK? It's just a sore throat!' I blurt and cough twice to make my point and redirect the conversation. 'Anyway . . . are you divorced, then?' He must be, or Dora wouldn't have set me up with him.

'Uh . . .' Confusion flashes across Theodore's face. 'Yes, I am; why?'

'Oh, no reason, just making chit-chat. I'm divorced, too.' I scratch at my arms and, without thought, give the dreamed-about fibbing answer. 'It's been a few years, but Rupert and I are finally on good terms. Which is super-duper important, don't ya think?' I haven't had enough to drink, so my fictitious past is tame. 'But my parents are still together, and going strong, God bless 'em.' I throw that in to show I'm grounded, in spite of the upset. Let's not analyse.

For whatever reason, the translator lady is still signing. Maybe that's the only way she gets paid?

'Libby, are you sure you're OK?' Dr Weaver asks with obvious concern.

'*Suuuper,* just grand!' I say, with an overabundance of en-thusiasm. I pare it down and try again. 'Really, I'm perfectly fine.' My own words cause a déjà vu prickling. I'd said almost the exact same thing before, but not to Dr Theodore and his *Weird Science* crew. It was to the EMTs inside the ambulance after my teenage car accident.

I shake the memory away, scratching again at my irritated arms, and notice them staring. 'How's your bun?' I ask Dr Theo, trying to spawn a real conversation, even if it's lame and about a bun.

'Great, thank you,' he says slowly, eyes narrowed and wary. He blinks. I blink. The translator lady signs. This is scintillating. Time to change tactics.

'So, Dr Theo . . .' That sounds creepy, just to note. 'Don't you find it all a bit wonky, this knocking-people-out business? Have they ever woken up?' Now we're talking. I lean on my elbows and look from Dr Weaver to the translator woman, who strangely hasn't said anything. Maybe she's hearing impaired? No, that wouldn't make sense.

'I saw this documentary once where, right in the middle of removing a massive tumour, I mean dead in the middle of surgery, *bam*!' I smack the table, causing the ice in the glasses to rattle, which rattles Dr Theo. 'The woman's eyes popped open. Has that ever happened to you?'

'That's impossible,' he says, furrowing his blonde brows and taking a quick drink of water as if the mere idea was too much.

I sit back, my momentary rush all but drained away. So much for fun conversation.

He wipes at his mouth with his unrumpled napkin, then throws it down like a gauntlet. 'An anesthesiologist monitors and controls the patient's vital life functions . . .'

'. . . heart rate, breathing, body temperature, blood pressure, body fluid balance . . .'

'. . . pain, the level of unconsciousness . . .'

'. . . no possibility of waking . . .'

When they've finally finished, I give a nod with an impressive, 'Wow, that's quite a responsibility.' My version of that conversation was much more appealing. At least he's good at his job. He's definitely putting me to sleep.

'The hives, Libby, is that a new symptom?'

Hives? Dr Theo nods to my – *oh.*

'Can I see your arm?' Dr Weaver reaches and turns it over. They're inflamed and swollen. Huge blotches of red cover every inch of skin. *What the –*

Sign-language lady motions to my jaw. A sign I understand to mean, you have food on your face. Reaching up self-consciously, I . . . *whoa.* My lip is ginormous. *What's going on?* I fumble inside my bag for my Goody pocket-brush-and-mirror combo, unfold and . . . 'Oh. *Oh* . . .' I start coughing. It's a dry tickle. Ugh, I seriously can't clear my throat. In fact . . .

I can't breathe.

'Do you have any allergies?' Theodore smacks my back as I hunch over in mini-convulsions. 'Has this happened before?'

I'm wheezing now. He smacks me again. My throat's constricted and people have turned to watch. I'm creating quite a spectacle. Or he is. Or the interpreter lady is. Why does she keep signing? *And stop smacking me!*

'Oh, I bet this is a re-enactment of *When Harry Met Sally*!'

I have no idea who said that or how that even fits, just that it was super-loud, and I'm seeing spots. Maybe I *do* have a brain infection.

'Are you choking on something?' Dr Theo doesn't wait for my answer. Instead he wraps spindly arms round my ribs, forms a fist and –

'Aaunk!' The force causes me to honk like a goose. He starts to position his hand for another go and – 'Aaunk!' I panic, squirming this way and that. *Oh my God*, let me go! For a skinny guy, he's surprisingly strong. I thrash left, then right, to no avail, leaving only one thing to do. I lean forward, then rear back in one swift movement.

'Ow!' Dr Theo says, rubbing his forehead.

I'd apologize, but really, I only clonked him hard enough to bruise his ego and – *cough-cough-cough*. Ugh, I hate this. And Dora. And her –

Oh, the shirt!

I stand and wildly point to myself, trying to hack out the words.

A pudgy fellow with unfortunate sideburns shouts, 'Oh, she's doing the *Harry Met Sally* bit where Billy Crystal fake-signs, remember?'

I don't, and seriously, people, get over *When Harry Met Sally*. I cough my objection, and again point to my sleeve.

'I think she's trying to tell us something,' sign-language lady says. 'You? You, what?'

Now she speaks? I wave to erase, in between wheezing coughs, and hold up one finger.

'One word?' everyone from surrounding tables yells simultaneously.

I nod-cough, while continuing to yank on the sleeve.

Dr Weaver leans in. 'Oh, arm? Your arm hurts?' He looks to Dr Theo. 'Well, that's understandable. It's inflamed, isn't it?'

'I think she's saying sleeve,' says Theodore drily, still rubbing his head.

Oh my God, now I really do need an interpreter. I hop up and down with breathless frustration. People start shouting guesses.

'Arm's length?'

'Is it a colour? White?'

'Yes, she's saying white.' The man two tables over confirms.

I'm hacking, pointing, apparently playing the worst game of charades of my life. Should I tug my ear, sounds like . . . I beat my fist on my chest for air, then wring the shirt in my hand as I gag.

'Shirt? It's shirt! Oh! Allergic reaction to the shirt!' Sign-language lady claps as if she's won a prize.

So does everyone else. Apparently the entire restaurant, including the staff, is playing.

With enthusiastic thumbs up, I dash, but not before swiping some Benadryl from a helpful nearby patron. Outside, the shirt's ripped off as I strike the standard pose to flag a taxi, which, considering I'm now exposed in nothing but cones of shame, is easily attained.

We'll call this Strike Three.

♫

I'm curled up on my couch with a freshly scrubbed, normal-sized face, and my hair pulled back in a sparkly purple scrunchie. I've downed half the bottle of Benadryl while waiting for Dora to call me back. She has Duncan tonight, so it may be a while; I guess he had a nightmare, and she's tired 'cause she's pregnant, and *blah blah blah*.

Serves her right, what happened to her shirt.

And since Finn didn't answer, I've resorted to talking with Ollie. I glance at the photo of us on my shelf as I do. In it, he's wrapped round me so his chin's tucked over my shoulder and we're laughing with big open mouth smiles. It's my favourite.

'Was it that bad?' Ollie asks, the syllables raspy with a hint of sleepiness.

'Worse.' I snuggle down into the couch and blow out a breath.

'It was a *group* date, and . . .' Running fingers through my hair, I tell him everything, from the brain infection to the shirt catastrophe.

He's laughing. Hard.

God, I love his laugh. I used to do anything to make him crack up. This time, I'm not even trying. 'Really, utter disaster, I mean what was your sister thinking, telling him all that? Oh, and he's already called to make sure I'm OK, which I guess is kind of nice, but he wants to reschedule with the team. He thinks I'm under-playing my condition. My *condition*. I mean, God, right?'

'Did he kiss you?' He moves, and his voice gets louder from the new position. 'I mean, with your super-sized plumped and ready lips, how could he resist?'

'Shut up, Ollie.' Now I'm laughing, too. 'And no, Dr Theo missed his chance, I'm afraid. Not that he ever had one.'

'Hmm, guess he didn't have the moves.'

'You mean like yours? What was it, Twizzlers?' I'm smiling. I can't help it.

'Hey, not only was it original, but it worked. So don't knock the Twizzlers, Shortcake.'

My stomach flips and I sit up, my smile even wider. He hasn't called me that in forever.

But God, it feels like yesterday.

Ollie and Finn had been forced to drag us along to the movies. He had to be sixteen or so, which would place Dora and me at about fourteen or fifteen. Ollie glanced at Dora and me in the rear-view mirror while he drove. Alanis Morissette's 'Ironic' blared from the front speakers of his little red Camaro. Unlike Prince's Corvette, it wasn't much too fast. It was used and sometimes didn't run, but it was red, and that upped our cool quota when we were seen in it. Being seen with us lowered Ollie's and Finn's considerably, or so they said. Repeatedly.

'We may be stuck with you guys, but there's some rules, got me?' Ollie said over the music. His hair was gelled back like Johnny Depp. So was Finn's, but being blonde, he looked more John Taylor new wave than Jump Street bad boy.

Dora rolled her eyes. 'Whatever.'

'First, we don't know you and you don't know us.'

Dora mimicked him, making me laugh. She slid open her gloss tin, dabbed her index finger in and rubbed it over her lips. 'Want some? It's strawberry,' she asked me, holding it out.

'You think some lip gunk will trick some dweeb into kissing you?' Finn turned round and smirked, and before I could react, he swiped it.

'Hey . . .' Dora lunged, swinging wildly over the front seat for his arm. 'Ollie, tell your geek friend to give it back.'

Finn was still out of reach, practically on top of the dash. The car swerved as Ollie tried to shove Dora away.

Finn sniffed the tin, then applied a gob with a series of lip smacks. 'Huh, it even tastes like strawberry and oh my God, it does make me want to kiss you.' He turned, grabbed Dora and went in for the kiss, while she squirmed and shrieked.

Ollie swerved again, and I laughed hysterically. When Dora safely retreated, Finn chucked the gloss at her. 'Bet neither of you have ever been kissed.'

'Have too,' Dora said, diving for the gloss under the seat. And it wasn't a lie if you counted Danny Stansky. He had just gotten his braces off and Dora was his first official metal-free smooch. Apparently it was a good one, 'cause they went together for three whole weeks after.

Finn readjusted his T-shirt sleeves so the second colour would show in the roll, then lit a cigarette, making Dora dramatically gag.

Ollie glanced in the mirror. 'What about you, Shortcake? You been lip-to-lip?'

I hated the nickname. One, I wasn't short, and two, Strawberry Shortcake was a doll I hadn't played with since I was, like, ten. Dora and I had all the characters. We loved their scented hair and dessert-named pets. One year for Halloween, I even dressed up as her. But now? Yeah, not cool. And I was desperately trying to be cool in front of Ollie.

'Oh my God, turn it up! Turn it up!' Dora yelled, bouncing on the seat. 'I haven't heard this in forever.' It was Modern English, 'Melt with You', one of our favourite songs from the Eighties.

We started singing, so Oliver cranked the volume, most likely to drown us out. Just as the chorus came up, my world stopped. I caught his eyes again in the mirror. He held my gaze, then smiled. A real full-on, crinkly-eyed smile, and it was for me. To say I melted was an understatement. I became a warm, syrupy mush puddle right there in the back seat. That became our song.

At least as far as I was concerned.

At the theatre, we went separate ways. They had tickets for Howard Stern's *Private Parts*, which was rated R, so we were left with the bogus PG kiddie flick, *Jungle 2 Jungle*. So embarrassing.

Also embarrassing was the fact I didn't have enough money for candy. In the middle of the movie, I made a snack run and came up short. I was holding up the line, digging in my bag, when Ollie appeared.

'Hi.' He ran a hand through his dark, slicked hair, then dropped his gaze to the assortment of boxes on the counter. 'No Twizzlers? Ya gotta have Twizzlers.' At the counter he asked for the guy to add a box and paid for everything without a word.

He ripped the top, tugged one out and took a bite as we walked back, but as we passed the mini arcade he stopped and stepped just inside the cornered wall. I, of course, followed.

'They're strawberry, just like you, so ya gotta try one.' He offered up an inch-long bite, but when I reached, he pulled away. 'Nope.' He held it right to my lips, almost daring me to bite it from his hand.

I smiled, confused, thrilled, in awe and burning up from the inside out. I'm pretty sure my ears were pink, and it wasn't just because they were adorned with multiple neon fuchsia hoops.

He leaned in more. 'Just hold it in your teeth, I wanna see something.'

What was he doing? This was the great and powerful Ollie, and he was talking with me? Like this? I didn't move. He tapped the liquorice on my lower lip, blue eyes never leaving mine, and for whatever reason, I opened my mouth and claimed it.

'Don't move,' he said, almost in a whisper, and leaned inches away.

Slowly, he bit over the extended liquorice; his lips gently pressed to mine, and after what seemed forever, he bit through and leaned back, licking his lips. 'Yeah, the gloss does taste like strawberry.' He handed me the box and left.

I stood there, stunned. He kissed me. That was a kiss, right? Yes, that most definitely was a kiss, I decided.

Looking back, I wonder if that was a test. Would I tell Dora? I didn't, of course, because I desperately wanted it to happen again. And after that night, when he called me Shortcake, I didn't mind. It was like we had a secret. The first of many, as it turned out.

'Libby?'

'What? Sorry, Ollie . . .' I shift on the sofa to shake away the memory.

'I'm sure your hair looks great, but why didn't you keep your curls?' His voice drops an octave so it's deep and breathy. 'You know I always liked your curls.'

Right, we were talking about the makeover. I sigh, still smiling. 'Well, thank you, but your sister and Finn were in charge, remember?'

'I remember lots of things . . .' It's almost as if he were lying beside me.

Does he remember that?

See? I don't need marriage, or kids, or their stupid intervention set-ups. I have love. I do. The kind that takes you over, sweeps you off your feet, and leaves you breathless. I always have.

'Mmm, I hope your next date goes better. You deserve a nice night out, even if it can't be with me.'

Maybe I'm breathless from chasing the past.

Rolling over, I stare at the ceiling. Dread fills me and sits heavy in my chest. The tears are right there, and I'm trying everything to keep them from taking over: reciting lyrics, then a shopping list of supplies needed for the store, even saying them backwards. I'm beyond tired, so why can't I just sleep?

Time passes this way. I have no idea how much. The clock doesn't work, and I can't manage the effort to move and look at the one in the kitchen.

Dr P.'s words rattle around inside my head relentlessly.

'Describe what it feels like, Libby,' Dr P. asked during one of our first meetings.

'What depression feels like?' I popped my eyes, at a loss for words.

He nodded. 'Since I don't experience it, how can I really know what you're feeling?'

He had a point. But how do you describe something so dense? Empathy is recognizing another's struggle, but true understanding only comes from personally living it. My eyes met his, and I shrugged.

'Just try.' He scratched under his fuzzy chin, waiting.

'Well . . . it's not like when you're sad, or upset with a friend or anything. It's not the same. It's . . .' I leaned back in the wingback chair and let it swallow me as I considered my words. 'When I'm upset normally, that's all it is. You get fired up about something or someone hurts your feelings and whatever, you get over it like everyone else, but . . . sometimes at night it's like a switch is thrown. I can physically feel it happen and everything starts moving in slow motion.'

Dr P. sat up. He was really listening, interested. 'How do you mean?'

'Um . . . I can think rationally, but the emotions are blown out of proportion and get distorted. They're super-heavy, and then . . .' I stopped, not wanting him thinking my Crazy Train was completely off the rails.

'This is a safe place, you can say anything. I won't judge you.'

'I judge myself.' It slipped out before I could filter it, so I quickly tried to explain. 'You know the saying, "the voice inside your head"? Yeah, well, mine has a nasty attitude and gets mean. Really mean.'

This was when I really fought for medication, anything to shut the voice up. I had been seeing Dr P. for a few weeks, and I was still not sleeping and beyond exhausted. 'If clinical depression is when your hormones get stuck and go out of whack, and I have borderline episodes, why not just send me to someone who can prescribe something to get it back in sync? I'd be set and it'd be done.' I was being stubborn, resisting his methods and really not seeing the point.

He rubbed under an eye and took his time to answer. Maybe he got this question a lot; maybe he was frustrated with me. 'Sometimes the meds are needed, for instance in postpartum . . . this is a chemical imbalance from a major change in the body, not from prolonged stress or emotional trauma. Medication is used to reset things, and it's temporary.'

My jaw clenched. Not what I wanted to hear.

'And you are functioning in the day-to-day; otherwise it would make sense to consider it, but only alongside treatment. Medication should never replace therapy. That's only treating the symptom of an underlying problem. If you stopped the meds and never worked it through, you'd be right back where you started the minute you came off them.'

My arms crossed. 'But talking can't fix the problem. Maybe it can relieve some of the stress, but what can it fix?'

'You're right. It can't fix or change the events that led to the trauma, but it can change how your body *processes* it, and this allows it to heal and move on. But you have to deal with it, let it out.'

I drummed my fingers. I didn't want to let it out. I wanted to bury it.

'Why do you think you wake up crying, Libby? You've pushed everything so far down for so long, your body *has* to release it somehow. And maybe it's only when you're not standing guard, it can sneak out. It's a natural process and it *must* be allowed.'

That's what he said back then, but I'm still dealing with it now. How much could there really be to let out? And is that even a good idea?

CHAPTER 5

'West End Girls'
The Pet Shop Boys, 1985

Lower East Side woman

It's Monday, early afternoon, and I'm at the store reviewing the legal notice I received from the property owners. Well, I was. I balled it up again, and this time chucked it at the wall. Now I'm staring at the wadded paperwork, knowing I need to pick it up.

I don't understand how they can make me vacate in thirty days. I've been here forever, and I have a lease. What if I refuse? Are they going to show up and physically remove me? I'm half-tempted to rally support and make a big fuss about it publicly. Maybe then they'd back off? At least I've taken the initiative and called Finn for legal counsel. We're meeting for lunch today.

I slap my palms on the desk so it rattles, stand, and shuffle to the restroom, passing Jas on my way. In spite of his rubbish clothing choices – today being no different, with his faded yellow Pac-Man T-shirt and ripped jeans – Jasper's somewhat brilliant. So after I meet with Finn, I'll have him weigh in on the situation;

55

but *only* if it's legit and I really have to quit, or move or whatever, which I won't because it's far from Hammer time. See? I'm being proactive *and* positive. Yay, Libby.

Leaning over the sink, I study my face. God, I look tired. I swear wrinkles have appeared around my eyes overnight. *And what are these?* Outlines? Leaning closer, I smile, then release. The paper-thin indents on either side of my mouth remain, and are a perfect match.

I pop the door and call out to Jasper, 'Do you think I'm wrinkly?'

A browsing teen in a grey skull hoodie and skin-tight black pants turns and looks in my direction. As if considering, his eyes scan the length of me.

'Don't you dare answer that,' I say, death-glaring him before he has the chance. Startled, he quickly looks down.

Jas is singing 'Come on Eileen' and dancing a bit while he organizes paperwork. He believes that Dexy's Midnight Runners fall squarely into post-punk new wave, so he likes them. They also slant pop, but it's not worth the argument. He doesn't get fired up like Ollie; instead he gets philosophical. I get frustrated.

'*Jas!*' I scream, my voice breaking the air, cutting through the music.

He turns in my direction. So does the teen, only to pretend he didn't.

'Sorry?' asks Jasper.

I take a few steps in his direction and repeat my question, impatiently. 'Do you think I'm wrinkly?'

'The lyric is do you think I'm *sexy*, and . . .' He eyes the slouchy hooded sweatshirt dress I have layered over stirrup leggings, and shrugs. 'I don't know, I wouldn't say in an obvious way.'

'Not *sexy*, wrinkly. Is my face wrinkly?' I lift my chin for his assessment, showing no expression, so I don't appear creased.

He steps to within inches of me, pushes straight blonde hair from his eyes and narrows them in consideration. Lifting a hand to my jaw, he turns me first left, then right, then locks his gaze with mine. His eyes are the colour of faded denim, where it goes light in the creases behind the knees. I've never really noticed before.

Just as I'm about to say something, he does. 'I'd say freckly, which I quite like.'

I smile. It's a nice thing to say, even if it's total crap. Stepping back, I reset a normal conversational space. 'Why can't men just say it like it is? Sorry, 'ol girl, but yes, at almost thirty-three you've gone completely south.'

'Because men like sex, and if we say that, we'll never get any.'

I laugh, knowing it's true. He's still looking at me. Well, my hair. 'What?'

'You're all smooth and . . . curvy.' He bobs his head and hand around in tandem to give the word a visual.

It's a weird visual.

'It was for the first Eighties intervention date. Not that it was a date, or that it matters.'

'And this first date that doesn't matter was into mermaid waves? That's a little kinky.'

'Brainwaves. He's an anesthesiologist, and more like creepy. It was horrible.'

'You could just go out with me.' Leaning against the checkout, he props his elbows behind him on the counter. When I don't say anything, he just keeps going. 'Right, I forgot. *That's* why you're doing their Eighties intervention thing. To *avoid* going out with me. Isn't that what Dora said?'

I meet his eyes – the washed-denim eyes that now hold too much truth. *My* truth. '*Why* do I tell you everything?'

'Because you trust me, might even fancy me, if you'd ever give it half a chance.' He offers a crooked smile. Deep-set creases frame it, adding to his appeal.

Why do we like this in men? How is this fair?

My lips purse and I glance away, pretending sudden interest in the latest *Popstar* magazine. I mean, what am I gonna say? It's all a bit J. Geils, isn't it? He loves her, she loves him, he loves somebody else, and you just can't win.

But I want to win. And yeah, love does stink. So does the teen who's circling round. In fact, he 'Smells Like Teen Spirit'. What is up with teenage boys and lack of deodorant and personal hygiene?

The hitched door grabs my attention. It's Finn. The beard's gone. He's dressed for work, with brown suspenders to hold the modern-cut dress pants, but missing the matching coat. It's probably at the office. 'So, did she say yes yet?' Finn asks Jas with a smirk.

'I'll be back in a bit,' I say, gathering my stuff, ignoring the comment. I also avoid Jasper's look. I don't have to see it to know he's giving me one.

♫

Finn taxied over from midtown Manhattan, where his firm's located. Here in the rinky-dink diner just down the street from Pretty in Pink, decked out in his proper business attire, he's certainly out of place. It makes me think of the Pet Shop Boys song 'West End Girls'; except I'm not a girl, and this is the Lower East Side. The place is quiet, since it's after the lunch crowd. Wish my mind was. It's buzzing from worry, and now with the lyrics, 'You think you're mad, too unstable. Kicking in chairs and knocking down tables' – which is what I'm gonna do, if he doesn't give me some good news already.

'Well?'

Finn's eyes dart from me back to the lease document. 'You know I don't practise commercial law, right?'

'Sure, but can't you pass it along to someone who does?' I ask in desperation.

'Yeah, I guess . . .' Finn sets it down to review the eviction notice, which I've folded into the popular Eighties fortune-teller game. His eyes lift questioningly as he slides his fingers into the slots and opens and closes the folds. 'Should I pick a colour or a number? Or better yet, ask a deep, meaningful question? Is Libby screwed?' He opens and closes with each syllable. 'Y-E-S.'

'Very funny,' I say, swiping it back to unfold and smoothing it flat. 'Just tell me this doesn't give them the right to officially evict me. Then I can burn it and be done with it all. I mean, I'm never late with rent, and I *have* a lease.'

His eyes narrow as he picks it up again and reads. I drum my fingers and wait.

And wait.

God, and wait. 'It's total crap, right?'

'Uh . . .' His eyes flick up. 'Looks like you *had* a lease, 'cause it was a sublease, and it's with a company that's dissolved, so—'

'So? So what?'

'So, sorry, looks like you're screwed.' He frowns. 'From the looks of this, they didn't have legal permission to subdivide the space. You're actually lucky the property owners are even letting you stay on in the meantime.' He takes a sip of tea, then adds, 'Have you contacted them? See if you can buy out the space or set up something with them direct? 'Cause then you could remodel – which I could help with, 'cause yeah, the space is hideously outdated.'

'The space is supposed to be, and yes, of course I called 'em. I talked with their attorney. Turns out they own commercial property all over the country with major retail chains established, and someone big is already in negotiations for the building.' I start folding my paper napkin into a micro-flyer, my nervous energy needing a release.

Finn glances out the window at the busy street. 'Well, it's a great location. I'll give ya that much. Lots of traffic.'

'I know, right?' I slump back in my seat and fly my plane. It's too heavy, and only glides a second before it nose-dives with a spin and crashes to the floor. 'That's why I'm not moving. And really, where am I supposed to go in thirty days? How is that even possible? I can't find new affordable space and move the store in a month. This is New York City, for Pete's sake.' I'd have to get packing supplies, actually pack, and hire movers. Years of stuff has accumulated there. I can't even fathom how long that would take me. And really, where am I moving it to?

Finn's face has crinkled into a frown.

'What?'

'You don't have a month,' he says drily, and motions to the document in his hand. 'This is dated from two weeks ago. You, my dear, have two weeks.'

My stomach plummets. I rip back the document and stare at the date. *Oh God*, he's right. I've been avoiding it, thinking somehow it would just go away or resolve itself. I shake my head and hand it back. 'It doesn't matter.' I wave a hand to dismiss the entire thing. 'There has to be something. Just work your magic and find a loophole.'

'Oh, honey, even I don't have that kind of power. This needs – *wait* – Seth Merriweather. He specializes in commercial law, and if anyone can pull this off, it's him. Plus, you're scheduled to meet him anyway.'

'Whattaya mean? Why would I meet him anyway?' I ask, fiddling with my half-eaten turkey and Swiss.

'He's your criminal date.' Finn takes a sip of tea and smirks from behind the rim.

'The criminal is a *lawyer*?'

'Aren't all lawyers criminal?' Finn places the documents in his messenger man-bag and slouches comfortably back in his chair, the small smile still playing with the corners of his lips. 'Besides, you might like him. He's a complete throwback. And he doesn't think you're mute, unlike Dora's Brain date fiasco.' He laughs softly and glances at the waiter while my coffee's given a topper.

I break off a small piece of crust and nibble, not really tasting anything. 'Seriously, Dora's gone mad, hasn't she? A mute? A brain infection? An entourage?'

'Yeah, but in her defence, she had no idea he was bringing anyone.' Finn stifles a laugh. 'But, oh God, it was *fantastic*.'

'Shut up.' I lean on the table and cover my face with my hands, but I'm laughing too.

His phone buzzes and he checks the screen, gives me an apologetic glance, then turns to take it. Big-shot attorney, so I'm used to his limited time. I'm just happy he managed to sneak out for lunch today. Even if Finn enjoys seeing me squirm, I like spending time with him. He reminds me of Oliver, of when we were all together, when things were simple and fun.

Once, Ollie's parents went on holiday, leaving him to keep an eye on Dora. Not their best judgement call as parents, I have to say. Oliver and Finn threw a huge party, and they were so smart about it, really clever. The guys moved all the furniture upstairs, locking everything valuable away so the house was completely empty. Ollie actually arranged for a cleaning service the next afternoon. The carpets and floors were spotless, so his parents never knew.

Dora and Finn never knew what else was locked away upstairs.

'What are you doing in here?' Ollie asked when he stumbled into his room that evening, red plastic cup in hand.

My heart jumped. I was hiding, wedged between furniture and boxes on the floor, watching *Late Night* on his small TV.

'You OK?' Ollie shut the door, taking long steps over chairs and end tables to reach my small cleared-away spot near his closet.

'Yeah, just, ya know, it's loud and . . .' I pushed back my hair and straightened some. The limited space meant I had to crane my neck to see his face as he hovered over me from disproportionately long legs. He was still a rock-star giant, and I was still his biggest fan.

'Hold this a second.' He handed me the cup and plopped down, practically falling on top of me. 'Whatcha watchin'?'

'Oh, ah . . .' I motioned to the screen, somewhat embarrassed that I'd rather be here than out there with all their friends. I had no idea why Ollie sat next to me in the dark, or why he stayed. We watched in silence for a while, then he burst out laughing at something on the show and spilled his drink in my lap.

'Oh, shit, sorry.' He grabbed a shirt from his laundry basket and started dabbing at me, but then froze with his hand resting on my thigh, his face so close.

I mean, if I looked up . . . God, what was going on? Ollie leaned over more, and put his arm round me. All I could hear was his breathing and my heart. It was going to explode from my chest. Was this really going to happen?

It was the Tiffany song acted out in real life. We were alone, no one around, and he did put his arm around me . . . I dared to hold his gaze, and then . . . this is when he really kissed me.

Soft at first, as if he were afraid of my reaction – he was, after all, seventeen, almost eighteen, which meant almost a grown man. I was almost sixteen. Ollie tasted of beer and Doritos. And God, I was in love. I'd been kissed before, but not like this.

My stomach swarmed with butterflies and when he moved to my neck, gently sucking against the skin, my body responded in ways I didn't know were possible. My fingers were clumsy but curious as I ran them through his hair and across the muscles of his chest. Without thinking, I dropped them lower.

'Whoa, whoa, hold up, Libbs . . .' He pushed back so he could see me. His blue eyes were bloodshot and inky. He smiled and shook his head. 'If you do that, there's no stopping. And you're not that kind of girl.'

There was a new texture to his voice, a rasp, and I'd put it there. I didn't want to stop, I wanted Ollie. I wanted to be that kind of girl. I tugged my hand away from his and –

'Libbs, I'm serious.' He growled a little. 'You're only—'

'I'm old enough,' I said, lifting my chin.

His head threw back. 'Please tell me you're not screwing arou—'

'No. God. Get real . . .' I wanted him to think I could, not that I already was.

'Good.' His voice settled back into softer tones and he pressed against the wall again, offering me space under his arm. 'I'd hate to think anyone was messing with you.'

I laughed. 'Aren't you messing with me?'

The corners of his lips quirked up and his eyes, although dewy from the beer, seemed to twinkle when he smiled. 'That's different. I'm not messing messing with you. I'm just doing, ya know . . . this.' His lips grazed my cheek, creating a trail of feather-light sensations. I turned, and this kiss was even slower, softer, better. God, it was better.

We stayed in his room all night, kissing and laughing. That's all we ended up doing, but it was perfect, more than enough, because it was more than anything I'd ever done. But what I really liked, more than anything, was how we talked.

He told me about his dad, and how much pressure he was under to live up to his expectations. Then he told me how I got him in a way that hardly anyone else did, and how special I was.

'Unlike anyone I've ever met. Way cooler than most girls,' that's what he said. No one had ever talked to me like that before.

I don't remember falling asleep that night, but I woke to the sound of voices and furniture being moved. It was early, or late for those that hadn't slept, and it was over. But really, it was only the beginning: a real turning point in our little story. I never would've guessed, some fifteen-plus years later, it'd still be unfinished.

I smile wistfully at Finn across the table as he pockets the phone.

He gives me a smile in return. 'OK then . . .' He pushes out his chair and busies himself with his bag. 'Need to get back, but I'll turn these over and get word to you straight away.' He stands and stabs a pointed finger in my direction. 'Start looking for a new place, though.'

'I won't have to if you guys do your job.' I stand too.

'Oh, we're helping Dora with wedding plans tonight, and tomorrow's the fitting, right?'

'That's the plan. Finally getting her bridal stuff sorted.'

'Trust me, she needs the help.' He pulls a face. Typical Finn.

I watch him leave, saying I'm gonna finish my lunch, but really I'm just postponing the conversation with Jas about Pretty in Pink – the one I can't avoid any more. The one I'm desperate to. Typical Libby.

CHAPTER 6

'Are We Ourselves?'
The Fixx, 1984

Unfortunately

In less than two weeks' time I'll be thirty-three – and without my store, unless I can pull off the impossible. I've hardly slept, so yeah, I'm in a spiky mood to say the least. Maybe that's why I'm dressed in layered brights. I'm trying to counter the gloom of my disposition. The green top has slashes across the front in perfect rows to showcase the underlying yellow. It matches the plastic shades I have holding back my wild hair.

'You're muttering,' Jas says from behind the register.

'No, I'm thinking, big difference.' I'm also refiling the discount CDs in my owner's Top Five weekly special display. No one gets what makes them special except for me, although Jas tries to figure it out. It's become a game of 'look inside my soul', a mix-tape poem using others' words and seemingly random factoids to express my feelings, with three rules to play.

First rule of Top Five: once solved, you do not talk about Top

Five. Second rule of Top Five: once solved, *you do not talk about Top Five*. That would be way too embarrassing. It's a look inside my soul, remember? And the third and final rule of Top Five: there must be a cohesive connection.

It's geektastic, and over time Jas has become obsessed. Last week he deciphered it within hours. Every song had something to do with my upcoming birthday. Way too easy.

This week's not as much about the tracks as the artist, although there is a common denominator with those as well, just to keep him guessing.

'That's an eclectic list,' Jasper says over my shoulder, reviewing each CD's tracks.

Nirvana, 'About a Girl'; INXS, 'Devil Inside'; Milli Vanilli, 'Blame It On The Rain'; Boston's 'More than a Feeling', and Crowded House, 'Don't Dream It's Over'.

'This one you'll never figure out.'

His smile pulls wide and quick. 'Oh, Libby London, I believe I will.'

I smile in return. But mine's forced. I need to tell him what's going on. Glancing round the store, I check whether we're alone and for the moment we are, so I begin. The knot in my stomach tightens as I explain losing the lease and the reason why; the two-week time-frame to find new space; how if we fail to leave the premises, I'll be slapped with fines. 'But I wouldn't worry,' I say, with abundant and zealous confidence. 'I've asked for Finn's firm to look into things to see if anything can be done. I really don't think anything will come of it. I mean, can you imagine moving Pretty in Pink?'

His brows pull down in thought, a significant crease between them. 'Have you started looking around?'

Panic gurgles from somewhere deep. Tiny tar bubbles between the cracks. The question holds more meaning than it implies. It asks: are you being proactive and smart about this? Have you put in the legwork? Am I going to be sacked? Will we stay afloat in an iffy economy if we move locations? Who's moving us? Should we start packing? When will you tell the staff?

I try to answer them all with a dismissive nod and calm composure. 'No, truthfully, I don't think we'll end up moving.'

'Well, maybe just in case, we should keep an eye out for available space.' The light whitewash denim of his eyes turns blue-canyon dark and uncharacteristically serious. 'There's a new building conversion with Now Leasing signs up a few blocks away; I can check it out when I leave.'

'Sure, if you want, but . . .' I shrug it away. This sucks. Telling him makes it real. His reaction makes it more so.

This can't be happening.

When I don't say anything, Jasper steps closer. 'Hey, you know what Bobby McFerrin would say – "Don't Worry, Be Happy".' His eyes relax some, but I can see the concern behind them.

'Right, and as Howard Jones would say, "Things Can Only Get Better".' I play along with a stale smile, knowing he's doing our Eighties song game to cheer me, but it feels more like REM's 'End of the World', and I think we both know it.

And if I don't get moving, I'll never hear the end of it from Dora. She expected me to meet her at the department store ten minutes ago.

♫

This is so not my store. I'd much prefer a consignment place with vintage baubles and treasures, and that's only if I absolutely have to shop. Not that I'm actually shopping. I'm following Dora around, acting as a human clothes-rack.

Glossy mannequins dressed in muted pops of autumn greet us in every aisle of the department store. Dora's low and wide heels click obnoxiously on the white marble floors, causing her to unconsciously follow the carpet runners. This is probably by design. A genius layout and marketing plan to guide the customers through elaborate high-end merchandise.

'So, this Nigel Harrington guy is a friend of Finn's? Isn't Finn supposed to choose my outfit, then, isn't that the rule?' I ask while trailing behind. I so don't have time for this. I should be looking for retail space, or harassing Finn so I don't have to. I haven't mentioned anything to Dora. One, I know Finn will open his big mouth soon enough; and two, she has her wedding and baby stuff. She doesn't need my stuff.

Another shirt's tossed over my arm. And I don't need all *this* stuff.

'Finn texted over his demands: something sporty and cute,' Dora says, turning, her eyes fixed towards my grey and white Converse All Stars. 'Do you have proper footwear?'

I glance down, pulling a face. 'I have shoes, isn't that proper enough?'

'According to Finn, Nigel is a top athlete and will probably take you somewhere fun, so you need to dress accordingly. Oh, and he's super-competitive, at least that's what Finn says, so bring your A-game.' She holds up a long-sleeved yoga cover-up only to cram it back, deciding it's a no.

'How competitive?' My brow furrows; I can hear the Athlete's words from *The Breakfast Club*. *You've got be number one. I won't tolerate any losers. Win, win, win!* 'So . . . are we going out to eat?' I have an A-game when it comes to that. I once won the hot-dog-eating contest in Times Square.

'Oh, I don't know,' Dora answers, half-interested, now eyeing a tennis-style skirt.

'I can't believe I'm even considering this again after Theo the Brain Pain.'

Dora stops short and eyeballs me. Her look flashes anger, annoyance, or maybe just baby-induced hunger.

'Do you need a twisty pretzel?' I ask before she can say anything, to distract her train of thought. 'You could get it without salt so you don't retain more – *what*, you're puffy, so I'm being super-duper considerate.'

'No, you're not.'

'You don't look bad, but you are a little—'

'*No*. Not about that. I know I'm waterlogged, I'm talking about Theo. Look, I get I made a complete cock-up of the entire situation, but Libbs, he's a really great guy.' She blows out a breath of frustration. 'I mean, if I didn't screw it up, maybe you'd know that, so I take responsibility, I do. But knock off the jokes at his expense, OK?'

My eyebrows drop low in confusion, maybe a little from guilt. 'OK. Sure, sorry.'

Satisfied, Dora again starts sliding clothes across the rack. This is where I should leave things, but when have I ever been known to do that? 'Soooo . . . what makes Dr Theo so great?'

She whips her head round, mouth hanging agape.

'I'm serious. I wanna know. I'm actually curious what you see in him. As far as looks, OK, not bad, but he was painfully awkward and cagey.' I shrug. 'So, what am I missing?'

The aggravation melts away from her expression as she considers. 'Well, for one, he's nice to me when I tag along with Dean to their racquetball games. He always asks if I need anything and seems really concerned about the pregnancy and with how I'm feeling.' Her lip juts out a little. 'Dean could take a lesson on that, if you ask me. A little pampering goes a long way. Oh, and he volunteers at that house charity, you know, where people give up their weekends to help build, and at the end the home's donated to a family in need.'

'So he's—'

'Kind. He's really a kind soul, who cares about people, and that's why he gave up his time to treat you,' she says, throwing another pair of casual trousers over my arm. 'Those are called boyfriends. They have lots of zippers, so you'll like 'em.'

My brows slant. 'I won't if my boyfriend can wear 'em.'

She ignores me and starts for the dressing room. Guess I'm supposed to follow. I slant my arms to the left and crane my neck to the right so I can see where I'm going. The view is still obstructed by the stack of clothes. 'OK, but Dora, a brain-infected mute? That was hardly kind of *you*.'

'I already apologized. It just . . . got away from me. You know how that happens sometimes. And the point is, *he* cared. Enough to call in favours, and get other people involved, and—'

'OK, right, I get it. I misjudged.'

She spins, a sly grin flashing across her face. 'Buy me a pretzel after we're done, and all is forgiven.'

'Deal.' I knew she needed a pretzel. 'So in this grand plan of yours, what happens if I like one of these guys? Do I still have to go out with the rest?'

'Don't be difficult.' She stops in front of an open dressing room, steps inside and hangs the clothes.

'No, really, what if I *adore* Nigel and his athletic ways? Why should I have to endure any more dates?'

'Look, if you really don't want to go through with all the dates, just go with Jasper. Then I'm happy, he's happy—'

'But I'm not. We've talked about this, OK?' I huff and disappear behind the curtain, dumping my armload on the stool. I'm *not* trying all that on. 'We work together, we're friends, he's younger—'

'He's hot, he's into you, and you really like him.' With a *whoosh* she pushes the fabric to the side, squares her rounded self and blows out a breath. 'That's the problem. I think it scares you. Look, things didn't work out the way you hoped with Ollie, the way we *all* hoped, but you can't just stop living because . . . well, you need to get out there, Libbs, you do. I'm beyond worried.'

I'm beyond everything. I *whoosh* the curtain back, so all that's left is her swollen feet peeping underneath.

'Libby . . .' Dora's voice softens as she talks from the other side. 'I know you still love my brother, and that's OK, but sweetie, you need to move on and let yourself be happy. It's—'

My phone rings to break the need of some meaningful reply on how I've tried, I'm fine, leave it alone. It's Jas, so I answer. '*Hello, is it me you're looking for?* And I'm seriously glad you called . . .' Grateful for the interruption is more like it.

'Lionel Richie, 1983. And why? Were you thinking of me? Have I become your "Obsession"?'

'Sure, and good try. Animotion, 1985. Now what's up?'

Dora's foot taps her irritation; then she swivels and disappears.

'I'm doing some location searches, but I need to know how much space you're wanting.'

'Oh, um . . .' With the phone wedged between my chin and shoulder, I strip from my jeans and step into the first leggings thing, trying to hoist them up by jumping on one leg in a small circle while mentally figuring my retail footprint. I need storage, an office, at least one bath . . . and the sales floor needs to be about the same, so . . . 'Maybe 3,000 square feet?' I already know I'll never be able to afford that in New York. The only way I've managed thus far is because it's a sublease, and Crafty Cathy's was struggling even back then.

Another jump, jump, turn, and I almost fall. This is the most exercise I've had in a while, and now seeing my half-naked body in the three-fold mirror as I bounce, I'm considering rejoining my gym; if I ever even cancelled the membership.

'What are you doing?' Jas asks.

'Oh, um, Dora's torturing me, remember?'

Whoosh. She slides open the curtain and stink-eyes me. 'Who are you talking to?'

'I gotta go,' I say to Jasper, knowing Dora will say something inappropriate if she knows it's him.

'*Wait.*' Jas shouts into the phone. 'The Top Five. All the songs charted on Billboard in the Eighties, except one. Does that mean something, am I even close? Yes? Say I am. I know I am.'

'You're half right. There's more. *Really* gotta go.' I click off the phone and toss it into my bag. 'Well?' I do a little sashay in my forced-upon outfit and turn for assessment.

Dora's lips curl in distaste as she eyes the half-skirt-half-leggings thing. 'Eh, I don't know . . . and they're on backwards.'

I look down. 'Who cares, I don't like 'em.'

'Try those.' Dora points to another selection, then slides the curtain closed again. 'We still have about an hour before my mom expects us, so I'm gonna see what else I can find.'

'Another hour?' *God.*

♫

Brooklyn Heights, where we all grew up, is only a twenty-minute commute from downtown in light traffic. The neighbourhood is neither overly trendy nor commercial, but hosts impeccable streets lined with proudly restored row houses. And Dora and Ollie's parents' home is one of the best. It's lovely, with a butter-cream wooden shingle facade and small-paned windows. What started as a project when they were first married has become a showpiece and a source of family pride.

Even the small back yard, fenced high for privacy and lavishly landscaped with flowers, is spectacular. I notice the deck's been freshly stained since my last visit. It lacks the weather-worn look that blends into the elements, and instead stands out as an unnatural red. I gently rock the small stand-alone swing, sip my iced tea and enjoy the breeze. This is nice, even if it means enduring everyone's constant gabble.

'Did you notice the new bloom of the month?' Mrs C. asks me, Finn and Dora, motioning to the hammered copper pot on the side table. 'It's an autumn mum. Last month it was yellow roses.'

'Did you plant them?' Finn asks.

'I did, yes, near the back gate. I wonder if the monthly flower deliveries will continue on past the New Year, or if it'll be the fruit club again. I much prefer the flowers.'

'Well, I liked the fruit,' Dora adds, then sips her tea. 'Oh, and the desserts year, although I probably gained a few pounds from all the chocolate.'

'The wines from around the world were very nice, too.' Mrs C. fans herself. 'I just wish I knew who keeps sending them. I'd send a proper thank-you.'

Finn laughs. 'Oh, Mrs C., you naughty girl, you know who it is.' His teasing smile causes Mrs C.'s cheeks to take on a rosy shade of pink. He always jokes she has a long-lost undisclosed admirer.

Dora likes to think it's her father, but it's obvious she loves it when Finn mentions the possibility of a secret, unrelenting crush. Her reactions are cute. I think regardless of age, women want to feel desired and beautiful.

I'm relaxed for the first time all week. I like it here. I always have. It's busy with family squabbles, motherly fussing, and rich in memories, especially ones of Oliver.

In summer, the gravel surrounding the patio became hot lava rocks. One touch and you'd die. The object was to move from one side to the other, in between the thorny shrubs, while saving the Doodle Bugs. Those were rocks we coloured faces on. We'd spend hours with Sharpies, drawing the eyes and expressions. Even now, if you kick around enough in the beds, you can find some.

The small gazebo at the back of the property became our pre-teen hangout. This is where Dora and I scribbled on notebooks and gossiped about what boy had smiled at us in the hall or said something awful. Oliver and Finn would skulk along the shrubbery to eavesdrop, or douse us with the hose.

I see Oliver everywhere I look. I can picture him standing at the porch door now. One hand over his head bracing the frame, the other casually propped on his hip. He's in jeans and an open flannel, with sleeves rolled to the crook of his elbows. He smiles at me, the teasing kind, where the eyes crinkle playfully.

Even this deck holds memories. How many times had we gathered round the small screened fire pit for toasted marshmallows, or watched the fireworks in the distance on the Fourth? This is home, even if it wasn't mine.

'So what do you think, Libby? Should we have the wedding here? Since this is Dora's second time around and she's with—'

'*Mom!*' Dora's brows furrow deep.

'Well, it's *true*, and we agreed something small and simple was more in order this time.' Dora's mom stirs her tea so the spoon clinks in the glass. She's just randomly doing that, she hasn't added any more sugar.

Finn nods. 'I think this would be absolutely divine, right, Libbs?'

He's on the *divine* bandwagon now? *Ugh.* I give a mental eye-roll. 'Definitely, the garden would be spectacular, Mrs C.' I've called Dora and Ollie's mom that since we were kids; she doesn't seem to mind. Their home always reminded me of the TV show *Happy Days*, where the parents were together and everyone was, well, happy. Maybe that's why I spent so much time here. That, and they fed me.

'Finn, I need some things moved into the attic. Would you mind helping before dinner?' Mrs C. asks, lifting her chin. 'You are staying for dinner, right?'

'As if you have to ask. Now what do you need moved?'

'Ask Mr C., he knows what needs to go, just don't let him climb the ladder. You know how he falls from everything.' She grimaces, lowering her voice as soon as Finn's up and out of sight. 'I'm so glad he shaved. I mean, really, what was he thinking? Did you like it, Libby? No, of course not. I do like your hair. That's quite new, isn't it?'

'She had a date.' Dora leans in. 'With an *anesthesiologist*.'

'Oh, that's wonderful, dear.' Mrs C.'s eyes are wide, looking to each of us, excited. 'So? Was he polite? Well-mannered? How'd it go? Did you like him?'

Before I can answer, Dora does. 'Disaster, utter disaster . . .'

Dora tells her mom everything, except how she personally caused the chaos. Of course, Dora's meddling usually does. She's responsible for Ollie's and my first break-up, too. Her plan, which was devised in about ten seconds, was for me to save face and Ollie to burn with jealousy. It only made him heat up in anger.

I smile to myself, lost in the memory.

We grew up without the internet, cell phones or any social media, so we were forced to communicate in archaic but highly skilled and creative ways. We basically were masters of origami note-folding and spent the majority of time in class writing the notes, folding them, passing them under the desks, and praying the teacher didn't discover the covert operation and confiscate.

Because, God, having them read out loud was the worst.

There were two types of popular note styles: the typical triangle, also used for finger-flick football, and the 'pull here' tabbed en-velope, the more personal of the two and preferred by girls.

While wearing Ollie's acid-washed denim jacket, I accidentally found a 'pull here' note, and it had a heart drawn on the tab. A heart, so yeah, I pulled. It was from Jeanie Styles, the little tramp. She hung out with us on occasion, had won Best Smile in last year's mock elections for yearbook, and had had her eye on Oliver since the beginning of the year. Everyone knew she crushed on him. Heck, she even told me once how lucky I was, and how tons of girls liked him. Whatever.

So yeah, it bothered me that she'd sent a note with a heart, but what upset me more was that it probably wasn't the first. I'm sure she flashed him her 'best smile' and flirted. And Jeanie was pretty enough, I guess. But she was completely unoriginal. I set my own fashion trends, she blindly followed everyone else's.

'Dora . . .' I leaned out from my desk and waved while Mrs McConnick wrote next week's speech assignment on the board. 'Dora,' I whispered again, only louder.

She looked up from doodling, blew a bubble and quickly sucked it back in. I held up the note to mean incoming. Tina in the next row took it and passed it to Deemer, who kicked Keith awake enough to grab and drop it over his shoulder with a fake stretch, but unfortunately a real yawn. It caught the teacher's attention. What a knob.

'What is that, Keith?' Mrs McConnick asked, already walking over with her hand outstretched.

Oh God. I looked at Dora in desperation, but it was too late. The teacher had taken possession and was holding it up over her head for everyone to see.

'Looks like Mr Fisher has a crush. The heart's a nice touch.' She smiled and pulled the tab as Keith protested that it wasn't his.

'Oh, right, you were passing it to Dora. In that case . . .' She handed it to Dora. 'Why don't you do the honours?'

'Um, I have laryngitis. So really, I shouldn't.' Dora's hand went to her throat and she gave a good throat clearing to prove her point.

The class laughed. I died. Dora had blown it. Why didn't she just make up something?

'I'll read it, Mrs McConnick,' Kelly Chambers said, hand held high.

Of course she would. Kelly reeked of Electric Youth, Debbie Gibson's perfume, and had hated me since the fifth grade because I wouldn't sit by her. Back then, she just reeked.

Kelly took the loose-leaf paper and began to read. 'Hey, Ollie . . .' She turned to look at me. So did everyone else.

Everyone thought it was a note from me to him, because well, we had been Together Forever. The 'I think you look cute today' comment and 'I'd love to see a movie this weekend' all seemed perfectly normal, until the dreaded closing . . .

'"OK, gotta bolt, luv ya cutie pie, your Jeanie-bean . . ."' Kelly looked up and smiled wickedly. 'Oh, and there's another heart over the "I".' She held it up and pointed as proof. 'So you and Ollie broke up?'

This is where Dora helped. Unfortunately. Her throat made a miraculous recovery. 'God, you guys. Libbs broke up with Ollie last week. She's dating Marc Leifer, so whatever.' She blew another bubble. It popped with the bell.

So did my world. We broke up? I may have been saved from responding, but really, it was only the beginning of my humiliation. Within five minutes, the entire school had heard of our break-up and new love interests, including Oliver.

'So you're into Marc?' Ollie asked, towering over me at my locker. He ran a hand through his slicked-back hair and glared at me with narrowed, accusatory eyes.

'So you're exchanging love notes with Jeanie-bean?' I threw back with an equal accusatory scowl. No hand through the hair, because, well, with so much hairspray, it wouldn't've made it.

'Whatever, Libby. I can't help it if she likes me.' His eyes dropped to his jean jacket. The one I was still wearing. The one I had no intention of giving back.

'You don't have to write her back. I mean, for real, Ollie.'

'What do you care? Aren't you into Marc now?'

'No.'

'No?'

'God, no. That was Dora. She said—'

'Yeah, I already got the 411, thanks.'

Poor Marc really thought I liked him too, and he and Ollie did fight after last period. Ollie claimed he'd won, but really it was a draw. Mr Oaks stopped it before a clear and concise winner could be called. After school, I babied Ollie's hand while he babied my ego, saying how Jeanie had nothing on me.

The memory ignites a flurry of flutters. It's crazy to imagine the feelings you have as a teenager could stay with you a lifetime. As we get older, every relationship is tainted by the ones before. You enter sceptical, wanting to be proved wrong. But with your first love, you aren't experienced enough to know any better. Your heart is wide open and unblemished. It's pure. That's why it stays with you.

Why Ollie's stayed with me.

'Libby, dear?'

'I'm sorry?' I shake my head to clear the past.

'Mom was just saying how everyone else is paired, so she was wondering if you were going to bring a date,' Dora says.

My eyes narrow. 'A date for what?'

'For the wedding, love.' Mrs C. refills her glass, then pauses. 'Are you OK?'

'Um . . . sure, I'm fine.' *More like lost.* I look to the garage, still seeing ghosts from my youth, still seeing Ollie.

I need to see Dr P.

CHAPTER 7

'If You Leave'
Orchestral Manoeuvres
in the Dark, 1986

I don't want to leave

'OK, I'm gonna get outta here, call me if anything comes up,' I say to Robbie, one of the teenagers who rotate the evening shift at the store. He has those doughnut earrings that deform the lobe to unnatural proportions. I can hardly stand to look at 'em.

My phone rings as I kick the door free and exit. I dig for it in my pocket and click connect. 'Hello?'

'Hey, you on your way? The guy's here now.' It's Jas. While searching online earlier I found some space nearby, made the call and made an appointment. I asked Jas if he'd meet me there to check it out.

'Almost there,' I say from the cab, knowing I'm already late. At least it's only three miles from our current location. Three miles doesn't sound like it'll make much difference, but in retail it's all about location. Right now, Pretty in Pink is just off a busy inter-section; we're visible and convenient, with street-side parking. It's perfect. And this? I glance round as we pull up, my early opti-mism already disintegrating.

Regardless of whether it's just around the block, this place seems 'A Million Miles Away'. And just like the *Valley Girl* DVD cover, where The Plimsouls song is featured, what's on the out-side doesn't match up. The girl posed with Nicholas Cage is not the female lead, just a random model, in case you were wonder-ing.

'Thanks,' I say, paying, then jump out. Wandering over, I squint up at the missing sign above the door. This used to be a phone store; I can tell because the missing letters are outlined by grime. Let's hope the landlord plans to paint.

Inside, Jasper's walking around with a man of about sixty. As I open the door, I'm struck by what they're walking on. Concrete. Where's the floor? Hell, where are the walls? There's no interior. I spin round, confused.

'Hi, you must be Libby London? I'm Carl Bonner.' His words echo in the empty space as he extends a massive hand. Every-thing about him is oversized, except his suit. It barely fits, and looks as if it may pop the two buttons that scream for release. He's also sweating profusely, and keeps dabbing at his forehead with a hanky.

'Nice to meet you,' I say, with a firm shake, but still stunned the place isn't finished. We have less than two weeks. 'When we talked earlier, you said it was ready for occupancy. There's nothing here.' I point out the obvious, then wipe my hand dry on my jeans, trying not to be.

'Oh, right, it's what we call white box. They all start this way.' Carl nods, his flappy jowls wobbling in different directions as if they disagree.

'But wasn't there a phone store here? Didn't they need offices and doors?' I ask, trying to reason. I mean, surely they had walls.

He laughs as if I've said something funny. I haven't.

Jasper rubs a hand over his mouth and jaw, the wince visible underneath. 'Yeah, I guess they rip everything out and start fresh for every client. I asked the same thing.'

'But this way you can build according to your brand.' Carl lifts his arms to showcase his point. 'Just imagine what you can do.'

'I can imagine this is costly.' Looking round, my stomach's on the floor. The unfinished one. 'And, well, if we really end up needing to relocate, which I'm hoping we won't, I need absolute, pull-up-the-moving-van, move-in ready. Not only do I not have the funds for a complete build-out, we don't have the time.'

'Well, unless you lease outside the city, this is standard.' Carl Bonner starts walking around, giving us his vision of how it could be set up, as if I haven't said anything. He shows us the corner and says how perfect it would be for an office. How the bathroom could be in close proximity, where we could divide for back storage options.

Jasper, seeing my frustration, interrupts the tour of empty space. 'What's ballpark rent and lease arrangements?'

'Oh, uh, for this space?' His face crumples in thought.

I have to hold my tongue from saying *no, the space next door*, which if it's finished and available, I'd rather go look at.

Carl dabs at his forehead again with his designated sweat-hanky. 'This is prime real estate and just over 1,800 square feet . . .'

Another dab before he shoves the hanky into his pants pocket. 'We'd need a five-year commitment, and there's a yearly grounds fee for maintenance, snow removal, trash . . .'

I stopped listening at 1,800 square feet. We have twice that now. I'm itchy to leave. I don't need to be sold. I need a dollar amount to see if it's even feasible, which I've already determined it's not.

'So, monthly rent?' Jasper asks again, stepping over Carl's words.

'Oh, well, you're looking at about thirty-six dollars a square foot, give or take, yeah, plus build-out. We'd give you a construction allowance of ten thousand to basically cover perimeter walls, bathroom and lights. You're welcome to use our contractors or your own, but anything over is your responsibility.'

I squint and mentally multiply the size and price. My stomach drops as I round up the answer. 'That doesn't even include build-out . . .'

Carl wobbles a bit as he readjusts his stance. 'Or common-area fees. CAM fees include snow and leaf removal, trash collection, repair and standard upkeep.'

I glance at Jasper, then step over Carl's words myself, knowing there's no way. 'OK, well, thanks for everything, we'll get back to you. Lots to consider.' I avoid another damp handshake and move towards the door, hoping Jasper's quick to follow.

Outside, I suck in a fast breath and blow it out so it plumps my cheeks. Right now, I pay eleven hundred a month plus utilities – that's it. Five times the rent, plus a yearly maintenance fee, utilities and build-out? Less than two weeks. Worse location. I may be sick. Finn better find a way for Pretty in Pink to stay put, or . . .

'Sorry. That isn't going to work, is it?' Jas says, catching my stride as I start to hail a cab.

'No, but I *really* appreciate you meeting me and . . .' I shake my head. 'It's just, I didn't deal with any of this last time. I bought it from the owner, just assumed the sublease. This is too much, there's just no way.' I glance back at the empty location and shake my head. 'Let's just hope we really won't need to move.'

'Yeah . . .' Jas runs a hand through his hair, causing spikes of blonde to jut up through his fingers. He leaves it there as if he's forgotten.

'Hey, I'll just look further out, and really, maybe we won't have to move. Don't stress it, OK?' I fake a smile, and wave the cab over.

'You looked stressed.'

'Yeah, well, I'm meeting Dora for her dress fitting, and I'm already late.' All I've been doing today is chasing time. I jump inside the cab, but Jasper taps the glass, so I roll down the window.

'Listen, you're right. Something will turn up. It's all good, OK?'

His eyes are warm and encouraging, and I'm grateful for his optimism, but nothing about this feels good.

♪♪

Mrs C., myself and Finn sip champagne cocktails and talk wedding details while Dora tries on yet another bridal gown. Yes, she's wearing white, and yes, they now make maternity wedding dresses. Who knew?

Finn wrinkles his beak-like nose and leans close. 'So are you ready to meet Nigel?'

'What's this about? Who's Nigel?' Mrs C. moves closer. She's wearing a plum-coloured mother-of-the-bride hat, for no other reason than she wants to. It's wide-brimmed, with a sloping edge and oversized feathers sprouting about.

The two of them are now huddled by my sides, leaving most of the horseshoe sectional empty and me squashed tightly between them. Finn's musk cologne battles Mrs C.'s floral and the combination stings my eyes. The last perfume I wore was Poison, which smelled good; their combination may actually kill me.

'Oh, Libby.' Mrs C. smiles with an excited nod, causing the feathers from her hat to graze and tickle my cheek. 'First a neurologist—'

'An anesthesiologist,' Finn says, patting her knee. 'Dr Theo is an anesthesiologist.'

'Oh, right.' She smiles affectionately. 'Well, it just warms my heart to see you getting back on the dating horse. You know . . .' Her eyes moisten and take on a gleam. 'I always imagined you would marry my Oliver, but I guess life doesn't always spin in the direction we think it should, does it?' She nods, with a wistful expression. 'Just nice to see you out there, really giving it a whirl.'

My stomach knots from her words. 'It's more like a dating merry-go-round, and honestly, it's making me dizzy,' I admit.

'Yes, well, you never know, maybe you'll be next?' Mrs C. motions to the surrounding bridal gowns with a quick nose-wrinkle.

Me? I glance at the sea of white ruffles, intricate beading and delicate lace. It could be fun to stand on the lighted platform with everyone gushing about how pretty I look. And I guess if marriage ever did suddenly become appealing to me, then I would've chosen Ollie. But God, no to the traditional white-pouffe gown. I'd opt for something with a bit more fashion flair, like Madonna's in the 'Like a Virgin' video.

In the video she's seen first in all black with a million necklaces dangling about, and then next, it's a dress with dramatic puffy sleeves. Hmm, maybe I don't like that dress after all. Oh, Billy Idol's 'White Wedding' video had . . . a coffin, and again, a woman dressed in black. Maybe it's a sign. 'I think I'll just pass,' I say, with a nose-wrinkle of my own.

The bridal assistant rounds the corner, arms full of something billowy and ruffled.

'Oh, Libby, this is the maid-of-honour dress I picked for you. I think it's perfection. It really screams your name, don't you agree?' Mrs C. stands, fans out the bulging skirt and fawns over it.

'Oh, that's divine,' says Finn, now standing to the other side.

She's lucky I don't scream. I mean, how much have they had to drink? My eyes widen as I take in the strange shiny mass of . . . 'What colour *is* that?'

'Salmon,' says the bridal assistant.

'You mean like the fish? Are they this colour?' I look to Finn. 'I always thought they were silver or greyish.'

'They're silver on the outside.' Finn nods, assuredly. 'On the inside, they're salmon.'

'So it's the colour of fish guts?' It just slipped out.

Mrs C. furrows her brows. 'Don't be difficult, Libby.'

'Mom? I need your opinion,' Dora says from behind the dressing-room door.

Mrs C.'s up and over, with Finn on her heels. I stay put, happily downing what's left of Finn's drink, since I've finished my own. I glance to Mrs C.'s, but she's emptied it. Being here makes me squirmy. This whole day has me squeamish, actually.

'Are you ready? Say you're ready!' Finn clucks, leaning out from the dressing room. 'Wait till you see her, she's . . .'

'*Divine*,' I say to myself, mocking him.

Dora walks out, her mom and Finn all smiles beside her. She lifts the train, stepping carefully onto the circular platform, and turns so she can see herself in the lighted mirror. She's beaming as the bridal assistant fluffs the material and makes adjustments.

Finn and Mrs C. chatter on about how beautiful she looks. They've swept her dark hair back and placed a small jewelled tiara on her head. It's quite lovely, and the dress . . .

It's dreamily suited to her, strapless, simple, flaring from under her bosom in an empire style. It's short, which is perfect to show off her spindly, although somewhat swollen, legs, and with the long train it still carries the elegance of a longer gown. She is divine. She's simply breathtaking. A vision.

A bride.

Dora's eyes meet mine in the mirror. I half-smile. My best friend's getting married again. She's found love twice, and I'm happy for her, ecstatic really . . .

Dora's brows crease. 'Libbs? Are you OK?'

Mrs C. and Finn spin round.

I flutter-blink to clear my vision. 'You're just really beautiful,' I say, shaking my head. 'Really. I'm just really happy for you, really.'

'That's a lot of reallys. How much bubbly has she had?' Finn asks, leaning close to Mrs C.

Dora ignores him, never breaking our connection. My lips contort to hold back the emotion. I'm plagued with it all of a sudden. My throat's tensed and my chest has swollen from the pressure to keep it all in.

Just seeing her like that, in that *dress*, and I'm . . . I'm . . . My face scrunches up. *Oh God, tears.* I have stupid tears. I'm a complete shambles; what is the matter with me?

'Oh, Libbs.' Dora gathers her dress and quickly steps from the platform, while the bridal attendant tries to keep her from falling over the train's excess fabric.

She sits beside me and takes my hand.

'You're beautiful,' I manage to get out again. 'Really, really lovely.' Glancing at Mrs C., the tears start afresh. 'My best friend's getting married. *Again.*'

'She's really snockered,' Finn whispers.

'I'm not snockered, I'm . . . I'm about to be thirty-three.' My voice cracks in a whisper. 'And I'm never getting married.' Now I'm blubbering. *Bloody hell.*

Dora buries me in her arms. I love her. I do. She knows I'm not intentionally being a prat. Maybe I have drunk too much. Maybe all this talk of dating, and Mrs C. bringing up Ollie and how she thought we'd end up together, is just too much. Maybe the thought of losing my shop location is. Or maybe I should have eaten something earlier; I *am* a bit light-headed. I sniff, and try to stop the blasted waterworks.

'Can you all give us a minute?' Dora asks.

Her mom and Finn walk towards the front shopping area, the assistant in tow.

My hands cover my face. 'I'm sorry. I've gone and spoiled your moment, haven't I? Typical Libby.'

'No. No . . .' She strokes my hair, then holds my head with a hand on each cheek. 'Aw, Libbs, since when do you want to get married?'

'I don't . . .' I'm still talking from behind my fingers, not that I have any choice; Dora's hands are still over them. 'I don't know, maybe I do.'

'You don't.' She leans her forehead to mine, and laughs softly. 'You hate the whole idea of it. Always have. Remember when you burned Bridal Barbie's dress?'

'Yeah, only because she didn't have a bra. I was making a statement.' I sniff. 'You know how much that'd be worth now?'

She laughs under her breath. 'Well, it proves my point. You've never warmed to the idea.'

'That's what I thought.' I nod with a taut look. 'But maybe I'd just like to know it was considered at least once. I'll be thirty-three and I've never even come close, so what does that say about me?'

'That you're independent. Don't need the stereotypical two-point-five kids, minivan and husband, and you're secretly in love with your manager. You just won't admit it.'

'Not funny.' I sniff.

'Libbs, are you sure you're OK? Is this about Ollie?'

I freeze, holding my breath. 'Your mom brought him up, said she always thought . . .' I don't need to finish, Dora knows.

'Have you considered going back to Dr Papadopoulos? He seemed to help last time, and I'm worried.' Dr P. is a family friend of Dora's; in fact, that's how I met him.

'I've been managing just fine, you know that.' Although I'm grateful for the initial contact, my on-again-off-again sessions aren't something I want to discuss.

'You have, but . . .' She releases a long sigh. 'Don't be mad, but Finn told me what's going on with Pretty in Pink, and I just don't want to see you go to that dark place again. I worry. We all do.'

I'm silent for a moment then sit back, freeing my hands to wipe at my eyes. *That place* is inescapable, it's not somewhere you can leave; but she doesn't understand. Most people don't. When you struggle with any form of depression, you have periods of coping, not the other way round.

'Well, the store thing, yeah, it's a mess, but it'll be fine. *I'll* be fine. It's just this whole birthday thing is always confusing, you know.'

'Well, technically I don't . . .' She grins playfully and bumps my shoulder. 'Because I'll still be thirty-two.'

I sigh. 'I hate you.'

'You love me. And I'll help with the store any way I can.'

'I know.'

A moment passes between us as we sit together, an understanding between friends. Sisters, really. Nothing else needs to be said. She knows and I know, and what she doesn't know I'm not ready to tell her, but it's fine, because it's enough. More than enough.

Although Dora's right to be worried. Last night I woke again, sobbing.

When I first started seeing Dr P., that's really all I wanted fixed. That's all I thought needed fixing. I mean, I didn't come from an abusive home, nor was I in a volatile relationship. There were no addictions or hallucinations. I wasn't a nympho, klepto, or pyro. I was tired. That was it; not exactly exciting cutting-edge psychology stuff, but he said we'd talk, and that's what we did.

Every week.

'So tell me something about you, Libby,' Dr Papadopoulos said.

I fidgeted across from him, questioning why I had come back for a second visit when I knew he couldn't prescribe me any meds. But there I was. 'Um, nothing really to tell, I have a business that I love and it keeps me pretty busy.' I half smiled then told him how I worked at the thrift store throughout high school, and right after, when they were about to close, I struck a deal to buy it by making regular monthly payments to the owner. No bank, no loan, just me. Nice and easy.

'That's a huge accomplishment right from high school. So, no college, then?' Dr P. asked as he leaned back in his chair. It was the kind that swivelled and rocked in any direction. It also squeaked.

I shook my head and eyed the clock, wondering how much time was left.

'Ever consider going?'

'You mean to college? Oh . . .' I laughed with a breath, because I was considering going home. 'Wasn't for me, I guess.' Another shrug.

'How'd your parents feel about this?' His words held intentions. He was baiting me.

'Um, they seemed to understand.'

He sat up, leaning elbows to knees. 'Didn't your friends go? At least some of them did, I'm sure. You never really considered it?'

My throat tightened as I thought back. And even now, I'm not sure why I said anything. Maybe because he was listening and I couldn't tell you the last time anybody was. They're busy. They have kids and spouses and lives.

'Well . . .' I scratched at my neck and looked past him, remembering, thinking. 'The summer between my sophomore and junior years, I got in a really bad car accident, and I didn't really snap back from it when the school year started.'

'Really? What happened?' he asked.

'Oh,' I shrugged. 'I don't know. My car was totalled, but I was OK, surprisingly.' My mouth opened and then shut again, the words lodged deep as a lump. I shrugged again instead, and flicked my eyes between him and the floor.

'You said you weren't hurt, but didn't recover from it. How do you mean?'

'Um . . . I don't know. It shook me. I started to question everything and school just didn't hold my interest, so I got really behind.' I looked up. 'But when I started to get things together in my senior year, I asked my counsellor, Mr Franks, what was available . . .'

'You mean for college?'

I nodded. 'Mm-hmm. I didn't know where to start, really.'

'And?'

And this is stupid. That's what I'd been thinking. This is stupid, and I'm making too much out of it, like always.

'Libby?' He leaned, the chair creaked, and I debated if what I was saying had any relevance. It didn't, but . . .

'It's not a big deal. He told me I didn't have any options left. I was too late, that I blew my opportunities.'

The vein next to his eye ticked. I only noticed because he

scratched at his brows and they were in need of a trim. I wasn't sure what else to say, or if I should've said anything at all.

'Huh.' Dr P. leaned back and shook his head. 'What a prick.'

My eyes snapped to his, not quite believing what he'd said.

'Even if you were failing, as long as you're willing, there are always options. What'd your mom say?'

'Oh, I don't think I ever told her.' His reaction was confusing; he appeared angry for me.

'Didn't she ask what you were gonna do after high school? Didn't you have some sort of plan in place?'

'No.' My skin warmed. I began twisting my fingers round one another. 'We didn't talk about things like that.' I didn't want to tell him why.

He paused, as if considering where to steer the conversation. 'OK . . . why didn't you just apply yourself?'

'I didn't know who to call, what to do, and was too embarrassed to ask anyone else 'cause . . .' Why were we discussing this? 'I don't know, he said I'd be lucky to graduate. I blew it.'

'And you believed him.' He shook his head.

I didn't have any reason not to.

Is that still the case? Have I done it again? Stalled to the point I've lost the opportunity to turn things around? The accident may have thrown me in high school and caused me to question things, but what's my excuse now?

The memory fades as Dora drops her head on my shoulder and rocks into my side a bit. Mrs C. and Finn can be heard chatting just outside the door, probably growing impatient. Or maybe not. Finn's wearing her hat, and they're laughing.

I sniff. 'Please don't make me wear that hideous fish-gut dress your mom picked out.'

Dora stifles a laugh. 'No promises.'

♫

Flipping through the channels on the TV, I pick at my late dinner and talk with Ollie. I'm somewhat distracted by the bathroom bears commercial. At least that's what I call them. I find them disturbing. The only way bears should be humanoid is if they exist in their own universe like the Care Bears with their happy belly-tats. I flip to another station and reposition my legs. The bottom one's fallen asleep. Wish I could.

'You there?' Oliver asks.

'In theory. Are you?'

He laughs. 'In theory . . . Hey, are you OK? You sound out of it.'

'I'm good, just tired, and I'm worried about my store. I think I've really screwed things up again.' Giving up on my makeshift dinner, I set the plate to the side and pet one of the cats instead. Lucky's back arches in his sleep as I scratch. 'I should call Finn, to see if he has any news.' I called him less than an hour ago.

'Have you looked for another location, then?'

'Yeah, of course, but . . .' I rub above my eyes, trying to quiet the panic that's working itself up. 'I went to see a space today, in fact, but there's a yearly fee and build-out costs; oh, and it's almost five times as much in rent, and in a worse location. Even Jasper was surprised.'

'Jasper's helping you? Are you sure including an employee is a good idea?'

'Despite appearances, he's quite clever, I assure you, and he's more than an employee, he's—'

'Look, you just need to be careful mixing business and . . . well, to be honest, I can't really see you two together. I mean, he and I are very different, aren't we?'

'Very different, yes.' Just mentioning Jasper to Ollie feels like a betrayal – which is stupid. I mean, he's moved on; shouldn't I?

Ollie's voice lowers so it's gravelly in his throat. 'Does he know to kiss you right below the ear, or—'

'Don't be fresh, Ollie,' I say, secretly thrilled and hoping he continues. The diversion is nice. Needed. Comforting.

'He doesn't, does he?' There's a smile in his voice. 'I knew there was a reason you liked me above all others.'

'And who says I like you at all? One, you have no taste in music—'

'Because I prefer something with a bit more substance than bubblegum pop?'

I half-laugh. 'Two, you dress like a gentleman—'

'Which we both know I'm not.'

'And three . . .' I'm mired by his comment. He's nowhere near a gentleman, in the best way possible. I learned that after prom. His prom.

The images flood through my mind, causing my skin to heat.

The hall was decorated with blue streamers and pearled balloons hung everywhere. And just like the prom's theme, 'Forever Young,' I could have happily stayed there, because things were perfect. I mean, God, I was with Ollie. And yes, I was young, really too young, we both were; but I was in love.

The real kind. The first kind. The only kind that mattered.

At almost eighteen, he was different than the boy of sixteen. The long dark hair was cut and cropped close, the one diamond stud was removed as if he'd never had it pierced, and on normal days, he'd dress in jeans and school-emblem hoodie. He was, after all, regularly visiting colleges with his dad and had to look acceptable. 'Like a gentleman,' his dad would say.

But that night? Decked in a black rented tux, he looked better than acceptable: he looked like a dream. One I've never really woken up from.

We twirled and danced under paper stars that sparkled from twinkle lights. Near my ear, he whispered, 'You look beautiful, Shortcake.'

'Yeah?' I smiled till my cheeks hurt. I really went all out. My hair was still a wild mess of red curls, but I had it pulled to the side so it waterfalled over my one bare shoulder. The other had a giant pouffe flower thing that covered the dress strap. I could only wear one oversized star earring because of it, but that was fine by me; I thought it was totally rad. The bodice was tight and carried over my hips, then flared at the thigh in an asymmetrical explosion of ruffles. Basically, I was a shiny, zigzagged mermaid. Oh, and it was pink. Completely awesome.

As we swayed back and forth Ollie whispered near my ear, 'What would you say if I told you we have a room for after?'

I leaned back to see his eyes, my own rounded and wide. 'Really?' We'd talked about it before, but face to face with the possibility it was terrifying and exciting all at once.

The rest of prom is only a blur. My memories begin with Dora and me getting ready, the limo ride there, the dance where he told me . . . and then everything else vanishes, until the point when we arrived at the room. Pretty sure that's all I thought of from the moment he uttered the words.

'We can just talk,' Ollie said once inside, a sly smile curling the corners of his lips.

For about five minutes, we did. He took off his tux jacket and set it on the chair by the small writing desk. 'Did you have fun?'

'Yup.' I hadn't moved.

'Are you sure this is OK?'

'Uh-huh.'

He stepped up and slowly took my clutch purse with the matching pouffe bow, and tossed it aside. 'What are ya thinking?'

About a million things ran through my head, but mostly that he'd be leaving soon. 'That I'm gonna miss you when you go.' It was almost graduation and then he'd be gone. Then what? During the prom scene in *Pretty in Pink*, OMD's 'If You Leave' plays in the background. This was prom and the lyrics – promise me just one more night, then we'll go our separate ways – haunted me. I couldn't bear the thought.

He stroked my cheek. 'Yeah, somehow I'm ending up just like the old man wanted, a yuppie wannabe attending law school. How's that for irony?' His eyebrows hiked.

'It's what you want too, though, right, to be a lawyer? That's what you and Finn always talk about.'

He shrugged. 'Yeah, but still, did it have to be so obvious?' He laughed.

'I like that you're obvious.' I smiled ruefully.

'You know what I like about you?' He jumped on the bed and kicked his shoes off. 'What I've always liked?'

Still smiling, I stepped closer to the edge, my thighs bumping his bent knees where they hung over. 'My great fashion sense and musical expertise? Or the fact that I put up with your lack of both?'

Sitting up, his hands grabbed my waist and pulled me closer. 'I like that you don't play games. It's real. You're real. And no matter who I'm trying to be for my dad or anyone else, when I'm around you, I'm real. It's always been that way.'

It still is.

A million years later, and his words still melt my heart. I blink and realize I'm smiling. Did I fall asleep? I think I at least zoned out pretty good. 'Sorry, Ollie,' I say to myself, then dig around the couch for the phone. I should call Finn. I know it's late, but I need to talk with him. I push the main button, accidentally summoning Siri, who asks what she can help me with.

'Flash me back to prom,' I say, and sigh.

'I'm not sure I understand.'

Yeah, me either. I select *favourites, Finn,* and wait for him to answer.

'Libby?' He clears his throat. 'Are you stranded somewhere?'

'No. Is that how you answer the phone?'

'It is at this hour, when I know it's you.'

'Did you turn over my lease and the eviction notice to your work colleague? Seth Merri-whatever.'

'Yes, I did, like I said I would. And it's Merriweather.' Finn pushes out a breath and moves, creating a rumpling through the line. 'He wants to meet with you sooner rather than later. Looks like they have every legal right to force you to leave.'

'What?' My heart slams my ribs. 'I really have to move? You said he could work magic.' Starr jumps into my lap to steal my attention from Lucky, but right now neither cat has it.

'No, I said *if . . .*' He yawns. 'I don't know what I said. Just what Seth did, and ya have to move. Sorry, Libbs.' His voice is crackly. 'Oh, he wanted me to ask if you've considered selling. I was gonna call you in the morn—'

'Sell *what*? Pretty in Pink?' I sit up, pushing both cats away, suddenly jolted wide awake. 'No!'

'Or we can talk about it now.' He clears his throat again. 'Look, he thought the property owners might be interested in taking it on, since it's already established on their lot and if it's profit-able—'

'Forget it. It's *not* for sale.' I'm shaking my head adamantly, not that anyone can see.

'Yeah, well, that's what I told him you'd say, but he wants to review your profit and loss and business plan just to be prepared. It might be worth seeing what they'd offer, right?'

'No, forget it.' My heart's beating fast in my chest. 'I didn't even think I'd have to move, and now to consider selling? Then what would I do?' Falling back onto the couch, Starr jumps and stalks away, miffed.

'Libbs, really, can we maybe talk about this in the morning?' he asks through another long yawn.

'Fine. At least one of us should sleep.' I click off and chuck my phone across the couch. It falls onto the floor and bounces once. I leave it there.

The shock of his words and my situation roll over me in a series of small, building waves. I know the tide's coming and I *have* to move or I'll be underwater, but I can't. No loophole. No escape.

I'd rather die than sell my shop.

CHAPTER 8

'True'
Spandau Ballet, 1983

Truth is overrated

After last Saturday's Eighties intervention spiel on top of the eviction notice, I found myself back at Dr P.'s. And now, learning I have to legally move or sell Pretty in Pink, here I am again not even a week later. So embarrassing.

I flip through magazines blindly while he finishes up with a patient. Maybe they've already left, I don't know. There are two doors. Patients wait in one area and exit out another. Privacy is valued, after all, and really, it's appreciated. I've left several times upset and emotional.

The door opens. 'Libby.' The smile pulls up, crinkly, making his eyes half-moon slits. 'Come in, come in.' It doesn't matter what the weather is; as always, he's dressed in trousers, button-up and sweater. Today's selection: long-sleeved burgundy with frayed sleeves.

What's new is the beard. I thought last week he'd just forgotten to shave, but I can tell now it's intentional. Maybe Finn's right and there is a men's movement. I still don't like it, and blended with his untrimmed hair, he resembles a lion. I stand, my smile fixed, and step inside, feeling every bit the sacrificial lamb. Yeah, within this den there's no escaping the roar of truth, but it won't stop me from trying.

Dr P.'s still smiling as he takes his seat and motions for me to take mine.

I sit across from him in the wingback chair, swallowed-up and small. 'Thanks for seeing me without an appointment,' I say, not sure how to begin.

'Sure.' His hands fold, one on top of the other, and rest on his plump middle. 'Do you have the *who am I* essay?'

With its mention, *The Breakfast Club* instantly comes to mind, and the line from the letter to Mr Vernon: *we think you're crazy to make us write an essay telling you who we think we are.* It is crazy, because I have no idea who I am. And yes, I realize I'm at a shrink's, but that still doesn't make me the Basket Case. 'Yeah, I don't have that yet.'

Instead, I tell him about Dora's fitting earlier in the week. How it affected me, how over-emotional I became. However, saying things out loud makes them seem trivial. I forgot that. My insides are jumpy, and it's stupid I'm here. *I should go.* I start to stand, embarrassed. 'I'm sorry, I'm fine . . . you're busy and—'

'Libby.' With both hands he motions in the air for me to sit back down, so I do. 'Have you been sleeping?'

Without meeting his eyes, I shake my head. It's probably obvious, what with my bloodshot eyes and dark circles. I'm a zombie from Michael Jackson's 'Thriller' video, specifically the one that's walking towards the camera and loses its arm. *Clunk.* It just falls off. Mine's actually fallen asleep. I shake out the pins and needles.

We sit in silence for a few moments before he starts poking around. That's his mode of operation. He digs until he finds something buried. 'So did you end up going out with any of the dates your friends set up?'

My eyes snap to his. 'Oh yeah, but . . .' I fill him in on the Brain and all the ridiculous details. I don't even have to embellish to make the story funnier; I mean, between Theo thinking I'm a mute with an infection and the sign-language lady, it's more than enough.

He's laughing until he has tears, and my overwhelming urge to shed my own subsides.

Whenever I'm in that dark place, it's as if my emotions are carbonated and I'm shaken. My chest and the back of my throat ache as the pressure builds and takes up every available space. Talking is the gentle tap that releases the trapped and distorted feelings along the sides. He knows this. It's a needed device. An effective technique. A weird analogy.

'Oh, and then I broke out in hives, which was crazy.' I'm shaking my head, remembering. 'Seriously, my arms were on fire.' I describe the charades, and get him going again. 'It really was that bad.'

Dr P. dabs at misty eyes, his laughter quieting. 'Has that re-action happened before?'

'The hives? Yeah, a few times after my accident. They just came out of nowhere.'

'And no allergies?'

I shake my head. 'Nope. None that I'm aware of, anyway.'

'That's interesting.' He leans way back in his chair, locking his hands behind his head. 'Did you know emotions can trigger allergic reactions, much like a panic attack?'

I didn't.

'Yes – in fact, it's a stress reaction.' After a pause, he switches gears. 'OK, well, how do you feel about your friends declaring that you need to change and setting you up, now that you've had some time to think about it?'

'I don't know. Part of me is annoyed, and the other part is . . .' I blow out a fast breath. 'Annoyed more. I mean, who cares what I wear, or who I date, or if I even do?'

Dr P.'s fuzzy brows are drawn.

I rub the permanent tension that resides above mine, then add, 'Anyway, I'm done with the whole thing.' I lean forward. 'I mean, come on, it wasn't even a real date. And I didn't know they meant the dates would literally be like *The Breakfast Club* characters. Dr Theo was too skinny, a total nerd, and boring. He went on and on and on . . .' So do I, because he's not saying anything. 'Although, Dora said under normal circumstances he's all right.' I stop my rant short and glance at Dr P. for a response.

He still doesn't have one.

'So yeah, I'm done. 'Cause what's the rest going to be like?' Actually Bender wouldn't be bad, but . . . I continue to fill the space. 'And even if he is a great guy, seriously, he didn't seem open to dating or really that interested. I mean, how hard is it to find a single, emotionally available man?'

'Are you emotionally available, Libby?'

And bam, he strikes. I swear Dr Papadopoulos is a ninja

shrink; somehow he always pulls up the past when I'm not looking and attacks me with it. I should've quit while I was ahead. This time it's me without the response.

'I have a theory on this. It's actually twofold . . .' Dr P. waves a hand to emphasize his thoughts. 'I think you keep everyone at an emotional distance as a safeguard. By identifying their quirks as flaws, it gives you the excuse to keep them back from yours . . . because yours are worse, right? So you push them away.'

My heart stutters. Forget ninja, he's an assassin, always going in for the kill. My eyes glance to the wall, trash can, bulletin board . . .

Dr P. lowers his voice, leaning forward. 'If anyone knew you, I mean *really* knew the true you, they might actually care about you. You might care about them. And they could leave, like Oliver did.'

That's going too far. I stare at nothing. Say nothing. I'm not ready to talk about this. I've had enough. With folded hands, I dig my thumbnail under another, pressing hard, the pinch a needed distraction.

'Do you still talk with Ollie?'

'Sure.' That's all I say.

'And do you think that helps you to move on?'

I stab a glance in his direction. 'So, what, I'm not allowed to talk to him any more? That's a bit severe.'

'I think in order to give a fair shot to any of these dates—'

'Dates? You want me to continue with my friend's intervention thing?'

He nods, brows arched high. 'Oh yes; in fact, I'm recommending it, but . . .' He lifts a hand and holds the gesture mid-air. 'To give yourself and them a fair shot, you may need to create some distance between you and Oliver.'

'I don't think there could be much more distance,' I mutter and look away, not liking this so-called suggestion.

'Tell me why you're really here.'

I flick my eyes to his. 'I told you: I'm not sleeping again.'

'Sure. You're under a lot of stress. You need to relocate your store. Maybe having to sell—'

'I'm *not* selling.'

Dr P. keeps going as if I haven't interrupted. 'You're about to turn another year older, and your friends are pushing you out of your comfort zone to date new and different people. Lots of changes, lots of stress. Now tell me why you're really here.'

God, isn't that enough? Lifting my chin, I hold his unrelenting gaze. He's waiting to see if I'll bite. It's like Rockwell's 'Somebody's Watching Me', only instead of the neighbours or mailman, it's Dr P.

I know what he wants me say, what he's waiting for, but . . . 'You said so yourself: if I'm not willing to have *that* conversation, therapy can't work. I'm not here to try that again. That's where we stopped last time.'

'*You* stopped.'

'Fine, I stopped. Whatever.' My arms cross to block his judgement. 'We started discussing things, and it backfired. You pushed and it failed. *Miserably*. Things just got worse, not better. So what was the point?' What *is* the point? Why *am* I here again?

'What triggered your hives, Libby?' Dr P. asked. 'What happened on the date that really set it off?'

My mind spins back to my own words. *I'm perfectly fine.* How it reminded me of the EMTs in the ambulance. How they kept asking me questions, how they wouldn't answer mine. Tears of frustration fill my eyes and I start to scratch my arms, only to notice him watching me.

Dr. P. narrows his eyes. 'Libby? *Why* are you here?'

'I just want to sleep, OK?' It comes out quick and staggered, but it's the truth. I need to sleep.

He doesn't like my answer. His jaw ticks. He knows it's only partly true.

The silence lasts longer than I'm comfortable with, so I fill it. 'Look, I just need some help sorting the everyday: like you said, lots of stress and lots of changes. And I need to sleep. I can't function without sleep.'

'No, you're right, you can't.' Leaning forward, elbows to knees, he softens his tone. 'Libby, what you need to understand is, your everyday is linked to your yesterday.' His fingers steeple and he narrows his eyes. 'So again, I ask . . . *why* are you here?'

Oh my God. I run my tongue over the back of my teeth. My jaws clench. The pressure builds again. 'Do you want me to leave?'

'No. I want you to come back on Tuesday prepared to do the *real* work this time.' He shrugs. 'Then you'll sleep.'

CHAPTER 9
The Athlete

Another sleepless night, and stressing over my financials has put me in a tizzy for most of the day. I spent the first half searching online for retail space that's move-in ready and compiling new overhead numbers based on the locations that met the minimum of my criteria: comparative square footage, decent enough location and low yearly maintenance fees.

With Pretty in Pink in our current location, the balance sheet is pleasantly fat and healthy. More comes in than goes out, and we're growing. I don't want to move, but if I legally *have* to, I need to see that it's doable with the added expenses. It's not.

For the rest of the afternoon I plugged in new numbers and rearranged what little expenses I have, but it didn't add up. It flipped my happy, healthy bottom line to a sick and dying dud. That's why this Seth Merriweather thinks the property owners may want the store. As it stands, Pretty in Pink generates a positive cash flow and, without rent, the profit margin is even bigger.

But *no*, the shop's mine. I bought it, built it and grew it. It's not for sale. But what's to stop them from slapping another name on the front and stocking with similar merchandise? Would customers follow me, or would they shop there from habit? This is why I need Seth *not* to mention a possible buyout. I don't want to give the property owners the idea. The problem is, I have no idea how I'm going to move in less than two weeks and keep my Pink in the black.

What a day. I'm frazzled and *God*, now I have a date. My shoulders drop with a sigh. I almost feel sorry for the guy; I'm in such a prickly mood. At least Nigel Harrington, the Athlete, appears better than Dr Theo, the brain drain. And he doesn't look anything like Emilio Estevez in *The Breakfast Club* either. I was worried he'd show up in a tank top and hooded varsity jacket, so I made Finn email me a photo.

Surprisingly, Nigel's quite a looker, with stunning hazel eyes and deep caramel skin, and in the pictures he's in normal everyday clothes. His hair's buzzed close, but it works with his square jaw. He's rather handsome, even noticed an indent in his chin. Go, Finn.

And according to Finn, Nigel's into extreme sports, a total adrenalin junkie, so I'm cautiously optimistic. Being able to tell Dr P. I went rappelling, bungee jumping or skydiving could paint me in a whole new light. It'll show I'm willing to try new things and open to new people, even if I'm not. Go, Libby.

Dora and Dean are here to cheer me on and send me off before they meet with Finn for drinks. They're up front watching the DVD I had in, while I change into my – I pull at the fabric and blanch – *whatever this is*. I'm grateful it's only them. Finn can be critical and I'm in no mood to deal with his *divine* opinions and commentary.

I hate the clothes from our power-hour of shopping, so I've improvised. They think I'm too Eighties? They really haven't seen anything yet. Stepping into the main sitting room, I stand with outstretched hands and twirl. 'Well? Am I date-tastic?'

Dora's mouth drops. 'Oh, Libby, *no*.' She waddle-walks towards me, mouth ajar. 'What'd you do?'

'What?' I glance at Dean, then recheck my ensemble. The boyfriend pants and matching jacket are on and facing the right direction, no tags are hanging about. It's fine. 'I'm fine.'

'You're a maniac. This isn't *Flashdance*, Libbs.' Dora shakes her head. 'Really, where do I even start? Pink sparkle legwarmers?'

'I'm just a small town girl on a Saturday night?' I smile cheeky, enjoying getting her riled.

'It's Friday, and we already think you're crazy.' Dora glares at my shoes. Her eyes pinch in dismay. 'I *asked* if you had proper footwear. What are *those*?'

'High-tops.'

She looks at Dean, who laughs, then closes his eyes with a truncated breath. I think he's enjoying this as much as I am.

'Is there a problem?' I'm really trying not to smirk. 'I did your makeover, and I'm in the clothes you selected.'

'Those are graffiti neon, and they have Velcro. *Velcro*. Are you going to start breakdancing?'

OK, I'm not *just* in the clothes she selected; I've added a few of my own. 'One, I used to be great at breakdancing, could even do the headspin, remember? And two, these are popular again—'

'If you're fourteen. Never mind, no time to fix. But it's a definite no to the fanny-pack thing. I mean, I'm gobsmacked, Libbs, it's see-through.' She glances at the contents. 'Do we really need to see your phone, a pack of gum and . . . a tampon?'

I shrug. 'You never know.'

'No one *should* know. But the worst, Libbs, I mean *really* . . .' She's shaking her head, eyeing my hair.

'What? It's just a ponytail.' I hold in my laugh. Seriously, what does she expect?

'No, you're off your trolley if you think that's just a ponytail. It's jutting out from the left side of your head like an antenna. You could pick up satellite with that thing.' She's sweating from her rant. Or maybe that's from the hormones too. 'And no to the sweatband, you're not Olivia Newton-John.'

'Maybe she wants to get physical,' Dean adds, trying to be funny.

He's not and I don't, at least not with Nigel. *Flash.* Dean sneaks a photo as Dora marches me back to my room. Within a minute I'm stripped of legwarmers, waist-pack and sweatband.

While Dora reaches for a brush, I snag the headband from the counter and shove it in one of the boyfriend pockets for later. If we do something radical, I may need it to keep the perspiration from my eyes, or my hair in place, or flag down someone for help. It's neon yellow, they'd see it.

'Here, turn about.' She spins me. 'And you should be excited . . .' She yanks my hair from the rubber band and starts to brush. 'Instead, you're being crabby and difficult.'

'How am I being difficult? I'm dressed and ready for an action-packed athletic date with a top athlete. *Very* excited.' *Very* worried.

'It's like you're intentionally trying to prove a point, Libbs. Fine, we get it. You're an Eighties girl, you don't want to change, but *come on*. You're the one who asked for help.'

'No, I asked for – whatever, it's complicated,' I say, knowing it's more than that. It's my store, it's my birthday and it's Ollie, so it's impossible. And I just need a good date story to show Dr P. I'm being open-minded – not a good date that could lead to another. '*Ow*, Dora.' I flip my hand to push the brush away instinctively.

She bats the hand away. 'Hold still . . .' With the rubber band in one hand, she grabs hold of the hair with the other, and secures it in the back. 'There.' She steps away with an approving nod. 'I don't understand why you can't just try, Libbs.'

She has no idea how hard I'm trying. 'After the first date, which wasn't a date, can you really blame me?' The bell chimes. My heart jumps. 'Have Dean answer.' Why am I whispering?

Dora cracks the door and shouts, 'Let him in, we'll be maybe another minute.'

We stay put, peeping through the door, Dora below and me craned above. I can't get a good look. All I see is the back of Dean's legs and Nigel's stout calves with bulging muscles and clean white sneakers. Let's hope he's in shorts and he's not naked. That'd be weird. Yeah, I'm not dating a nudist. That's *not* an adventure date I'm willing to consider.

Dean sidesteps to allow him in, and—Oh, *hell no!*

I shut the door, swinging round to face Dora abruptly.

Her face contorts into a smile.

'It's not funny.' I hold my hand to my chest to demonstrate the obvious problem. He may not look like the athlete from *The*

Breakfast Club, but they do have something unfortunate in common. 'He's *this* tall.'

'OK, I didn't know that.' Dora blinks, inhales sharply and lifts her delicate chin. 'Maybe just slouch a bit?'

♫

Nigel Harrington is lovely; he is obviously taking his health and fitness seriously. Although he's square. And I don't mean in a Huey Lewis and the News kind of way. I glance over. Yes, definitely square, almost as wide as he is tall.

His chest is broad, his neck thick and corded and his thighs are huge masses of veined strength. His arms don't even hang at his sides; they sort of splay out, like a child packed into a snowsuit. And no wonder – his biceps are bigger than my head.

How does he zip his pants? Or, for that matter –

'You OK?' He hollers over the music as we drive. It's loud classic rock, and giving me a righteous headache. His squeaky voice isn't helping. Maybe he's hyped on steroids. I've heard they can shrinky-dink men, but would that alter him to a soprano?

'Yup, just enjoying the ride,' I say, my own voice sounding strangely baritone. For the record, I heard Nancy Reagan in the Eighties, and I said no.

Nigel's truck is barely street legal. It's shiny blue with red flame decals along the sides, and colossal wheels that suspend us high above the vehicle's body and everyone else. I had to climb actual steps to get inside. And it bounces. The hydraulics are insane; every bump sends me airborne. A sharp turn causes me to clutch my seat belt with both hands. 'Whoa, look out for—'

He swerves, just missing the motorcycle, clips the curb and

pulls into a parking lot. I'd say this adventure date's in full swing.

He pops his door and leaps out as if jumping from a plane. We're that high off the ground. I hear a *thump*, but don't see him walking round. Where'd he go?

Climbing down the two metal steps I look left, then right, and . . . no way, he's walking *under* the vehicle to my side. Wow. Our height difference again stares me in the face – well, the boobs. He's just above them. I have to resist the urge to pat him on the head like a puppy.

He smiles, revealing perfect white teeth and pink healthy gums, 'So are you ready to kill it, Libby?'

I'm ready to kill Finn. I smile, now thinking I should have flossed, or brightened, or maybe brushed again. At least I have gum. I swiped my waist-pack on the way out.

'Let's go.' He motions towards –

Oh, come on. This is the high-adrenalin, action-packed date he's planned? What happened to zip-lining, bungee jumping, or indoor skydiving? Not that I would've done any of those, but High Adventure Seven Sea's *Mini-Golf*?

The course is fashioned around a crazy pirate theme, which explains the name. Huge pirate ships touting heavy artillery and busted hulls sit in pools of shallow water to make up the course. It's like a mad battle took place, leaving a shipwreck graveyard. Each hole is connected by wooden boardwalks and bridges, and the course is illuminated by football-stadium spotlights. I actually have to squint to look round.

'Doesn't this remind you of *Pirates of the Caribbean*?' Nigel asks, as he digs through his wallet to pay.

'I was thinking more *The Goonies*.' I mumble this because One-Eyed Willie's staring at me from behind the register.

'Here ye go, pretty Lass. Now ye're ready for th' high seas,' the eye-patched man in pirate garb says, as he slaps a huge tricorn hat with skull and crossbones on my head. My ponytail makes it skew forward, so it rests just above my eyes. The elastic hangs under my nose, and he reaches over to snap it under my chin.

'Really?' I look from the man to Nigel, but he's not paying attention. He's too busy picking one out. Glancing round, I notice everyone's wearing pirate attire. I hope they wash these. My phone's vibrating from the waist-pack. A quick unzip and I answer while I wait. 'Hello?'

'Hey, it's me,' says Jas. 'Some attorney stopped in from Finn's office and was looking round. I have his number if you wanted to call him right back.'

'Um, no, not right now. Can you leave it on my desk?' I'm somewhat preoccupied watching the assortment of hats Nigel's modelling for me.

'This one? Arggggh!' Nigel tips the crow's-nest hat and smiles. It bends in the front and juts super-wide on each side for unob-structed views. Or so we're told. The history lesson from One-Eyed Willie is for our educational benefit. The fake green parrot now pinned on Nigel's shoulder is for his amusement. The employee is maybe all of twenty, and I have to wonder if his jug o' grog doesn't have some real merriment mixed in. My next thought is whether he'll share.

'Where *are* you?' Jas asks.

'Oh, sorry. Ah . . .' I glance round. 'Pirate golf?'

'Oh, you're on one of your *dates*—'

'OK, must go.' I can't click off quick enough. This is embarrassing. Jas is gonna tease me good about this one.

Walking towards the first hole, we pass the grub hub and barnacle arcade, and the smell of burgers and chips is heavenly. As always, I'm starving. 'Doesn't that just make your mouth water?' Maybe he'll get the hint. I'm a girl who has an appetite, after all. You date me, you feed me.

'Oh, almost forgot.' Nigel digs in his pocket, produces two protein bars and hands me one. 'We need fuel if we're going into battle.' He rips open his bar with his teeth, quirks an eyebrow and inhales his in two bites. 'Eat up,' he says while putting on a golf glove.

We'll call this Strike Two. The obvious first: I'm wearing a pirate hat, he has a parrot, my dinner is a mushed protein bar, and *a golf glove*? At *mini-golf*? Looking round, I don't see anyone else wearing one. Is he going to moonwalk? He already has the voice.

Actually, forget King of Pop: Nigel's the king of swing. He can hardly clasp the club, let alone do a full rotation. He's like a hulking T-rex with mini arms, using little wrist flicks to flip the putter back and forth.

'Oh, come on already,' the guy behind us says as Nigel lines up his shot using the club like a telescope. The man's stout, with white-grey hair peeking from his Captain's cap. He's like a bullfrog, his neck and jaw connecting as one, and his lips stretch wide into a thin frown as he waits.

My stomach rumbles, loud enough that I'm sure everyone hears even over the *yo-ho-ho* music blaring from the hidden speakers. I carefully peel open my bar and chomp a bite.

Ugh, bleah – total crap. *What is this thing?* I half-chew and hold it in my mouth, not sure what else to do. Swallowing is out of the question.

Nigel looks back. So does his parrot. 'You're up.' He sunk the ball in two shots. *Great.*

I smile with tight lips, the gunk firmly held above my tongue. Placing my ball in the mat's groove, I tip my hat up so I can see and swing hard. Too hard. It flies up and over the laughing Captain Hook and onto another green, almost hitting an elderly gent dressed in a waistcoat. 'Sorry!' I mumble.

Nigel sets off to retrieve it.

I look left, then right, searching for a trash can. *Do they not have bins?* My eyes swivel down to the open treasure chest at the end of the green. It's either there or my bumbag, and that's clear. Without another thought, I spew it from my mouth, then rid the hideous taste with a few lip smacks.

Oh, gum. See, I knew my bag would come in handy. Popping a piece in, I look up, and my face flushes hot. The toady man behind me stares with a confused look. I crumple the gum wrapper, then drop it into the chest as well to assure him it is in fact a bin. My glare defies him to challenge me on it.

'You're up, Libby.' Nigel says, ready to move on. He's petting the bird.

Instead of swinging full-force, this time I tap. I make it just left of the hole. I tap again, and this time it rolls to the right. This is ridiculous. *Tap, tap, tap.* Oh my God! *Tap, tap.*

Captain Croaker behind us decides to skip, and jumps past. I didn't know you could do that. When Nigel's gaze follows his direction, I push the non-conformist red ball in with my foot.

119

'Score!' I enthusiastically raise my arms like goal posts, almost knocking off my hat.

'She cheated!' a snot-nosed whelp on the next green shouts, pointing his fake hook hand.

Why didn't I get one of those?

When Nigel looks from my mini-accuser to me, I step close and whisper, 'She did. His Grandma's not very good.' I nod towards the silver-haired woman by his side and narrow my eyes with disapproval.

Three more holes, and it's the same thing. I'm just pinging the ball around. I'm also running out of ways to get Nigel and the bratty tattle-tale to turn so I can nudge the ball with my foot. I keep gasping and shouting things like, 'Oh my gosh, a real parrot!' Or 'Isn't that Johnny Depp?' He must think I'm the most easily amused person ever. I even got him to look up to the sky by shouting, 'What *is* that?'

Actually, everyone looked up. I may have shouted too enthusiastically. When Nigel asked, 'What is *what*?' I looked blank and repeated 'What?' And that was that. I'm now out of diversions and back to *tap, tap, tap*.

I hate golf, the stupid costumes, and really, this whole date. And if Nigel keeps making his parrot talk, I'm going to ram a cracker down both their throats.

Tap. I follow the ball to the left.

Tap. It passes over the hole and continues on.

Tap. 'Seriously?' This time it stops inches in front.

'Here, let me help.' Nigel gives up the scorecard and steps behind me. He reaches round, but instead of holding his hands over mine, his hulking mass only allows him to guide my forearms. We flow back and forth, back and forth. So does Skully, the parrot. Yes, he's named him.

'Just nice and easy, see?' Nigel says into my back, because he can't see above my shoulder. Oddly, Skully can. His beak keeps nicking my ear, making me cringe. It tickles. Nigel says something about control, or direction; I don't know, I can't hear him.

He rocks, so I rock, trying to be a good sport, trying to decipher his words, and more importantly, trying to hold in mine. Did he just grunt? I've had enough. I mean, he isn't an athlete, and this isn't an adventure date, he's just – the parrot jabs me. I flick him hard so he bends backward, and then I swing full-force. 'Tally ho!'

The ball just misses Granny's head, pings from Captain Scallywag's hat, and *whoa*, uh-oh, it's coming back. I duck . . .

Nigel doesn't.

♫

No way am I asking Captain Birdbrain to drive me home, so I sit outside on the wooden metro bench, waiting for my cab. I don't like buses. The truth is I've never ridden on one to understand how they work, and now, in my thirties, I'm too embarrassed to ask. I mean, exact change or credit card? How do you know your stop? Is there a thing to pull, or do you just stand and shout *stop*!

A cab's easier. I give them the address, they take me and I pay; but there aren't any cab benches, and I want to sit. I'm also using the time to give Dora and Finn a piece of my mind. Well, their machines, or voicemail, or whatever.

My foot taps under the bench, keeping time to my words '. . . and you know what else? You can forget the rest of your Eighties intervention *Breakfast Club* dates, cause yeah, not gonna happen, Bucko. I'm done. With *all* of it.' I huff and fume into the phone, even though I'm aware that I have an audience.

A young guy in a fedora sits beside me and pretends not to listen. Why a fedora? Or the better question, why *that* one? It's too small for his head. I look right at him. 'Blind dates suck, right?'

He shrugs.

'See?' I say into the phone. 'Even the fedora guy next to me agrees. Here . . .' I push the phone near his mouth. 'Tell her.'

'Blind dates suck?'

'Exactly. Nice hat.' I show him mine. Yes, I kept it. I tried to kidnap the parrot, too, but I only succeeded in ripping Nigel's shirt when I swiped for him. 'And you guys can forget the party too. I don't celebrate birthdays, and you bloody well know why. I'm skipping it all. Screw birthdays and screw the Eighties intervention thing.' I press *end* and plop the phone in my lap. *Screw everyone.*

The guy looks at me sideways. Well, not him, he's way too young; and that hat, I mean, really.

'I once tried to skip Christmas.' I cross my arms and shrug. 'That didn't work out either.'

And that's all I have to say about that.

I drum my fingers. 'You have any chocolate?'

I'm safely at home, happily tucked in for the night, and talking with Ollie as usual. I understand what Dr P. was saying about distancing myself, but I can't help it. I've just finished telling him about my misadventures with mini-man on the seven seas, and he's cracking up.

'So how did you leave things?' Ollie asks.

Squeezing my eyes tight, I cringe. 'I told him I had cramps and had to leave that instant.'

'*Libbs.*' He busts out a laugh.

'I know.' Maybe I should've faked an injury, but I glanced at my waist-pack and, well . . . 'I just couldn't take him seriously. The nurse's station iced him and gave him an eye patch. A ridiculous eye patch, but the worst part is *he wore it*. And he kept talking pirate. Everything was *arghhh* and *shiver me timbers*. When he said he loved booty and looked at mine, I told him to walk the plank. The whole thing was disastrous. I *hate* golf anyway.'

'You like golf courses.'

I look up to consider, then smile. 'That's different. We didn't actually play the stupid game, we just, well . . .' Ollie and I would park in the course's lot. It really was pretty, and at night no one was there.

'There's still three more dates ahead, right?'

'It should just be you.' I clench my teeth, waiting for a response. Silence fills in the blanks.

'You know what? Forget I said that. Sorry.'

Between losing my store location, my deteriorating youth and after tonight, my sanity, I can't bear to rehash losing Ollie too. I don't want to think about it, or anything.

I'm already in Davy Jones' locker.

CHAPTER 10

'Shout'
Tears For Fears, 1984

Oh, I'm gonna

It's Saturday, and everyone except Finn is gathered round our usual table at Shermer's. I have no idea where he is, but I'm pretending I don't care. Just like Dora's pretending I've accepted her apology about their second date fiasco, which I haven't.

The diner's filled with the normal clamour: rattling dishes, bits and pieces of casual conversation and the outside bustle of traffic whenever the front doors opened. I keep glancing over to see if it's Finn. It isn't, and I'm growing restless and bristly. I'm really ready to just let him have it. I've been building my case since last night, and I don't care how good he is at prosecution: today, he's gonna need a good defence.

In preparation for the diner drama that's about to unfold, and since I'm self-represented, I thought it best to self-express in the truest of colours. I'm Libby Lauper, Cyndi Lauper's distant third step-cousin, twice removed.

My hair's tied with a black headscarf, my black T-shirt layers over a longer white one, and I'm sporting three long necklaces with different pendant charms, since I was thinking about Madonna the other day. I was half-tempted to wear a netted glove, but decided to heed the wise words of Coco Chanel: before you leave the house, look in the mirror and remove one accessory. So *voil*à, no glove.

The door opens again. Not Finn. Maybe I should summon him by phone.

'Oh, speaking of your dress . . .' I say, because Dora was. 'I dreamed about it last night.' This is surprising, considering what little sleep I had. 'It was *my* dress, *my* wedding, and I couldn't button it up. So I'm walking down the aisle holding the blasted thing together while straining to see who's at the end waiting for me.'

'Who was it? Nigel the Athlete?' asks Dean, forgetting himself.

My eyes narrow a warning, but then I shake my head and laugh. 'Worse. It was my cats, in mini-tuxedos.'

Dean's lips pull into a dramatic frown.

'I know, right?'

'Oh, there's Finn,' Dora says, looking towards the door.

He's in jeans, a pullover sweater and another man-scarf, this one blue. In other words, he's not dressed for the occasion. Maybe he doesn't realize he's about to stand trial. He gives a wave and ambles over in his slow, leisurely gait. 'Sorry I'm late.' He pulls out a chair, forcing everyone to scoot round.

I don't move. I'm not going to.

'Libby, budge over,' Finn says, practically sitting on my lap. He glowers with an eye-pop.

I unleash my death stare and his head jerks back from the impact.

'God, Libbs—'

I'm still staring when the waitress arrives. My heart's thumping, my stomach sour. I could spit acid. Like a llama. Well, if llamas could spit acid. Finn avoids my glare while orders are taken, then keeps everyone chatty with friendly banter. Dora and Dean's baby plans, Dora and Dean's engagement, Dora and Dean's wedding, how fabulous and divine he is, *blah blah blah* . . .

'Libbs? Libby, you OK?' Dora nudges Dean's shoulder. 'She hasn't blinked.'

I flutter my lashes, bringing them into focus, then turn to the accused. 'Aren't you going to comment on the message I left you, Finn? Ask me about the *fabulous* date you so nicely set me up with?' I lean on the table, daring him to begin his pitiful defence.

He blows out a slow, calculated breath and lifts his cup of tea. His left brow quirks, arching high into his blonde pompadour do. 'Are you going to apologize?'

'*For what?*' My jaw unhinges and literally sits on the floor. I may need to scoop it up just to form coherent words. '*Me?* You think I should apologize? Seriously?' I give questioning looks to the witnesses, which would be Dean and Dora, as if to say, *did you hear what I heard? Is he out of his bloomin' onion mind?* OK, no one actually says that, but I have a craving and kinda wish they served those here.

'And really, Libbs, how could I call you back when I was on the phone all night with sad Nigel? Yeah, I heard all about it.' Finn shakes his head in disapproval, then takes a deep breath, leans back, and calmly begins to state his case. 'Nigel's funny, fit and always fun. So, I don't see what you're complaining about—'

'I have plenty to complain about!' My eyes widen. He's just unleashed the Kraken. The original one from 1981, not the remake, so he's been bound up for a while and is raring to go. 'Nigel's three feet tall, drives a ridiculous monster truck, and took me to mini-golf. Mini *pirate* golf!' I break out my best pirate speak. 'It was all, *ahoy ye scurvy dogs* this, *shiver me timbers scallywag* that, and there was no rum. In fact, there was no meal. He fed me a mushy-gushy *protein bar.*'

Dora looks confused, Dean entertained. Hash-Brown Harry, the old guy to Finn's left, looks somewhat distraught. He's stopped eating, leaving his fork to hang in mid-air.

'He got the bar from his pocket, Finn. From. His. Pocket,' I repeat for drama. 'I mean, *God*, what were you thinking?' My voice steadily gains in volume, and now almost sings theatrically. 'So, yo ho *no*, Finn. Just *no.*'

Dora and Dean throw glances between us, knowing things are just getting started. It doesn't take a *Real Genius* to figure it out. Even the twentysomething couple in matching grey sweats at the next table are leaning over and taking an interest.

Finn gives me a long-suffering look while propping an arm on the back of his chair. 'I was thinking maybe you'd give him a chance. He's a really nice guy.'

He's wearing his 'I'm a superior lawyer' face, the one that stays cool and unruffled, and makes me want to smack it and hurl food in his direction.

His eyes pinch. 'Did you even ask him anything about his life, Libbs? Do you know *anything* about him? One thing?'

I slump a little in my seat as he glances to the jury, which now includes Dean, Dora, the matchy-match couple and Hash-Brown Harry. The waitress even rubbernecks as she passes by to offer refills.

My mouth opens, but Finn doesn't let me respond. 'Did you know he's a full-time professional bodybuilder, and even won the strong man contest in Vegas last month? You didn't, did you?' He looks round, building his case and tearing mine down. 'Or that he works with last-chance troubled teens three days a week at the gym?'

He's playing the good-guy sympathy card. He drives it home with a grand, sweeping gesture of his hand. 'For *free*. That's right, and that's where I met him, at his gym. The one he *owns*. Did you even know that, Libby London?' His eyes narrow, smugly. 'Did you *even* know *that*?'

That last repeat was a bit overly theatrical, but *whatever*.

Finn slaps the table, gaining more attention. 'In fact, might I persuade you to name one thing you *do* know?' Finn gazes deep into the jurors' eyes, lingering on each one. Each juror, not each eye, 'cause that would take forever.

'So, I ask again . . . Name one thing you bothered to learn about this charitable and highly accomplished man, who only wanted to take you out and show you a fun-filled evening.'

Now all eyes are on me. Except Hash-Brown Harry's. He's back to gumming his potatoes.

'I object,' I say, holding my ground. 'You're leading the witness. All of them.'

Dean lifts a finger. 'Technically we aren't witnesses, because we weren't there—'

'Overruled,' I say.

'You're overruled.' Finn declares with self-appointed authority. 'Just answer the question, Libbs. Name one thing you know about poor, dear Nigel Harrington.'

'Nigel Harrington from Get Slim Gym on 26th?' asks one of the Doublemint joggers. 'He's a superb trainer. A *really* fantastic guy.'

Great, he has a character witness.

'Well?' Finn pushes. 'Then I rest my—'

'He likes parrots!' I all but yell.

'You *killed* his parrot,' Finn says, pointing a manicured finger in my direction. The room gasps.

'You killed his parrot?' Dean repeats, mortified, his face screwed up. Dora pats his arm in comfort.

'*No*. No!' I protest, looking around at my accusers. 'I didn't *kill* it, because—'

'And –' Finn blurts, totally grandstanding the situation, 'she ripped his new shirt he specifically bought to impress her, in the process.'

'The bird wasn't real, OK?' I shout, pleading my case. '*Not* real. It was a stupid fake parrot pinned to his shoulder, and he kept making it talk.' I eye-pop everyone, then backpedal a little, remembering. 'But yeah, the shirt may have ripped when I *accidentally—*'

Finn tuts.

'*Accidentally* bumped him,' I finish, knowing Finn's far from done.

'Oh, there was an accident, all right.' Finn waves a hand in the air and scoffs. 'Little Miss Mayhem over there swung her club all willy-nilly, causing her golf ball to ping throughout the place. It actually zinged back and struck him! He almost lost an eye. Poor guy had to visit the doc, ice it, and wear a medic eye patch.'

Dean gasps. Dora's hands are over her mouth. The couple at the next table gawk.

'He liked the patch,' I mumble, but no one's listening.

'Is that what you told yourself when you *bailed* on him?' He spins to address the entire restaurant, nodding as he makes his closing argument. 'She did. She just ditched him and the parrot, leaving them wounded and alone. Said she had *cramps*.'

A universal gasp ensues.

'Using the cramp card's pretty low, Libbs,' Dean says in a whisper.

The back of my neck warms, and I'm sure my cheeks are pink. My head smacks into my hands. *God.* How in blazes did Finn turn this all around? Lesson learned: never argue with a court attorney. I never stood a chance, even if his idiotic date set-up was an inch tall, with a parrot and . . . I peek over my fingertips at my accusers and sigh.

Finn has his arms crossed, shaking his head. Dean and Dora are just staring; they may be in shock. The matchy-match running duo stabs me with their glares. Even Hash-Brown Harry is eye-balling me. Or maybe he's looking over my shoulder. I'm not really sure he can see.

Regardless, it's a hung jury. Mine.

Finn knows he won. 'If anything, Libbs, *you* owe *Nigel* an apology.'

'Hear, hear,' everyone agrees.

Their words slap me across the face, and my cheeks burn from the strike. The whole thing's embarrassing. I open my mouth to say one thing, but something else comes to mind.

The truth.

They're right. The minute I saw Nigel Harrington the Athlete was mini, I ruled him out; and *wow*, I *was* kind of awful. He never stood a chance, did he? I mean, he's not Ollie. Ollie, with that warm laugh and rogue smirk when he thinks he's clever. Or the stare that lingers, unblinking, and you think surely everyone in the room will notice.

After a moment I drop my hands and admit apologetically. 'OK, fine, I get it. I'm guilty.' I look to the eavesdropping couple. 'Guilty as charged, OK? I sentence myself to formally apologize.' I shrug to Finn. 'Do you have his address? I'll send him a card, maybe a new shirt—'

'And he had to pay for the hat you stole.' Finn's brows arch.

'*Libbs* . . .' Dora says, aghast. Then the waitress appears with our food, stopping my persecution.

Too bad I'm not hungry any more.

It's late, and although I did manage a few hours of shut-eye, I'm in my TV room staring at the wall. More specifically, at the small crack that runs diagonally through it. I follow its line with my eyes until it splits and ends near the baseboard. Does it breach the foundation, or is it merely surface? Without hiring an expert, I have no way to determine the extent of damage.

Earlier, all I did was shout, and now I'm wracked with tears and fears. Both things I can do without. So pathetic. Thank God people don't know what a massive cry-baby I am. I'm not sure they'd believe it if I told them. And they certainly wouldn't under-stand it. I'm not sure I do. It's weak and pitiful, and I hate it.

I blow my nose and fold my knees up to hug them, which used to be easier when I was younger and minus the squidgy middle.

I keep thinking about Pretty in Pink, and Ollie, and the un-fortunate Athlete date. I really was all kinds of awful. I didn't even see it that way until Finn flipped the script on me. First thing tomorrow, I need to purchase Nigel a new shirt, and I'll send it with my hat. Maybe he can get his money back from the mini-golf place.

And I should send him a parrot.

CHAPTER 11
The Criminal

The better part of my morning and afternoon has consisted of shopping. I've found the perfect replacement shirt for Nigel. It's a sporty long-sleeve, non-wicking compression thing. At least that's what the salesman said (minus the 'thing' part). I packed it with my pirate hat and a nice apology card. Then I drove to his gym to personally hand-deliver it all, because I also got him something that can't be mailed.

A mid-size, blue and green, *real* macaw parrot.

His name is Bluebird. Not exactly original, but he does in fact have blue markings, so it fits. Although, I'm calling him Blue*beard* and he doesn't seem to mind. Maybe he thinks I have a strange New York accent where instead of dropping my r's, I twist them.

When Bluebeard said 'Hi, pretty lady' in the pet store, he completely won me over. And after sharing my sad, pathetic story, I won the shop keeper over. He practically gave him to me for free, so how could I refuse? Nigel would forgive me at once and my guilty conscience would be absolved.

Fat chance. I'm still being punished.

Bluebeard talks, all right: he also does non-stop super-loud sound effects. I learned this in the car when he shrieked police sirens the entire ride, which explains why the pet store owner was so quick to be rid of him. By the time we got to Nigel's gym, my nerves were completely raw and frazzled. The staff looked at me like I was crazy. Can't say I blame them. I was dressed for my legal meeting at Pretty in Pink with Seth Merriweather, the Criminal, and, well . . .

Regardless of whether Seth and I like each other enough to go through with a real date at a later time, I need him to take my store situation seriously – which means taking me seriously – but I really didn't have anything appropriate to wear. It's not like I own a proper suit. So I made do with what I found crammed in the back of my closet.

It's a polyester-blend black skirt set with football-sized shoulder pads. And it's not exactly cheer-worthy; in fact, it's rather bleak. I hoped that adding a bright yellow tank, matching bangles and my signature one star dangle earring would negate its sad aspect and poor fit. The last time I wore it was in high school.

It's not my best look. The parrot didn't help.

So, yeah, the strange looks were understandable.

'You can't leave the bird,' Body by Jake said when I waddled in. 'No one's here after five, and—'

'But he's a gift.' I hoisted his cage up higher, which was no easy task. The bird doesn't weigh much, but the cage is at least ten pounds, what with its multi-tiered ladders, bells and bottom pull-out tray. 'Oh, and he talks. Say hi, Bluebeard.'

He whistled a loud catcall, causing several fit women to turn and look at Jake, who then smiled.

'See? He likes you,' I said hopefully, really needing to put everything down. Between the oversized cage, bird and gift bag, my arms were shaking.

He shook his lug head. 'Lady, you can't leave the bird. I'm sorry.'

'But he's no trouble, and I brought all the stuff. Nigel doesn't need to get *anything*.' I'd spent a small fortune on food, toys, even a 'how to care for your parrot' book. 'Look, I know for a fact Nigel really, really likes parrots. *Please*, just take him.'

'Wait . . .' His eyes pinched, then went wide. '*You're* the bird killer?'

'What? No. Well, yes, but that one was fake.' Does everyone know about this? 'And see? I'm trying to make it up with Bluebeard here, so come on, whaddya say?' I shook the cage, causing the bird to catcall again and laugh, which sounded freakishly human and evil. *Who in the world taught him that?* This again caused looks, and not in a good way.

'Yeah . . .' Blockhead scowled. 'You both gotta go.'

So I left the other stuff, and I still have the bird.

'Hi, pretty lady.'

'Hi, yourself,' I mumble back.

In the small office at the back of my store, I sit hunched over my computer, waiting for Seth. Boxed merchandise is stacked near one side of the door, almost blocking the entrance. Paper towels and office supplies purchased in bulk are stacked near the other. The space is cluttered and could use a good sorting, but the desk is large, and I have more than enough room. Plus, I rather like the seclusion and quiet.

'Hi, pretty lady.'

Well, I *did*. I eyeball Bluebeard as he head-bobs, and sigh.

Online, I scour the internet for locations, but nothing lines up. I just can't imagine Pretty in Pink anywhere else. *This* is my store. My whole life is wrapped up in these walls. How is any other site going to feel like home?

Well, at this rate, I won't need to worry about that. I can't find anything. Everything's the same: major build-out costs, common area fees and high rent. The far and away districts have some move-in-ready lease options, but even those are double what I pay now. I swallow hard and glance at the financials that are spread on my desk.

What I need is a hot bath, a bottle of wine and a new life – or no life, because if Pretty in Pink goes under, so do I. Rubbing at the side of my neck, I try to release the taut muscles, to no avail.

'Hi, pretty lady.'

'Hi,' I say back half-heartedly, and continue browsing.

'Karma Chameleon' is cranked through the speakers, and the song's fitting. I'm getting my karmic justice for everything. If Nigel doesn't call, I'm returning the bird first thing, come morning.

The overhead fluorescents flip on with a blinking buzz. I jump, and the bird gives a bloodcurdling shriek.

'Sorry,' I call out. It's Jasper, in his normal attire of frayed jeans and concert T-shirt. Maybe going deaf is another thing I should tack on my 'crap things to look forward to' list. I didn't even hear him come in, and after the bird's shrill scream, I may never hear again. 'What are you doing here?'

'Have some work to catch up on.' Jas tosses his keys onto the filing cabinet. He looks from the bird to me. 'I thought you killed the bird. Don't tell me you whacked the pirate king instead?' His lips are curled in a dangerous smile.

'Of course not.' My head jerks back. 'Wait . . . how do you know about the bird?'

'Finn called earlier, looking for you.' Jas leans in the doorway, eyeing my clothes. 'So if not the bird, who died?'

I look down at my outfit self-consciously. 'Funny.' Just as I'm about to launch into a full blow-by-blow of the disaster date, I stop myself, remembering yesterday's scolding. 'The bird is a gift for Nigel, the Athlete. Turns out he's a decent enough date. Even if I wasn't.' The last part's mumbled.

'I heard about that, too.' Jas's face screws up. 'So you bought him a bird?'

'Not one of my better ideas.'

My phone vibrates on the desk. 'Hang on.' I glance down. It's Seth. 'Hello?'

Jas watches me curiously.

'OK, sure.' Now he wants to meet for *dinner*? 'No, no, I'll meet you there, it's fine . . . Yeah, I know where it is.'

'You have another date?' Jasper asks in a whisper.

'Sounds great. See you in about an hour?' I disconnect and regard him. 'I didn't. We were supposed to meet here to go over the lease stuff. That was the attorney from Finn's firm. He's also the Criminal.'

'Wait.' Jasper makes a face as if he's tasting something bitter. 'The Criminal's your attorney?'

'I know . . .' I roll my eyes. 'He works with Finn. I'm hoping he'll have some good news about the shop.'

'You think they've changed their mind?'

'No; I said *hoping*.' I motion to the screen. 'I'm looking, but really, nothing fits. I need to either convince the attorney to convince them, or we need to think outside the box. Like mall kiosks or something; I don't know.' My stomach drops just saying that option out loud. I don't care if it's doable; it's a cart, not a store.

'Hi, pretty lady.'

I glance at Bluebeard, then back at Jas.

'No,' Jas says, already knowing what I'm about to ask. He's shaking his head. 'Forget it, Libbs.'

'Then what am I supposed to do with him? I have cats, the pet store's closed, and I can't just leave him here alone.'

Jas shrugs. 'Take him.'

'Take him where? On my date?'

He scoffs. 'I thought this wasn't a date.'

'It's not, I'm officially done with the Eighties intervention thing, but . . .' I lean back, distressed.

'You're done?' Jasper shakes his head. 'Libbs, you have to be willing to put yourself out there if you want the big gesture.'

'Big gesture?'

Jasper smiles crookedly, but it's only half-cocked. 'Ya know – the big gesture, when they do something so huge, so out of character, that you know it's sincerely from the heart. But you have to meet them halfway. Give 'em a chance.'

'Oh, and they're gonna give me a chance?' If my words weren't clear enough, my screwed-up expression is.

'Look, just be yourself, and they'll either adore you just as you are—'

'Hi pretty lady.'

Jas stifles a laugh. 'Or they won't.'

God.

♫

Parked outside the River Cafe in my car, I take in the view and try not to worry about what I can't help worrying about: Oliver, my stupid birthday, the shop, the Eighties intervention and what the heck to do with this blasted parrot. I bribed the valet to let me park myself (most likely illegally) near the front. I explained, quite dramatically, that the bird was endangered and rare and required a special life-saving medication, so I would need easy accessibility in order to check on him. When he asked what was wrong with it I said 'bird flu' without thinking, then quickly recovered by stuffing a few more bills in his hand.

'Hi, pretty lady.'

Bluebeard's cage is beside me, secured with the seat belt. Tilting back, I glance round. It really is lovely here. The restaurant's waterfront location offers indoor and outdoor dining with full views of the East River and the Manhattan skyline. Lights dot the far horizon in fuzzy colour blobs and dip mindlessly beyond the Brooklyn Bridge.

My nerves are in a tizzy and nausea overwhelms me, so I roll the window halfway down to feel the breeze. There's something different about wind coming off of water. It's dewy and scented and because we're at summer's end it carries the crisp promise of fall. I inhale deeply, comforted by the scent, and enticed by the ones coming from the restaurant. At least I get to eat this time round.

'Hi, pretty lady.'

'Bye, annoying bird.' Time to move. 'The window's cracked and I won't be long,' I tell Bluebeard, as if he understands. He head-bobs his response.

I slide out, lock the door and try to take another calming, deep breath, but my ribs are constricted. The pinched puff-sleeved jacket cuts into my air supply. Walking in this getup also proves to be a challenge. The skirt's tight around my knees so my thighs can't separate. Good thing we won't be walking, I just need to get inside and strike a pose.

I regard my reflection as I approach the restaurant's double doors. I'm Joan Collins in *Dynasty*. I'm Julia Sugarbaker from *Designing Women*. Hell, I'm Tess in *Working Girl*. Just like them, I'm independent and strong.

The door sticks, and I can't pull it open. Maybe not that strong. With both hands, I lean into it and work it open an inch at a time.

'I'm meeting Seth Merriweather?' I say to the lithe blonde greeter behind the hostess stand. It comes out sounding like a question.

She's wearing a face that shows she's trying to put me with him, or him with me, and it's not matching up. Or maybe she's constipated. Same face. 'Right ... ah, this way, please,' she says at last.

I totter behind the prune-deprived woman with mini knee-bend steps, trying desperately to match her brisk pace. My black ensemble is a bold contrast to the sea of stripped serenity, and everyone turns as I shuffle past.

Raising my chin, I smile slightly. Stay confident, stay focused, stay *upright*. My bowed ballet flats are slippery on the restaurant's wooden floor. Thank God I wasn't foolish enough to attempt heels.

She motions to the small linen-clad table, the one with the man facing the other direction, and turns to leave me to it. *OK.* This is it. I move so I'm in sight and give my brightest, razzle-dazzle, please-have-good-news-and-save-my-store smile.

'Seth?'

'Libby?' Seth stands. 'You *must* be Libby. Finn described you perfectly.'

Really? He said I'd be in a too-tight black-poly suit? Too bad Finn didn't describe him as anything other than 'throwback', which I took to mean he'd resemble the criminal Judd Nelson from the Eighties. He did get the decade right, I'll give him that much.

Seth Merriweather is Phil Collins. The groovy kind, with straggly mullet and reverse-horseshoe combover. And maybe there's *No Jacket Required . . . But Seriously*, an appropriate shirt is. Why is he dressed for 'Another Day in Paradise'? He's in a loosely buttoned, monochromatic Hawaiian shirt with a gold chain proudly displayed in the collar. Well, I guess it is the weekend, but still.

I do my best to maintain my smile, because really, it doesn't matter. 'I Don't Care Anymore', because I'm 'In Too Deep' and I need his help with my store, even if it is 'Against the Odds'.

He smiles, the kind that's held long after the initial reaction, and motions for me to sit. I wedge myself into the chair across from him. There's a rip. The cool sensation of vinyl against the back of my thighs confirms it. The skirt's just split in back.

♪

This is supposed to be a work meeting to discuss my financials and options, but it's been thirty minutes of Seth talking about his ex-wife and how they have a decent relationship for the sake of the kids. How he tries to see them every chance he can, and thinks he's a better dad now than when they were all living under one roof as a dysfunctional family unit.

I've heard that one at least a dozen times. My observation is this: when the parents are together, lots of dads are present for the important things like soccer and football games or choir concerts, but they aren't present in the everyday. The quantity isn't quality. On their own, the time spent with their children is scheduled. It becomes a manageable priority, a compressed block of time with a clear beginning and end.

Does it make them bad fathers? No, of course not. It just means they perform better in the 100-metre dash than cross-country. And truthfully, most of us do. The endurance needed for day-to-day relationships is exhausting. *This* is exhausting.

While Seth gabs, I'm politely bobbing my head because I'm, well, eating: wild North Atlantic halibut with roasted mushroom and green peppercorn sauce, garden peas and pickled spring onions. 'So good,' I say, dabbing my mouth with a napkin. We have yet to discuss my store, so I'm confused, but I'm also hungry. I can't remember when I last ate, or ate so *well*. The food is incredible.

With a final swallow, I take a drink of tea and ask, 'How many children did you say?' Then I take another bite while he answers. Seriously, so good.

' . . . the oldest, Marcus, is sixteen, and the youngest, Ruth, is twelve. Rand's in the middle at fourteen. They're a good group, somewhat mouthy, but weren't we all?'

'Yeah, teenagers.' I say this like I know, which I don't. I mean, I was one, I'm around them at the shop, I still feel like one . . .

'What about you?' He takes a few short, fast nibbles of his yeast roll.

'Am I mouthy?'

He half-laughs after thinking about it. 'No, I meant do you have kids?'

Rupert comes to mind. Our messy separation and divorce, the custody battle over the Great Dane that I never wanted but now must have, and all the other vivid tales of our fictional life; but I stop myself. He knows Finn. 'I never quite got around to kids – or, really, marriage, for that matter.' I add the last part because I know that'd be his next question and I don't want to get into it. I shrug. 'I have enough to handle with my business.'

'Oh right, the business.' He taps the table with his knuckles as if he only just remembered. 'That is, after all, why we're here, isn't it?' He smiles sheepishly. 'And here I am just going on and on about personal matters. Forgive me, Libby, you're so easy to talk to. I should only bill you half.'

Or not at all. 'So, did you discover a loophole that allows us to stay?' *Say yes. Please say yes.*

'I thought Finn informed you,' he says, chin dipped. 'The eviction's legal. Your lease doesn't hold up. It dissolved with their bankruptcy, so the property must be vacated next week.'

Finn may have informed me, but that doesn't mean I've accepted it. I take a minute to readjust my tactic. 'I can't move the store. I've looked. Everything's overpriced with tacked-on fees, so . . .'

He shakes his head incredulously. 'Surely something's available.'

'Surely you can find a way for us to stay.' I set my fork across my plate to signal my ravenous appetite's now exhausted. In fact, the bloat in my gut is making me uncomfortable. 'Look . . .' I reach into my bag and pull out my financials, desperate to show him the healthy bottom line and how it sickens with the new adjustments.

He quickly takes them and begins thumbing through. Flipping to the profit and loss, his eyebrows hike. They climb high into his missing hairline. 'Oh, yes, OK then.' After a moment they drop, slanting heavily. 'Mmm . . .'

'Mmm? What does that mean?' A strong, unsettling prickle crawls over my skin as I watch him.

'Another tea?' the waitress asks, peering into my near-empty glass.

'Only if it's a Long Island.' I pull a face to show I'm serious, because I am.

She collects a few plates, then disappears. I can't stand the wait any longer. 'Do you see what I mean? My expenses are so low that—'

'They are.' Seth glances up. 'Do you mind if I take these? I mean, if I know your bottom line and exactly how much wiggle room you have, maybe I can help. I have a few resources I could tap for possible quick and ready move-in opportunities.' His face opens with the suggestion.

Mine opens with hope. 'Yes, of course. If you think they may be able to find something in such a short time, that'd be utterly fantastic.' I'm grateful for the offer, but it's short-lived and my mood deflates as I realize there most certainly has to be one. I must, without question, relocate Pretty in Pink.

In a week.

God.

'Or maybe you can ask for an extension?' I try one last-ditch effort. 'More time would be helpful.'

'I'm doubtful they'll concede to that, but I can try. How about I get back to you sometime tomorrow, or Tuesday at the absolute latest?' He stacks my financials neatly and places them inside his satchel. 'Oh, and as I mentioned to Finn, there may be some interest from the property owners to purchase if you'd con—'

'It's not for sale.'

'But it might—'

'Not for sale.' I hold his gaze to hold my ground.

'To be honest, Libby, I don't think they'll grant an extension, and if my realtor connections don't come through, then selling is your *only* option.' With just a twitch of his brow, his entire demeanour shifts from groovy to gangster, instinctively causing my insides to bristle.

'Excuse me . . . someone's alarm is going off. Excuse me.' The hostess is running from table to table, inquiring to guests. 'It's an older grey sedan with a bumper sticker that reads, ah . . . "What if Stacey's mom was Jessie's girl and named Jenny?"' She doesn't have a clue what that means.

And I don't have an alarm.

Bluebeard.

God.

145

CHAPTER 12

'Tainted Love'
Soft Cell, 1981

Tainted life

It's Monday, and although I called to reschedule tomorrow's appointment with Dr P., he somehow convinced me to come over immediately, saying I sounded stressed. Well, *yeah*, so here I am back at his office. Same dim lamp on the same dated end table. Same story. Mine. And I'm sick to death of it.

I'm almost thirty-three. A good portion of my life is over, and what have I actually accomplished with the years I've been given? Dr P. asked me to write a 'who am I' essay. The better question is, 'who am I without my store?' And I don't know. I just know this can't continue. *I* can't continue. Not like this. Maybe I really am the Basket Case. At this moment I can definitely relate. I pick at my nail.

No, forget it; if I were Allison, aka the Basket Case, I'd be chewing on my nail, not just randomly messing with it. Bender said if she kept chewing on her hand she wouldn't be hungry at lunch, and she spat it at him. I mean, *God*, like I'd do that. So, I'm hold-ing on to Claire. Yeah, I'd rather be Claire because she kissed Bender and – well, Ollie's Bender.

'Libby?'

'Sorry?' I snap to attention. I know this is where I need to be, and yet I'd rather be anywhere else, and it's obvious. It's like I'm in detention for real.

'I asked about the *who am I* essay? Did you bring it?'

'Nope; I haven't finished it yet.' Haven't even looked at it. 'I did meet with the Criminal, not that it was a date. He's a work col-league of Finn's, and trying to help sort the must-move-my-store debacle. I told you about him.'

'And?' Dr P. leans back, rocking his chair by flexing his feet as I explain in detail the latest non-developments.

'I just can't find anything to work within my margins, and the attorney doesn't feel an extension is possible. He's recommend-ing I *sell* – can you believe it?'

'Libby, if it's not feasible to move, and you must vacate, and this attorney feels there may be an interest to purchase the store, why not consider it?'

All rational and good points, but the question lances through my heart. How do I explain it's not just a store? That it's my life, my life *support*. The minute I sign it away, it'd be like authorizing them to pull the plug. There'd be nothing left of me. If it's gone, I was never here.

I don't answer. When it's obvious I'm not going to, he changes the subject. 'Is there a date tonight? Am I remembering that correctly?'

I just want to forget. 'It's tomorrow; the Princess. I did have one with the Athlete, though.' I regret the words the minute they leave my mouth.

'How'd that go?' He rolls his neck and straightens in his chair, ready for my story.

'OK, so . . .' I don't disappoint, launching into Version One: mini man, monster truck, majorly annoying.

Dr P.'s laughing.

But then I explain Finn's version: mad woman, mayhem, majorly judgemental. 'I tried to make up for it with my apology gifts, including Bluebeard, but he still hasn't called me back.'

'So you still have the parrot?'

'Not exactly.' I explain how I was practically forced to take him with me to meet my attorney, and left him in the car. 'With the window cracked,' I say, to make sure he knows I was being responsible. Regardless of how irritating the dumb thing was, I have a soft spot for animals. 'So he was really OK and the meeting wasn't that long, but . . . he talks and does siren sounds and, well, he disturbed the diners.' I leave out how I bribed the parking attendant due to the rare bird flu disorder and need of life-saving meds, which explains (in my hypothetical world) why the vehicle simply had to be in close proximity to the restaurant at all times.

'So what happened to the bird?'

'Seth kind of loved him, so Bluebeard has a new home, but now I'm wondering if I made a mistake. Seth is kinda, I don't know, questionable. He probably won't take good care of him, or clean his cage enough, or give him the treats I bought. Oh God, what if he gives him to one of his *kids*? I bet he does . . .'

My mind is racing round the imagined scenario. They would come by for a visit and be so impressed with Bluebeard's tricks that Seth would hand him over, feeling like the part-time-dad hero. They won't take care of him. I just know it. My insides are guilt-stricken. Poor Bluebeard. What have I done? Instead of a pretty lady, I'm pretty lame.

'Libby?' Dr P. has a half-smile plastered on his face. 'I'm sure this Seth Merriman—'

'Merriweather.'

'Merriweather is capable of caring for a parrot. You should try and have an open mind. Give him the benefit of the doubt. Is he someone maybe you could see yourself dating?'

My face says it all, which is good, 'cause what do I say to that? I compress my lips and swallow painfully.

'So, that's a no?' Dr P. shakes his head. 'Can you think of one date you've been on in the last five years where the man didn't have major flaws?' His hands interlock and fold over his middle.

I scratch my head as my mind churns through anyone and everyone I've gone out with. 'Keith. He was fun, although he had a gap-toothed smile that went way beyond signature or sexy, so . . .' I look up and to the left as I scroll through the last few years. '*Oh* – no, he was divorced twice. That's problematic, times two. And Terry was nice-looking and decent, he just, I don't know, everything was football; and he smelled of cheese.' I pull a face.

'What about your friend, the one you mentioned works with you?'

'Jasper? He smells nice, actually.' I knew that wasn't what he meant, but . . .

'Would you date him?'

'He's asked several times, but he's probably not serious, and no, we work together. Plus, I consider him one of my best friends, so I don't want to ruin that.'

'Why would that ruin your friendship?'

'Because things are great. He's super-clever. You wouldn't think it by looking at him, but under the grunge is a really great guy. And if we dated, I might find out he's annoying, or worse, not all that bright.'

'Or what if he got to really know *you* and changed *his* mind?'

I shrug, still undecided how to change the conversation effectively into something else.

Dr P. does it for me. 'I'm curious: have you ever told Oliver how you feel?' Using his toes to push against the floor, he swivels the chair back and forth like a cat's agitated tail.

My chin lowers. 'Sure, I guess.' I flip my hand in the air, dismissively. 'Maybe, I don't know.'

'Have you ever told *anyone* how you really feel? Even once?'

'I can tell you I don't feel like talking about this. Does that count?' My gaze falls to the chair arm and I pick at a loose thread. The off-white jacquard pattern could unravel with just one firm tug.

He stretches and leans forward. 'Libby, I have no doubt you had and still have very real feelings for Oliver, but that may be the problem. He's moved on, and you haven't.'

My tongue scrapes the front of my teeth, pushing out my lip temporarily. I get what he's implying, but anger wiggles under my skin, making it crawl. My toes tap inside my Chuck Taylor high-tops, trying to pacify it.

'I think you hide behind a barrier of humour and sarcasm.

150

That way, no one can see your vulnerability. And yes, I understand it's a survival mechanism; but when is it off?' After a beat, he lifts his chin. 'So I have some homework for you. I'd like you to really try and get to know this next date. Let your guard down.'

Is everyone in on this? I stab a glare in his direction. He's seriously grating on me. I'm on the edge of my seat, ready to leave.

Dr P. lowers his voice. 'I'm not attacking you.'

I tut. 'Really?'

'Really. I said come in ready to work. Well, it's time to work. And I'm going to be frank with you, put it out on the table, because I want to make sure you understand what you're dealing with—'

'I get what I'm dealing with, trust me.' I fall back into the chair with a huff, somewhat peevish and uncomfortable in my own skin. It's tight from restraining the emotional bloat.

'Yeah?' That's all he says. Dr P. kicks his head back and looks to the ceiling, lowering only his gaze to fix it on me.

'Yeah,' I say, clipped, somewhat sharper than intended. Again I readjust my feet.

'So you're angry with me? Ollie? Your friends? Who?'

'I'm not angry, I'm—'

'Angry. That's what the feeling's called.'

I'm back up again. 'I don't care what it's called. I don't wanna feel it, OK?'

Dr P. sits forward, too, motioning with his hands. 'You feel it because the ineffective crutch you've created in Oliver is being pointed out. You feel it because the one thing you honestly have a sense of accomplishment in, your store, might slip away. You feel it—'

'I don't care why I feel it. I want it gone.' I wave my hand. 'And you don't know everything, OK?'

'So tell me.'

'Why?' I lean back, staring at the wall. 'It just gets worse. We talk and everything gets worse. That's what happened before, so maybe starting up again is a huge mistake.' There, I've said it, and in this moment, I mean it.

I'm ready to quit. Him, me, everything.

'That's the process, Libby, and I promise you, it works.'

My gaze slides back to his. 'Yeah, well, the process sucks.'

'It does. Yes. You've heard the saying, *if you're going through hell, keep on going*? Well, don't stop now, 'cause it's about to get good and hot. But you're the one who has to do it. I'm only a tool to help you. This is all you.'

I glance at the clock, wondering if he knows how pretentious he sounds. *This is all you, Libby*. As if I don't know that. I mean, *duh*.

He wets his lips. 'I want to try something different, but I need your commitment to be here Wednesday, Thursday and Friday, no exceptions.'

There's a sharp silence. The pause is pregnant, further along than Dora and carrying the Thompson Twins.

'So, do I have your word?'

'Sure,' I say, meaning *maybe*.

His eyes are locked onto mine, cutting through my nonsense. 'I need you to promise, Libby.'

That does me in. Trust is everything to him. We spent an entire session talking about it. I rub the back of my neck, already hating this. 'Yeah, fine, OK. I promise to be here. But three days in a row? Is that *really* necessary? I have a lot on my plate right now.'

'It is. And with everything going on, it's perfect. You'll have to trust me on this. I'd like to try something called EMDR. It stands for eye movement desensitization and reprocessing.'

I cringe. 'That sounds painful.'

'It's not.' He tilts his head. 'Well, not physically, anyway. But if we do it right, it'll allow you to release the emotional kind. I'm hoping this will help unlock some repressed memories. Make sense of those bits and pieces that are surfacing. The things you're refusing to deal with.'

Goosebumps speckle my arms at his words. There's nothing I can say, so I'm silent.

'OK, we start Wednesday.'

God.

CHAPTER 13

The Princess

It's less than a week until my party. My birthday's chasing me down, sprinting in brand-new running shoes, and I'm a bit out of shape, practically wheezing with side stitches as I try and stay ahead.

The first two dates were disastrous – and yes, I'm now openly claiming *some* of the responsibility. And while the Criminal one wasn't really a date, it was equally uncomfortable and even more disappointing. He looked nothing like Judd Nelson. At least Dr Theo did look like the Brain, Anthony Michael Hall; and Nigel was a jock and short like the Athlete; so what happened to Seth? And tonight is the Princess? Although if he looks like Molly Ringwald, I'm done. I'm not going out with anyone prettier than me. At that, I draw the line.

Since this is Finn's choice again, he made me promise to behave. And I'm trying, really. I'm not even overdoing my Eighties vibe to prove a point. But holy hell, I'm failing miserably. I used the salon's styling goop, and I've utterly screwed it up. It's slicked, shiny and stiff, but only at the sides. I swooped it back, and the top flopped forward in a cascade of curls, and it froze like that.

Froze.

I'm the lead singer of A Flock of Seagulls, and my date is going to run, run so far away if Dora can't fix this. She's currently en route to my apartment.

Taking a sip of wine, I stare down at my wardrobe choices: leather skinny pants, which take at least fifteen minutes to get on and another ten to shimmy out of; a linen shirtdress in pinstripes that's too tight, which Dora said was the point; and yoga pants that pair with the lightweight sweater. Or maybe the shirt goes with the skinny trousers in grey. And why's everything *skinny*? I'm not skinny.

The buzzer rings. *Finally.* I swing open the door.

'Oh God.' Dora's expression drops. She turns to Finn. 'She has *wings*. Literal wings.'

'Why is *he* here?' I ask Dora, who ignores me while eyeballing Finn. But I already know the answer. Dean couldn't make it, and probably insisted she didn't travel alone in her condition. She also can't drive due to her growing belly. Dora's short, so she has to pull the seat up close, and her baby bump is starting to get in the way of her steering. It's kind of funny, but inconvenient. I suggested she rig up some pedal blocks. She suggested I reel in the commentary.

Finn rushes past Dora, mouth agape, phone in hand. 'Oh, honey . . . no, just no.' *Snap-flash.* He's laughing, leans close, gives an open-mouthed smile next to my cheek and clicks one of us together. *Snap-flash.*

Dora's shaking her head. 'Shower. You absolutely must start again.'

'And what's she wearing?' Finn says to Dora, as if I can't hear him.

'I was in the middle of changing, so . . .' I say and turn, moving to the kitchen. *Forget it.* I look around, forgetting why I came in here. I grab my glass of wine and regard Finn. 'Have you talked to Seth?'

He perches on my couch arm. 'Did you *like* our smooth Criminal?'

'Not so much, but he has Bluebeard, and I'm worried.'

'He has a blue beard – what?' Dora forehead-bunches, confused. She has one shoe off to rub her swollen ankle. 'Is this another men's movement thing?'

Finn snorts a breath. 'Hardly. Are you ready for this? Bluebeard's a *parrot.* Our dear Libby gave Seth a parrot.'

'So did you talk to him or not?' I ask, ignoring their side conversation.

'Wait.' Dora holds her hand up. 'I thought you killed the parrot, and that was with the Athlete. Why does the Criminal have a parrot too?' Dora looks back and forth between us. 'Seriously, what's up with all these parrots?'

Without answering, I disappear to de-wing. I'm determined to make this date count. And maybe make myself a sandwich, since I have no idea if dinner's included. Oh yeah, that's the reason I went into the kitchen.

♫

Inside the cab, I fidget with my handbag, a bit nervous for what we could possibly have in common. I mean, look at him. At least I *think* Adrian's a he – the name does in fact go both ways. But as I explicitly expressed to Finn, I don't.

Although I can see why Finn pegged him as a princess, Adrian's a bit androgynous and either a pretty 'he' with feminine qualities, or a 'she' with unfortunate ones. There's a five o'clock shadow. There's also blue eyeshadow and eyeliner, so I'm utterly confused. I also like the shade: a bright robin's-egg combo is hard to find these days.

'That's a great replica,' Adrian says, glancing over.

'This?' I hold up the small Fendi baguette, the one item I didn't update. 'It's actually vintage.'

'Oh, brilliant.' His face brightens at the discovery of common ground. 'I love searching for retro treasure, where'd you find it? No. 6 in Little Italy? Amarcord in SoHo?'

'Oh, it was a while ago, so I don't really remember.' I smile with a head-shake. I don't mention it's because it wasn't vintage when my mom purchased it in the Eighties. I loved raiding her closet as a teen.

At least he has taste. We'll call that . . . what's the opposite of Strike One? Should I give gold stars? See? I'm thinking positive, and looking for the good instead of a way out. One shiny lucky star it is for us both.

We turn onto Washington Street in the Meatpacking District of Manhattan and pull alongside the curb.

'Here we are.' Adrian pays the cabbie, then reaches over to pop the door. I step out and . . . my newly cheerful disposition spirals. Hip twentysomethings are gathered in front of a bright red building. This isn't a restaurant. 'This is Cielo's,' I say, turning to face him.

He quirks an eyebrow with a nod. 'Right. This is where I dance.'

Where he dances? Has Cielo's incorporated poles? I'm either going to learn if Adrian prefers Jack or Diane, or –

'Finn mentioned you like to shake a tail feather?'

'Sure, but it's usually at Culture Club.' Culture Club is a midtown venue owned by Debbie Gibson that plays Eighties music I'm familiar with; but in truth, I haven't been there since the reopening in 2011.

Adrian begins chatting up the bouncer, who could be Nigel's younger and much taller brother, while I consider my moves. I can 'Walk Like an Egyptian', 'Bust a Move' or drop and wiggle the worm. *Ugh* – my stomach crawls like one. We're waved right in. Great.

Immediately I'm assaulted by the techno beat and flashing lights. The bass thumps against my ribcage and the matching strobe blinds me. Well, now I can see – nope, dark again – *oh* – 'Sorry,' I say, running into a girl. I *think* that was a girl; the lights are gone again.

The lasers overhead flash different colours, revealing a massive wave of reappearing gyrating movement to a song I vaguely recognize. *But how do you dance to this?* It's not even music. I squint to focus. *Is that even dancing?* I think it's a sampling of Janet Jackson's 'Rhythm Nation', and they need some 'Control', 'cause this 'Escapade' is a sexcapade.

'What?' I turn back to Adrian, but he's not talking to me; he's chatting with Boobzilla and her friend, Forgot-my-skirt. This places him firmly in the *he* department for sure, which is a good and positive development.

Adrian says something, the trouble twins giggle, then he turns to me. 'What are you drinking?'

'Lots,' I say, and smile. I'll need it. Happy juice is essential if I'm to survive the night.

'Coming right up.' And he's off, stopping every few feet to flirt with . . . well, those are men, and now I'm confused all over again.

Forget it. This is already a complete catastrophe. Moving from the flow of traffic, I whip out my phone and text Dora.

Help, at Cielo's! Princess has twinkle toes. Mine are MC Hammer. He's going to have broken ones!

Actually, I've never been able to do Hammer's fancy footwork. Whenever I try, I look like I'm in seizure. I do own some drop trousers, though, which would have been more comfortable than this too-tight shirtdress thing. I should've just listened to Jas and gone as myself. Instead, I'm the creation of Dora Finnstein. My phone buzzes in my hand.

What? DO NOT HAMMER! I repeat, It's NOT Hammer time. Just bob and shuffle.

Bob and shuffle? 'What the blazes is that?' I ask no one. Maybe I *should* ask someone. Looking around, I study the moves and try to inconspicuously copy in mini-version. OK, lots of bum shaking. I can do that. Shake, shake, shake. Now, lift the hands, wiggle down and repeat.

There doesn't seem to be any pattern to this, though. I half-smile to a man who's glanced my way. Maybe I shouldn't practise. *Where's Adrian with that drink?* I'm trying to think joyful thoughts. Be positive. Make an effort. Blah blah blah.

I turn, scanning the mob and – *no way*. He's with Booblicious, a drink in each hand, and he's tearing up the dance floor. Well, if you can call what they're doing dancing – the girl's basically mauling him. So is that guy. Really confused.

OK, Libbs. I'm doing homework for Dr P., and more importantly, I need that damn drink. I undo the top three buttons of my shirtdress, shake the girls and start bobbing my head to get the beat.

I'm going in. Lucky gold star for me. And move it, lady, 'cause I'm coming through.

The lights flash in sporadic bursts as I hobble-strut towards him, confidently, on fire. Look out. Adrian smiles. I don't. I take my drink from his hand, tip it back and it's going, going, *gone*. And then I finish his while I'm at it.

'Whoa,' I say loudly with a head-shake, handing him back the empty glasses. I stab a challenging glare to the date thief and the hairy guy, then start to get my groove on. Shake-shake-shake, hands up, wiggle down and repeat.

Boobs moves along Adrian's body, an arm on either side. She shimmies down to a squat, throwing her head wildly back and forth, creating a crazy whip effect. I snort a breath. *You can't out-Devo me, cupcake.*

I punch my arms round Adrian from the other side and go low, almost hitting her while she comes back up. *How low can I go?* Watch me. *Ha!* I'm practically on the floor.

I am on the floor.

I can't get up, Hairy Guy's too close. I reach and grab his arm with a yank, almost pulling him down with me.

I'm up. I'm on. *This* is how it's done. I clasp my hands and jut them out, only to wind them back. My hips work in tandem. Say hello to the cabbage patch. *Oh, that's right.* I bite my lip and crank faster, forcing Boobs back, back, back and away from my date.

I twist my left foot, then the right, jump and turn towards Adrian, who smiles. It's the safety dance. Nothing safe about it as I flounce about with wide, wild arms. I almost knock Hairy Guy over again.

Boobs tries to move round me, but I'm not done. My hand jabs forward in a *stop* motion, the other cups behind my head and slowly rotates with a stop-start hip-shake, only to speed it up. *Oh!* She's been hosed with the sprinkler!

Adrian laughs . . . Time to bring my victory home with the running man . . . that's right, can't catch me, I follow it with some pop and lock and . . . *stand back* . . . it's Michael Jackson's side slide. Ta-dah!

Adrian's cheering sets off a small bit of applause. I smile, quite proud of myself and give a see-ya nod to my competition. Gold stars all round.

Adrian shouts into my ear, 'That was wicked! And here I thought I was the one with the moves! Another drink?' He holds up the empty glasses.

Like he has to ask. I strut past the defeated dancing duo to follow my prize towards the bar, feeling vindicated, on top of the world, out of breath. I think I pulled something. Really, my side hurts and my left knee is throbbing.

'Tequila slammers,' Adrian calls to the bartender as we sidle up and claim some stools.

Within a few minutes we each have small glasses of yellow in front of us. 'What's in it?' I ask, leaning over to smell.

'It's just lemonade and Tequila – ready?' He lifts his, and we tap glasses. 'Cheers.' And it's down. Then another. And another.

Whoa.

I flutter-blink to get focus. We didn't eat anything. Is this a new dating trend? No dinner out? 'So, Adrian, ever been married?' Look at me making small talk, being social, trying to figure out his gender.

'Sure. Been divorced for about three years now, you?'

'Me? Oh, yeah, of course. Rupert. *Ruuu*-pert. Charming man, sweet like Andrew McCarthy, you know, from *Pretty in Pink*? He had the same squinty eyes and fake hair. You did know Andrew wore a wig in the last scene, right?'

Adrian's brows pull down. I take that to mean, no I didn't know and please continue, so I do.

'Yeah, I guess they had to reshoot the ending, the audience wanted Molly Ringwald's character to end up with him instead of the Duckman, complete and utter crap if you ask me, but anyway – Andrew had shaved his head for a play, so he had to wear a really bad wig, like my Rupert. Unfortunately, all he did was play video games.'

'Andrew McCarthy?'

'No, Rupert, *Ruuu*-pert, and I swear, he was completely useless. Then he lost his thumbs—'

'What?' Adrian's head snaps so he's looking directly at me. 'He lost his thumbs?'

I meant to say lost the *use* of his thumbs because of the gaming, but whatever, I go with it. 'Horrid accident.' I almost laugh. 'What's your ex's name?'

'Terry.'

That's helpful. 'Kids?'

Adrian leans closer. His guyliner has smudged some, but actually looks better, creating a dramatic smoky Adam Ant eye. 'Two, how about you?'

'Nope. Rupert had . . .' My eyes drop to his crotch. 'Well, like I said, *horrid* accident.'

His eyes pinch. 'Oh, *oh*.'

'Yeah,' I say, and finish off my drink. I'm not sure this is what everyone had in mind, but I am trying. 'I have all my parts, though.' I flash the thumbs up and snort-laugh.

In my thirty-two years, I have learned one thing for certain: I am not a sexy drunk. You know how women in the movies drink and get all sultry and flirty, wildly losing their inhibitions to have steamy one-night-stand sex?

Not me. Not once. Definitely not now.

I become a comedian, and I'm usually the only one laughing at my useless jokes. But let me tell you, I think I'm *hil*arious. In fact, I can't stop laughing now.

Adrian looks confused. 'Wanna dance?'

I flash him another thumbs up.

I've no idea where Adrian is, or how long I've been dancing. Everything blinks on and off. The guy I'm dancing with is facing me, now he's backwards. Trippy. He's back. 'Hi!' I laugh, and spin round and round. I've no idea what moves these are, but I'm . . . *oh shit*, I'm dizzy. Not only am I earning gold stars, I'm seeing them.

Staggering from the dance floor, I try to locate my so-called Princess date. Time to go, Cinderella. Maybe I should call my own coach, 'cause it's way after midnight. I look to the corners, trying to see over people's heads for the washroom. *There*. I'm off, weaving through – OK, more like into people. 'Hi,' I say, and flash the thumbs up again . . . OK. Right.

There's a line but I walk right past it, a hand up to silence the protests. When a girl has to go, she has to go. And I need to go . . . home, so I need a quiet place to call a cab. Reaching in my bag for my phone, I notice my wallet is MIA. How do I not have my wallet? I smack my forehead. I switched bags. I click through my phone's favourites, deciding who to call.

Dora? No, I don't want her to know I lost Adrian, and Dean wouldn't let her drive anyway. Can't call Finn, he'd never let me hear the end of it. Crap, what if the princess left *me*? That's embarrassing. No, I ditched him. I'm the original Dancing Queen. At least, Rupert always said so.

Jasper.

At Cielo's, snockered. Ditched date guy who is maybe not a guy. Need ride. No cash for cab.

I let my arm fall, still holding the phone, then lift to add . . .

Am also Hungry Like the Wolf. Feed me?

Outside the club, I dance while waiting for Jasper. In fact I'm singing 'Dancing With Myself', 'cause that's what I'm doing. A couple of guys out to have a smoke cheer me on. I give them all thumbs up.

It actually feels good out here. The brisk night air fills my lungs with every belted note. I wobble, stepping too near the curb, and almost stumble over.

'Libby. Libbs, hey . . .' It's Jasper. His hands are on my back to hold me upright.

I stop mid-note and turn, causing my adoring fans to boo.

'Yeah, all right, show's over.' He looks back at me. 'You OK?'

'I forgot my wallet 'cause I switched bags . . . so I need a ride.'

'Come on, and yeah, I got that from the string of non-stop car song titles you texted. Billy Ocean, "Get Outta My Dreams, Get Into My Car", Prince—'

'"Little Red Corvette", oh who who . . .' I can't remember any other lines, so I sing it again, then somehow morph it into 'I Would Die for You', complete with hand motions.

Jasper opens his car door for me and I fall into the passenger seat. He leans over to help me with my belt, because I'm all thumbs. *Oh God*, now I'm in a fit of laughter. He can't get the belt fastened.

He's super-close, and – 'You smell –' I sniff loudly, never really coming to a definitive conclusion of how to finish the statement. Then it's just awkward because I paused too long, which I think is funny. 'I just said you smelled.' I'm now in hysterics, folded over.

Once buckled, he closes my door, walks round and cranks the ignition. 'You good?'

'You smell *good*. That's what I meant to, yeah . . .' I let my head hit the seat back, and flash another thumbs up.

CHAPTER 14

'Talking in Your Sleep'
The Romantics, 1983

Wide awake now

'Ah,' I say in a hoarse whisper while reaching for my head – my aching, bloated melon of a head. I cough to clear my throat, and roll over . . . *whoa*. Holy moly mother of pop, I'm *rocking*. So is the room. Am I on a boat? I blink, trying to bring everything into focus. I'm surrounded by a deep, murky blue. How much did I drink that I'm seeing – *wait*.

The logic in this truth tries desperately to wiggle its way through my fog. Squeezing my eyes tight, I hold for a moment then re-open even wider . . . still blue. My bedroom walls are yellow. I blink and stretch my eyes wide, propping up on my elbow, but it sinks into the mattress.

Oh my God, it's a waterbed. Who has a waterbed any more? Why'd I get rid of mine?

In a rush of panic, I sit up, causing a tidal wave. I look left and right: exposed brick on the far wall, orange guitar leaning in the corner, nightstand without a clock, window covered by black shades. My stomach churns. *Where in blazes am I?*

Gathering the sheet tight to my chin, I slink back with a panicked heart. Is this Princess Adrian's castle? Must remember. We were dancing, and then . . . I was dancing with someone else and there was that horrid hairy guy. Did I ditch Adrian, or am I at Adrian's? *Oh, please don't let this be Hairy Guy's place.* Not good, Libby, not good at all.

Scanning the room for clues, I try and decipher my next move. My heart stops. My shirtdress is draped over a chair. If that's over there . . .

Glancing down, I confirm I'm in my intimates. Which are mismatched and worse for wear. Charming.

A buzz sounds from the other room, then footsteps. *Oh no.* Leaping up, I swipe my dress and . . . more footsteps. *They're getting closer!*

I dive back on the bed, but I'm on top of the covers. I kick to dig under, but can't manage to – *ugh.* Using my legs like scissors, I grip the comforter and roll once then again, my dress still held to my chest.

It's silent. The only sound inside my blanket cocoon is my laboured breathing.

'Libby?'

My eyes pop wide in recognition. *Nooooooo.* No, no, no, it couldn't be. *Could it?* 'Jas?' How am I here, like this? The memory hits me at once. *I texted him.* I seriously cannot hold my drink. I peek over the blanket. 'Morning.'

He laughs and sits beside me, causing me to semi-roll into him. He's freshly showered. His hair hangs damp and is darkened to a deeper blonde. The scent of soap still clings to his skin. 'As requested, in song I might add, I'm waking you up before I go-go.' His smile spreads wide.

I blink as a faint recollection of a strip Wham performance comes to mind. Whatever inhibitions I have were eased by alcohol and completely dismissed. I put the boom-boom into the room. I cringe. *Oh God.*

'I brought you coffee, aspirin and a bit of tequila to burn off the bite.' He motions to the nightstand where he placed them. 'You OK? You were completely on the piss, never seen you that way.'

'You've seen quite a bit now, haven't you?' I force a laugh and clear my throat. It's gritty, like sandpaper.

'Quite. You're a wild one, Libby London.' He tilts his head and quirks a tiny half-smile.

My mind whirls with a hundred images of Jasper and me being, well, wild. Not that I remember anything, I'm only imagining. My cheeks now burn as if on fire.

He pushes the hair from my face, then wipes under my eyes. Black smudge comes away on his fingertips. His denim-washed eyes hold my gaze, but after a beat, he breaks the connection. 'You had a nightmare, I think,' he says, glancing back. 'Yeah, I woke up and you were thrashing about and mumbling.'

'Mumbling?' My stomach knots. 'What'd I say?'

'Something about Ollie.'

My breath stills as I watch the tick in his jaw, waiting to see if he'll say anything more.

'You, um . . .' He starts as if going in one direction, but pulls back and redirects. 'I don't know, you settled down after a minute and were out again.'

I'm not sure I completely believe there isn't more, but right now, half-awake, I'm happy to play along. 'Sooooo . . .' Yeah, this is awkward. I wrinkle my nose and wait. If I woke him, does that mean he was beside me? I blink, studying his face again for clues.

His blue eyes narrow a fraction, as if he's studying mine. I quirk a grin. I don't want to smile, but the way he's looking at me. *God.* It can't be helped.

'What?' I ask, feigning innocence.

'You're wondering if we . . .' His smile is slow, but flirty. 'That's what you're thinking, isn't it?'

'*Nooo.*'

'Ahhhh!' He points to my pinked cheeks, the smile now epic.

'Shut *up*, God.'

He laughs. It's warm and radiates from his chest. 'You passed out, Libby. I slept on the couch.'

My shoulders drop with a truncated sigh. 'I knew that—'

'But, ah, you did kiss me.' Jas looks away, but then regards me with a sideways glance. 'If you can call it a kiss.' His expression is playful and spirited.

Mine's aghast. 'What do you mean, I *kissed* you? I didn't kiss you. I remember no such thing.'

'Well . . .' His lips quirk sideways. 'It was more an attack, and just so you know, you missed.' The rogue smile's returned. 'Yeah, think my chin's bruised, actually.' His hand rubs over his jaw.

'Shut up.' I smile. His widens. Yeah, he's completely messing with me. I think.

'Anyway . . .' He motions to the night table, where the coffee and shot are positioned, then stands. 'Drink up, and feel free to stay as long as you want. I need to get to the store or we won't open on time.' He moves to the door, but stops in the frame. 'Oh, I left the cab number on the counter with a few bills, but really, stay as long as you need. And Libby?' His expression falls and becomes unreadable.

My heart speeds up a little. Between the Wham striptease, missed kiss and talking in my sleep, I'm afraid of what else he's going to say.

'I'm glad you called me.' He gives a thumbs up, smiles and disappears into the hall.

I disappear under the blanket. *God.*

I'm dressed and sipping lukewarm coffee in Jasper's flat. His words echo in my scrambled mind. 'I'm glad you called me.' Glad? I was a mess, it was super-late and completely inconvenient, and yet at a moment's notice he was there. But I knew he would be, didn't I?

That's the thing about Jasper: I can count on him. Had I called Dora, she would've made a major fuss about the time and would've made me find Adrian to take me home. Ollie isn't available, and Finn might have come, but he'd complain – or worse, make me stay so he could dance.

But Jasper? Not only did I know he'd be there, but he completely looked after me. And he's *glad* I called him. I snuggle deeper into his couch and let the feeling resonate. I'm afraid to move, on the chance I'll lose it. Even though my head's in a spin, the mental exhaustion I usually wear like an ratty old robe has been replaced with something else, something lighter, something almost like *happy*. I haven't even thought of Pretty in Pink until right now.

My phone rings beside me, and I debate whether I should answer. My eyes squeeze shut to hold the feeling just a second longer. But it could be the Criminal with news, or Finn with news, or . . . I blink them open, and reach over. 'Hi, Dora.' Bet she wants news.

'You didn't call me back. Adrian said you ditched him. What happened?' She's entirely too chipper for this time of – I've no idea what time it is.

'Is that what he said?' My fingers rake the top of my head and snag on a tangle.

'He also mentioned you were utterly bladdered, lost him, and when he found you, you'd already called someone for a ride. I think you may have scared him a bit too, Libbs. He mentioned something about horrid accidents and missing body parts? You OK?'

I laugh, remembering. 'I'm fine. Jasper came and got me.' I shake my head, then regret the movement. 'I'm a bit hung over.' I sit up and take a full breath. 'Yeah, I need to get home.'

'What do you mean, get home? Where *are* you?'

I bite my lip and look to the ceiling, wishing I'd kept my big flap shut.

'You're at Jasper's, aren't you?' Her voice jumps three octaves to rattle my oversensitive brain. 'Oh my God, that's great! That's the most incredible—'

'Can I call you later?' I rub at my temples and cringe. 'Yeah, I'm not feeling well.' I wait till she says OK, then disconnect. Clicking over to last night's exchange with Jasper makes me smile. To say

I text-bombed him is an understatement. And there are four missed messages: two from Dora and one from Finn. Wait, that's three. Wake up, girl. I select Finn's and read.

> **We need to talk tomorrow. It's about the store. Can you come my way around noon?**

I knew he'd figure something out. I type 'YES' in shouty caps, then add I'll meet him at 'wichcraft, a tasty grab-and-go cafe near his firm's building. Wait, tomorrow is today, and he sent that last night. I retype another message to say 'Make that one', and hit send.

Setting my empty cup in the dishwasher, I wander around Jasper's being a nosy hen. I can't help it. I'm dumbfounded. I'm not sure what I expected – maybe a dingy hole with framed Nineties grunge posters, a hodge-podge of furniture and really, a bit messy.

Definitely not this.

For one, the apartment is spacious, which isn't the norm in New York City. And for another, it's quite stylish, which isn't the norm for Jas. How can he afford this place on what I pay him? The main sitting room is urban and cool in blacks and greys. The oversized sectional with perfectly placed scatter cushions sits atop a white fluffy rug. The back wall has built-in shelves and everything's organized and neat.

Neat.

Jasper's not neat. He's dishevelled with his flyaway hair, arm tats and questionable T-shirts. How'd I peg him so wrong? My stomach drops. Maybe Dr P.'s right. I don't really ask or allow myself to get to know anyone.

Stepping closer, I eye the books and black and white photographs set with purpose on display: Jasper with some friends at a concert, another surfing, and the last photo is maybe his family. I squint and regard it closer. It's him with, I assume, his brother, and a woman who might be their mom. She's pretty, with shoulder-length blonde hair and a tiny frame. Returning it, I sit down to process. I really don't know him outside of Pretty in Pink.

What *do* I know about him? He's from LA, moved to the Big Apple on impulse and considers himself a forever bachelor. Oh, and he can play guitar and has a decent singing voice. I've heard him belt it out more than once at the store.

But what was so bothersome in LA that he had to escape? Does his family still live there? I don't think I've ever asked. Maybe I should. Or maybe I should keep my mouth shut. Apparently I've already said quite enough.

He heard me say something about Ollie.

CHAPTER 15

'Burning Down the House'
Talking Heads, 1983

Adding fuel to the fire

After I manage to get home and grab a shower, I dial Dr P. to cancel tomorrow's session, only to remember that he was expecting me in later today. Just as I'm about to hang up he answers.

'Hello?'

'Hi, it's Libby. I was calling about rescheduling tomorrow, but—'

'You promised you'd be here today, as well as tomorrow and Friday, and I take your word to heart, Libby,' he lectures.

Guilt instantly percolates. 'No, I know. That's just it. I was thinking it was Thursday—'

'We also have an appointment on Thursday.'

'You're right. I know. I screwed up the days, thinking today was Thursday, and a meeting popped up for the store, which is actually today, and then I realized it's only Wednesday, and we changed the times, so, yeah, I'll be there. Sorry.'

'You OK? You sound . . .'

Drunk? 'I'm fine.' I switch the phone to my other ear and hunch over the table.

'OK, as long as I can count on you for all three days. Remember, you promised to be here and do the work this time. I know EMDR can seem intimidating, but it's a means to an end.'

The end is what I'm most worried about.

♫

Waiting for Finn at 'wichcraft, I'm lucky enough to grab some stools near the front. I check my hair in the window's reflection. Yeah, I look hung over. It used to be I'd tie one on, and other than a slight headache from dehydration, it didn't even faze me. My body has no recovery any more. My focus shifts from myself in the glass to Finn approaching on the other side.

I give a little wave to get his attention and he smiles. It's a good one, the kind that pulls everything up and must mean he has good news. Yes, that's a good-news smile if I ever saw one. He sits beside me and the smile falters.

Uh-oh. 'Hey,' I say, suddenly thirsty and taking a drink of my water.

'Hey, yourself.' Finn leans up on his elbows, his gaze gliding over my hair, making me at once self-conscious.

'It's fine, Finn.' My optimism taints with annoyance. Sure, it's a curly mess and maybe I should've tied it back or something, but with pending news on Pretty in Pink, I don't have to be pretty. 'So?'

'Let me get a tea, first,' Finn says, adding that he really can't stay, but this is of the utmost importance.

Longest five minutes of my life.

When he returns, I bombard him. 'Are we waiting on Seth?' My fingers nervously fiddle with the salt and pepper shakers. I've rearranged their placement twice. 'And I'm really hoping you have some fantastic news.' My eyebrows hike. 'You do, right?' Between waking up at Jasper's and this lingering headache, I could really use some.

'I do, yes.' He smiles, then reaches into his tan briefcase.

He has good news! I knew it. My heart floats high in my chest like a balloon, no, make that 99 red ones, just like the Nena song. I'm soaring that high.

As he sorts documents, Finn glances up with a twisted smile. 'First, you have to explain the parrot.'

'You already knew about the parrot.'

'Yeah, but Libby . . .' He laughs. 'Seth has it in the *office*. And sure, it was a novelty for about an hour. But seriously, Libbs? He won't shut up.'

'Bluebeard, or Seth?'

He rocks his head as if considering, then severely scowls. 'Both.'

I launch into the short and fast version of my 'how Seth ended up with Bluebeard' story, desperate to return to his how-to-save-my-store one. 'OK, what's up? What is all this?' I ask, thumbing through the stack of documents.

'It's a complete prospectus based on the financials you gave him. This clearly shows Pretty in Pink's worth, profits, projected growth and fair market asking price. And, you ready for this? You, my unfortunate frizzy friend, have an offer.' His smile pulls wide.

Mine completely disappears. 'How do I have an offer?' My eyes dart from the paperwork to Finn's. My toes squeeze inside my yellow jelly shoes. There's an uncomfortable unease that bristles under my skin and fizzes through my veins. 'Why would someone make an offer? I didn't provide a—' I look down at the neatly secured document's index: P&L, growth analysis, comparative market, and yeah, it's a professionally organized prospectus. Anger creeps up my spine, one vertebra at a time.

'What's the matter? Thought you'd be thrilled. I would be. The offer's substantial. Now you can refurnish your apartment. Look . . .' He taps the paperwork. 'Page three.'

Lips pursed, I death-stare him a moment, then snap my gaze to the paperwork and quickly peel back pages until I land on three to see the magic number.

Wow, it is a good offer. My eyebrows lift. My anger doesn't.

'Keep reading.' Finn chin-nods.

I scan the stipulations, my finger tracing each line, but stop dead on line 16, item b. 'They want the name too?' I glance up, appalled. 'They would keep the store as Pretty in Pink? Then what do I do?'

'Well, that's why the offer's so high.'

'Are *you*? There's no way I'm selling.' I slump low on the stool and eye him with suspicion. 'In fact, I never ever said I wanted to sell. I gave Seth my financials because he said he had real-estate connections and it'd help to know my bottom line.'

Finn's brows furrow deep, and his mouth hangs slightly open in confusion. 'Wait, I thought . . . Are you telling me you didn't ask him to—'

'Ask him to stab me in the back? No! You need to call him and get him here right now.'

'Oh, boy . . .' Finn wets his lips and glances away momentarily.

'Oh, *boy*?' I tilt my head. 'Oh, boy *what*, Finn?' My heart's racing, knowing he's about to say something I won't like.

'Due to the conflict of interest, Seth's stepped away from you as counsel. I thought—'

'Stepped away?' I repeat, as if the words will make more sense if I say them.

'Yeah.' Finn's face tightens. 'He's been placed on retainer with the Lander Property Group.'

'The Lander Property Group?' I do it again.

He leans back and taps the counter with a knuckle. 'They own the commercial property Pretty in Pink is on. They're the ones evicting you, Libby.'

'I know *who* they are, I just . . .' My jaw hangs open as his words sink in and resonate. 'That's not legal.' My voice is shrill, rising with each point. 'Seth had all my financials, he's already reviewed everything. It was already a conflict. How could he legally *share* them?'

'Oh, shit.'

My heart stops cold. Oh, shit is definitely worse than oh, boy. 'What does that *mean*?' I may have said that too loud. The gentleman seated beside us glances over. 'How could Seth *give* them my financials without *my* consent, Finn?'

'Did you sign a confidentiality agreement?'

'No.'

He slides one hand over the other, brushing at imaginary crumbs. 'What about a formal contract authorizing him to represent you legally?'

Oh God. I slowly shake my head.

He squares his shoulders and pulls his game face. 'Then *oh shit* means just that. Legally you never secured him as counsel. So it's technically not a conflict. That's why I thought—'

'Technically, that's *total bull!* I mean, are you kidding me?' My voice has reached inappropriate decibels, but I don't care who I disturb; I'm disturbed! 'How would I know to ask for one? Isn't that why you seek out an attorney? For advice on these things?' My entire being shakes.

Finn scoots his stool closer and leans in with lowered voice. 'You said it wasn't a date, so didn't you discuss roles and proceedings?'

'You wanna know what we talked about on our non-date?' I lean back, flustered. 'His stupid ex-wife and kids. He did ask if I'd consider selling, but I said *no.* Then he said he had some real-estate contacts, and having my financials would help him understand . . .' I shake my head from the enormity of the situation. 'You know what? *Forget it.* He completely swindled me. I knew something was off.' I smack the counter, attracting dirty looks. 'I knew it.' Maybe the voice inside my head isn't crazy after all. It's mean, but not mental.

Finn lets me stew a moment. Good thing, because I'm about to lose it. He drinks his tea. I push my water away, feeling weary to my core.

I shake my head, still unable to wrap it round the turn of events. 'Seth Merriweather certainly lives up to his name as the Criminal, doesn't he?' The look I give Finn is more wounded puppy than ravaged pit bull. 'How could you put me in this position?'

'Me? Oh, no no no no *no* . . . I didn't know anything about this. This is an unfortunate—'

'Unfortunate?' I spit the word. '*Unfortunate* is missing the elevator, or getting the wrong take-out order and not realizing it until after you're home. Unfortunate is what's gonna happen to *this* guy if he keeps gawking at me.'

The man sitting nearby huffs, but looks away.

'*This* is criminal, Finn. Pretty in Pink is mine.' I built the name and grew the customer base. But it's not even about the money, it's really not – it's about me, and the one thing I've done with my stupid life. My fingers drum in quick, angry beats. 'Well, it doesn't matter if they've seen it; I don't have to sell, do I?' My chin lifts in defiance.

'You forget I've reviewed the numbers, too, Libbs. You're profitable, but only in your current situation.'

I don't say anything.

'I get that Seth played you, I do.' Finn rests his manicured hand on top of my agitated one. 'And I'm *sorry*. I feel awful. You know I wouldn't intentionally allow anyone to take advantage of you.'

I know Finn wouldn't, but Seth did.

'Look, regardless – you have a good offer on the table. At least consider it. If it's what you decide, all you have to do is adjust the list of tangible assets. This was only a guesstimate. And if—'

'How would they even know what to guess?' My eyes narrow, then round. '*Oh my God*, Seth was at the store, that nasty bastard! Jasper called and said an attorney from your office was at the shop the other day. He was there snooping.' I shake my head. 'This whole thing was planned.' *I'm an idiot.*

Finn drops his shoulders with a sigh and runs a hand through his hair again only to leave it there and rub, seemingly in thought. 'OK . . . OK, well, like you said, you don't have to sell, but . . .'

'Yeah, but what's to stop them from replicating my exact business model in my space? They have everything they need to do it now, don't they?' My heart's lodged in my throat as my mind runs scenarios. 'Finn, even if I find a new site, why would a customer follow me when the store's still there? Even the name would be the same.' I shake my head. 'I'm basically dead in the water.'

This is the first time I feel like I'm drowning in the daylight.

'Sorry, Libbs. I am.' His eyes meet mine. 'But at least there's an offer, because like you said, with forcing you out, they could open a duplicate store anyway, right? And it's quite a lot of money. You could take some time off, or start something else.'

My hands knead my forehead. The headache's returned and throbbing. I look up. 'That's what you don't understand. There is nothing else.'

Mindlessly I flip magazine pages while I wait for Dr P. There's a physical tension in the air. Well, at least in my neck and shoulders. They're corded tight, adding to the colossal pressure that radiates under my skull. Agitated energy travels in random paths, lighting me up from head to toe because every nerve, just like my hair before the trim, is frayed and split. I don't want to be here, and yet, it's exactly where I need to be.

'Hi.' I say when he finally opens the door. I offer a half-hearted smile as I pass him, the kind that says *I'm not sure about this, or you, or anything, but here goes*. I take my seat in the white wing-back and take a deep breath, trying to get a grip. It's definitely slipping.

'Thanks for making it in.'

Dr P. is wearing the same sweater from last time. That explains why they're so worn out, or maybe it has sentimental meaning, or he's superstitious, or doesn't like to shop.

'You OK?'

'I guess.'

'Any improvement with the sleeping?' he asks, leaning casually back in his chair, the one that squeaks with the smallest movement.

'No.' That's a lie. I slept really well last night at Jasper's. I may have had a nightmare, but it didn't wake me. It could've been because of the waterbed, I don't know, but it's not something I want to analyse with him. I have yet to pick it apart myself.

I shift so one leg's folded under the other, and eye him. I don't care how relaxed he appears, he's not fooling me. He's ready to pounce. I'm ready to bolt. I mean, really, why three days in a row? And with everything else going on, it's just too much. My world is compressing, and if I wasn't claustrophobic before, I am now.

'How'd the homework assignment go?'

'Which one? The *who am I* essay, or the get to know your date thing?'

'Both.'

'Not so much with the essay, but this happened . . .' I unload, aggressively filling him in on Seth Merriweather the two-bit Criminal, the illegal conflict of interest and the forced offer to buy my store.

His brows knit, making one long furry line over narrowed eyes. 'And you don't want to sell?'

'No,' I say with a flustered breath. 'But I may not have a choice, and then what?' The question's weighted with meaning. 'Everything's changing.'

'Libby, I give you my word, if you'll just trust the process, trust *me*, eventually, it'll get better. Things will feel back in sync because you will have changed as well.'

Change – it's the stupid theme of my life as of late. Doesn't it matter that I don't want to? At least I can change the subject. 'I did make an effort with Princess Adrian.' On autopilot, I fall right back into my familiar rhetoric, telling him about the dance-off and the bar conversation, but leaving out how I called Jasper for a ride and crashed there. The story lacks my usual animated flair and humour, and comes out flat. 'See? I tried. I put in the work.'

A small smile forms on his lips as he nods. 'Good. This is good.'

I half-smile in return, believing the words, but knowing there's more. We sit like this a moment. Dr P. deciding if the conversation should go further, and me standing my ground because it shouldn't.

'OK . . .' He sits up, pushing against his thighs with his palms. 'Are you ready to try what we talked about?'

My smile drops.

'Do you know what this is?' Dr P. holds up a metronome, used to keep musical time. He places it on top of a small table and moves it between us. 'I'm going to have you not only focus on the pendulum, but physically shift your eyes back and forth to follow it.'

A slow smile forms. 'You're serious? Is this, like, a hypnotism thing? 'Cause I can tell you right now, it won't work. I was once pulled up on stage for this show and while people clucked like chickens and did idiotic dances on command, I pretty much just sat there giving the guy a hard time.'

'It's not quite the same thing.' Dr P. rolls his chair closer and leans in. 'EMDR, eye movement desensitization and reprocessing, rests on the principle that traumatic events with high levels of toxic stress are stored wrongly in the brain. These experiences are never processed. They're just shelved, and like all memories, certain things trigger them, but they're distorted and overwhelming.'

'Wasn't that what we were doing by talking? Working through stuff and sorting it out?' Maybe he's getting desperate.

'Yes, but only what you'll allow to surface. By engaging in bilateral stimulation such as lateral eye movements, it keeps the gatekeeper busy, so to speak. Then, as I ask questions, impressions and memories materialize. And we finally can reprocess them together and store them back away correctly.'

Sounds easy enough, and yet the muscles in my back are pulling so tight, my spine's going to separate.

'Are you ready?' A simple tap starts the *tick, tick, tick.* 'Follow the metronome's pendulum with your eyes.'

I watch – left then right, left then right – feeling absolutely foolish, like there's a hidden camera and this will end up on YouTube or something. I mean, who does this?

'Concentrate on the sound, and imagine a well.'

'Aren't you supposed to say, "You're getting sleepy"?'

His lips pinch. 'Concentrate, Libby. Follow the pendulum with your eyes and imagine a well, made of grey fieldstone. It's in the country, set within a field of prairie grass, and stands alone. Every click lowers the pail deeper and deeper inside.'

And just like that, I see a well, I'm picturing a well.

185

Tick, tick, tick.

Dr P. doesn't say anything for the longest time. I'm bored with the vision, so I've embellished and added a butterfly flittering about near the top. Yellow wings flutter against the warm breeze and it hovers almost in place, never gaining momentum. Now I see Bluebeard. He swoops down and swallows the butterfly. Gross. Pretty sure parrots don't eat butterflies, but what do I know? I didn't read the parrot care book I purchased.

Tick, tick, tick.

'Tell me about your accident. When was it?'

I glance up.

'No, no. Keep your eyes moving with the pendulum, Libby,' he says with hiked brows. 'I'd like to know about your accident.'

Of course he would. My eyes swivel back to follow the swinging arm, but I'm annoyed. 'I can tell you about the accident without this. It's not like I don't remember.'

'Just trust the process, Libby.'

Fine. My insides knot even tighter. I follow the swinging arm with my eyes left, then right, left, then right. The sound rhythmically punctuates the movement. Again I see the field, the well, and imagine the pail lowering on each *tick, tick, tick.*

This well is endless.

After some time he starts again. 'Your accident. Tell me anything that comes to mind.'

'I was in high school and it completely totalled my car.' That's all I say, still self-conscious and unsure. I mean, really, what else does he want to know? How I remember thinking, life flips like a switch? One moment I'm Libby London driving along, singing to my favourite jams, and the next, I'm Libby lost?

'Keep your eyes moving.'

Left, then right. Left, then right.

'Do you remember what caused it?'

'Me.' I shrug. 'And um, loose gravel along the shoulder.'

'OK, I want you to picture yourself in the car. Say anything that comes to mind. Just tell me what you see.'

My eyes continue moving back and forth, back and forth, but I no longer see the pendulum or the well. Instead I see the road, two lanes in both directions and normal traffic. 'I'm driving. It was afternoon and I had on my new sunglasses. They were Ray-Bans with thick black plastic and neon-pink sides.' They were a gift, and I liked them. Such a silly thing to remember, but this experiment is what's really silly. I remember the accident. It's not suppressed.

'Good. Keep going, Libby. Concentrate on the details. What you hear, smell – be as specific as you can.'

I picture myself driving. The vision's like Max Headroom, glitchy and distorted. I see my hands on the wheel. I have black netted gloves on, and I'm tapping them along to the song on the radio. I think I still have those gloves somewhere, actually. 'The music's loud but I can't remember what was playing, just that I was sing-ing to it.'

'Keep your eyes moving and keep telling me what you see.'

Left, right, left then right.

I concentrate harder, and can see my hand reaching out and messing with the – 'No, it wasn't the radio, it was a tape. I was changing out the cassette, and when I looked up the car in front of me had stopped to turn left.' My heart beats faster. 'I swerved onto the shoulder.' I can hear the gravel under the tyres, but the sound's not in sync with the image. 'The tyres spun out and I . . .'

Another long pause.

'Don't stop. You've swerved to the shoulder, and then what?'

'I lost control.' My eyes continue to travel left, then right, seeing the scene as if I'm outside of my car, watching myself. The sound plays again. Hundreds of pebbly rocks kick up in clouds of dirt and dust. 'My tyres hit the gravel, and my car turned into oncoming traffic, and . . .' I watch the car spin, watch myself panic.

'And?'

Watch my life change forever.

'Libby?'

'I'm trying to straighten the car, but I may have overcorrected.' I see my hands rotating the wheel round and round. 'There's a truck. I can see the man driving it and . . .' I knew he was going to hit me. 'Shit!' I squeeze my eyes tight and brace for the impact, as if it were happening all over again.

'Talk through it. What's happening?'

It's in slow motion: the wheel, the tyres, the spin, the scream. My own added to it as metal struck metal. Tears stream down my cheeks. 'I fishtailed so he hit my passenger side. It was a truck.'

'A semi?'

I shake my head. 'It was, um, the tall and boxy kind. A delivery type.' *Bam.* I feel the impact again, every bone jolted, and the momentum spinning me round and propelling my car off the other side of the road. That's when my head hit the glass.

The click of the metronome suddenly fills the space. *Tick, tick, tick.* My heart keeps time, but I don't want to see any more. I blink and look at Dr P.

'Is that all you remember?'

My teeth lock hard against each other and I stand, needing to leave.

That's all I want to remember.

Back at the store, I dig through the cabinet in the break room for aspirin. What a horrendously long and taxing day. Between Dr P.'s tick-tock-ya-don't-stop Color Me Badd hypnotism thing and learning Seth truly is a scumbag criminal, I'm at my official Libby London limit. My head's going to explode. My heart already has. I keep hearing Finn's words over and over, but it's chaotic and modulating up and down over the skid of tyres and gravel.

'. . . Seth's been placed on retainer with the Lander Property Group . . .'

'. . . You didn't sign a confidentiality agreement . . .'

'. . . No formal contract authorizing him to represent you legally . . .'

Stupid, stupid, stupid.

I pop two extra-strength, sit at the small table and wash it down with bottled water while eyeing Jasper out front. How is it that dishevelled Jas has such a cool bachelor pad? So weird.

This whole day.

My whole life.

'What, Libby?' He doesn't even look my way, just keeps refiling records one after the other as if in a trance.

I straighten in the chair and lean my elbows on the table. 'What do you mean, what? I didn't say anything.'

His eyes regard me from their corners, but only for a second. 'You're staring, so just out with it already.'

I'm both Kris and Kross, so I jump-jump up and over. You know I'm disconcerted when my mind pulls Nineties bands. Spying the *Purple Rain* album in Jas's hand and seeing where he's filing it doesn't help. 'He doesn't belong under T, I don't care if he is *The Artist Formerly Known As* . . . everyone always looks for Prince.'

'Maybe I'm doing them a favour.' Jas rolls his eyes and places it there anyway. 'Are you going to tell me what happened at the meeting?' He files the last album and locks eyes with me. 'You look like someone stole your Zingers.'

'Trying to steal the store is more like it.' I push my hair back, shrug and walk to the register. 'And my Zingers better still be in the break room.'

'I left ya one.' He follows me. 'What do you mean, steal the store?'

It all comes out: Seth 'the Criminal' Merriweather, Finn 'the Guilty' informant and Libby 'the Stupid' stooge.

'What a knob,' Jas spits out the words, his crooked smile curled into a definite vexing snarl.

I look right at him. 'I don't know what to do, Jas.'

He regards me with cool blue eyes. 'I might. Remember how you said "think outside the box"? Well, I have an idea. It's definitely outside the lines, but might just work. Seven o'clock, OK?'

'You have a plan?'

Jas nods.

'Then it's on like Donkey Kong.'

CHAPTER 16
'Should I Stay or Should I Go?'
The Clash, 1982

Consult me later

I'm chatting with Dora over the phone, trying not to let on that I'm in a mood. Pulling the phone down, I eye the time: ten to seven. Maybe Jasper wasn't serious about having a plan, or forgot. It was a flippant comment, and one I've taken too seriously.

'I'm back, sorry,' Dora says over the line, but then yells again to Dean. Something about how she can't find a screwdriver.

My eyes pinch. 'What are you guys doing?'

'He's putting together this baby swing – well, re-putting it together. He had it backwards, and now he can't find the hexy thing it came with. It showed up at Mom's from her secret admirer with a note that read, "for your new grandbaby". I know it's Dad, it has to be. Who else – Duncan, *stop it*! Hang on again . . .'

She's off yelling about something. Then Dean's voice can be heard, followed by a kid's wailing. At least I hope that's Duncan.

It's always a circus when she has him for the weekend. I slouch at my desk, eye the time again, then pick up my Magic 8 Ball. I no longer trust my mind to make logical decisions.

'Will a miracle happen that allows me to keep Pretty in Pink?' I whisper, then jostle it about a few times. There are twenty different answers, but I only need one and *Reply hazy, try again* isn't it.

'Will I find perfect space, then?' I give another shake. *Don't count on it.* 'Shitastic.'

I set it down and instead check my emails while waiting for Dora. She may have forgotten I'm still on the phone, who knows? I click through the spammers and delete-delete-delete, then pause on a message from the Basket Case. He emailed me? I glance at his address and smirk. It's from basketcase@yahoo.com. *At least he's funny.*

Dear Libby,

Sorry for the late notice, but I'd love to take you out on Saturday. Will seven-thirty be OK?

See you then,

BC

Consulting the Magic 8 Ball, I squeeze my eyes shut and ask for enlightenment. 'Should I give this last, pathetic blind date a chance?' Shake, shake, shake – I pop open my eyes, and . . . *Definitely not.* 'Well, that *definitely* settles it.'

Besides, Saturday night is my party. *God*, Saturday's my birthday. With Dora, Dean and Finn's set-up track record and my rotten luck, it's safer to attend alone. I'm already on the ledge. I don't need the push.

I type up a quick response saying I'm under the 8 Ball, at least its influence, and I'm not sure what my future holds (which is entirely true). So thanks, but maybe some other time.

Knock-knock-knock.

I walk to the door, phone tucked at my shoulder since Dora's still blathering on about something to Dean, and swing it open with too much force. It startles Jasper, but I'm the one taken aback. He's here – and somewhat dressed up. Still in a T-shirt and jeans, but the shirt's plain, black and tight. He looks impossibly fit, and the deep V fiercely displays his tats on both arms and chest. I've seen the arm ones of course, but didn't realize they carried over onto – 'Sorry, come on in.'

'Who's there?' Now Dora wants to talk. 'Wait, do you have a date tonight? Is he *there*?'

'No, it's Jasp—'

'Jasper? Oh my God, you're going out with Jasper?' She's entirely too excited. I can almost feel her bounce from here. 'Dean, guess what?'

'No, Dora. You've got it wrong, it's just . . .' Explaining will take entirely too much effort. 'Look, I gotta—'

'Go out with Jas! Abso-bloody-lutely.' Dora babbles on about how fantastic it is for me to get out there, and how much she likes him and *blah blah blah* . . . I'm only half-listening because she's not saying anything new, and I'm busy watching Jasper look round my apartment. Maybe I should've picked up more, but I didn't really expect him to show.

He glances over, so I wave my hand in a small circle to visually help Dora wrap up.

'Oh, oops,' she interrupts herself, then laughs. 'The hexy tool was in my pocket the whole time. I gotta go, but call me after and have fun, OK? Dean, um, is this—' The phone goes dead.

I just hope Jas's plan hasn't.

♫

I was under the impression Jasper had found space; not that we'd be travelling through it. We've flashed to the past and landed at Starcades Retro Arcade, right round the corner on 10th Street.

Does he think this is a date?

'Why are we here?' The question, and my annoyance, are lost in the *blips* and *beeps* as Jasper pays the cover. It's a one-time fee for unlimited play. No tokens. Too bad, I always liked them.

'Come on,' Jasper says, and guides me through with a hand near the small of my back. It's an unexpected small thing and somewhat nice. Still not a date.

Inside the narrow space, large flat screens blast classic MTV from when they actually played videos. If 'Video Killed the Radio Star', then reality TV killed video. 'Ladies and Gentlemen, rock 'n' roll,' I mumble the iconic first broadcast words. Yeah, I miss my MTV.

My mood's lifted slightly as we move deeper inside. The place veers to the right and is bigger than I originally thought. Asteroids, Space Invaders and pinball machines cram together in orderly rows atop dark carpet that sparkles like stars with interwoven fibre-optic lights. The ceiling does the same, creating a cool galaxy ambiance.

Jas steps to the side of foot traffic, guiding me to follow – then again, as people move from the restroom in the other direction. We're like Frogger trying to keep from being flattened. Right now,

I'd prefer to just stand still and allow the splat. It's nice of him to try and cheer me, but . . .

'What do you see when you look around, Libbs?' Jasper's lop-sided smile pulls straight and wide. He doesn't wait for an answer, which is good because I don't have one. 'This company has over thirty locations, and they're growing. They're always packed, and guess with who?' He motions to the crowd and somehow smiles wider. '*Our* customers.'

I glance round, taking in the mix of indie teens that consider anything retro cool and adults who grew up in or around the Eighties. They're the collectors with buying power. I shrug. 'OK, so we share the same clients. And?'

'And here's what I'm thinking . . .' Jasper spins so he's facing me. 'Since we can't find space within the same budget as our current location, and you have an offer, why not sell?'

My stomach drops. 'Jas, I don't want—'

'Wait, wait, wait, hear me out.' He pauses to make sure he has my attention; I widen my eyes to show that he does. 'OK, if you sell, you're sitting on some serious capital, right?'

'Yeah, but they want to keep Pretty in Pink open, remember? They'll get the name, location, everything. So what I'm really sitting on is my—'

'Ask me why it doesn't matter.' He leans closer, lowering his voice, but speaking fast and not waiting for me to respond. 'Because they don't have *you*, Libbs. You're the reason it stays authentic and cool. You love it and it comes through in all the details. Business models don't succeed, *people* do. It's your passion that has grown the store into what it is. You're the heart of Pretty in Pink.'

His words swirl warm inside, like steam from hot cocoa. It's sweet; maybe the sweetest thing anyone's ever said to me. But it doesn't change anything.

Jas nudges my arm. 'So I say, *sell*. Let them have the store. We can open with a new name. A better name, because we have you. And you're Pretty in Pink.'

My heart lifts from his words. 'Thanks, Jas, but . . .' I push out a breath, flattered that someone actually gets it and understands, but it's so frustrating because . . . 'I don't want a different name.'

'OK, I know, but just think about this. Starcades has over thirty locations serving our target and shared customer base. Here's what I propose: we piggy-back here. It would be low overhead, and offer real growth potential.' He shifts his weight to rock on his heels as he waits for my reaction.

My brain's still in a fog, and I'm not getting it. 'Piggy-back?'

'A small-footprint build-out *inside* Starcades Retro Arcade, like the sublease we had before. Only they get a small percentage of net sales. That's what the department stores do in the mall. They lease floor space for their designer brands.'

That's what the kiosks in the mall do, too. I still don't say anything, mulling over his words, the possibilities. *Maybe*?

'Look, Libbs, it's much cheaper than white-box build-out – and the best part is, the customers are built in. Our customers are already here. And with multiple locations, the growth potential is huge.'

My mind continues to cycle through his proposal, then stops abruptly. 'OK, wait . . . What's in it for you? Because there's always a catch; this is business. Nobody gets money for nothing and the chicks for free.'

'Partners. We grow the new concept together. That's what I want.'

My eyebrows lift. 'You deserve ownership for the idea?'

'Well, yes, that . . . and for already having pitched it to them.'

My mouth opens in surprise.

'I didn't want to get your hopes up if it wasn't feasible.' He smiles brightly. 'But it is. In fact, I have preliminary paperwork to share with you.'

My eyes narrow, the wheels spinning behind them. 'It's clever, Jas,' I say, giving a genuine smile. And I mean it. He always astonishes me with his business savvy. 'It's also a lot to think about.' Something I can't do right at this moment, but I will. Oh my gosh, *I will.*

'Hey, Jas,' says a guy, maybe in his early twenties, with lip ring and Nirvana tee. 'Think you should know I knocked you down the board.'

'What? No way.' Jasper glances towards the far wall where a Ms Pac-Man machine sits. 'Come on.' He leads me through the crowd, and within seconds has a new game set up.

The guy and I situate on either side to watch.

'Hey, Jasper,' a girl with pink hair says, hovering. She reminds me of Jem and the Holograms. She places a hand on Jasper's shoulder and leans in. Truly outrageous. Does she not see me? What if we were on a date?

They both appear comfortable with the contact. I find myself curiously watching them instead of the screen. I've only ever seen Jasper with one or two girls. Rachel was a cosmetologist and pretty in an edgy sort of way. Lots of black eyeliner and a small diamond nose stud. He dated her off and on, but she had two kids, wanted more and began hinting about a ring. Jas, like Hall & Oates, like me, 'Can't Go For That', so 'She's Gone'.

People always struggle with this, as if something's wrong with you if you don't want to reproduce. They never consider that it's a choice. Not everyone's equipped, or should take it on. And believe me, there are many I think should have reconsidered. I mean, you're responsible for a *human being*. My cats are tricky enough.

More people surround us to watch and cheer as Jasper continues to play. My mind continues to wander, allowing the small possibility he presented to take root. I should consult my Magic 8 Ball later for a final verdict. Out of the twenty possible answers, seven are positive, and I'm overdue for a win.

'OK, now bring us home, Libbs,' Jasper says, jolting me from my thoughts. With a tatted arm on either side, he locks me in front of him to face the screen.

'Jas, no, I'll only botch it up.' I wasn't even paying attention. I try and step away, but he stops me by lifting my hand to the controller and pressing his firmly over the top.

I'm drawn to how it completely covers mine. The smooth skin of his palm contrasts with the calloused fingertips from years of playing guitar. Having him leaning over my shoulder, breathing near my ear, and his arms wrapped round me is . . . I'm not sure what it is. Maybe nice. Maybe I just needed a hug.

'Keep her steady. Easy, easy, and . . .' Jasper pulls the lever left as together we guide Ms Pac-Man through the neon maze.

'Yes!' he says, as the screen flashes black and an animation of Ms Pac-Man and the ghosts floats across to a strange happy victory song. 'Well done, you.'

I tilt my head up and manage a smile, but quickly pull my head back. He's *this close* and isn't moving. The screen blinks for the winner to add in their three initials. With his hand still over mine, he taps the control to rotate through the alphabet, then twice more to fill the three slots. 'There we go.'

He's added *J* + *L*. 'Jas plus Libby?' With a smirk, I turn slightly.

He shrugs with his crooked half-smile. 'It's for Jasper *and* Libby, but sure, plus works, too.'

I glance out the car window, not really saying much on the drive home; not that I've said much all night. I have to admit, the idea of teaming up with Starcades has potential, but to lose Pretty in Pink and take on a partner has me panicked. It's a lot of change all at once – and yeah, like Exposé sang, 'Seasons Change', but I don't want to.

My mind's swimming in decisions, which is better than drowning in despair, but even the prospects are weighty and complicated, and I'm tired. It's been a long, problematic day.

'You've been really quiet.' Moving into the turn lane, Jasper pops his blinker after the fact and slows to wait on the arrow.

I lock eyes on his. 'Yeah, you've just given me a lot to think about.'

'Off the top of your head, what's your biggest concern?' Reaching over, he turns down the radio.

I blink, my thoughts indexing through the list of many. 'What if the new owners of Pretty in Pink require a non-compete? That's a standard request when selling an existing business, right? That protects them from us competing directly.'

'Well, yeah, usually it's about distance.'

'Starcades is right around the corner, Jas.'

'Thirty locations, remember? There's one in LA, and I wouldn't mind going back home. Only a few reasons I stuck it out here anyway.'

My stomach twists several times to wring out the truth. 'So we start over in LA? Just pick up and go?' I know I've glossed over the deeper context of his words, but I pretend I haven't. Moving is enough to deliberate.

'Yeah, why not?' With a sideways glance, he asks, 'What's keeping you here?'

My hand rubs at my neck as I sit back, letting the question crystallize. This is home. Pretty in Pink is home. And Dora, Finn and Dean . . . but if I'm honest, Dora's about to become absorbed in marriage and motherhood again, Finn's just absorbed, and my parents moved years ago. And the store? The store is all but gone. My heart sinks. 'I guess . . . nothing. Nothing's keeping me here any more.'

Except maybe memories. I'm haunted by them.

I turn and stare out the window again, unable to articulate the overwhelming urge I have to flip open the door and roll out, ninja-style. It's all unravelling. My heart beats wildly and my hands go damp. I don't want to sell, or move, or anything. I don't.

'Hey . . .' Jas bumps my leg so I look over. 'Let's talk about something else. Tell me something I don't know about you.'

Something he doesn't know? Like what? Does he mean something trivial and odd like my irrational fear of crickets, or something deep and secret like my crying jags at night? I pull a face. 'Nothing exactly worth sharing and pretty sure there's nothing new to tell.'

'Not true.' The light switches green and Jas starts forward. 'I didn't know you couldn't handle your drink, or that you have nightmares.'

'Yeah, well, now you know.' Should've gone with the crickets. I shrug. 'Usually they wake me up and I can't get back to sleep.'

'And Oliver's in these nightmares? You screamed out to him.'

Another shrug. 'Like I said, I don't really remember 'em.' I can feel Jasper peering over at me, but I concentrate on the road, how the pavement changes to blacktop in sporadic patches. Why not repave it all at once? Fix it at the same time? 'And besides, you're the one with all the mystery.' I peer back over.

'Me?' He taps the steering wheel and half-smiles.

'Yeah, *you*.' I shift in my seat, so the belt cuts sharply into my shoulder, and regard him. 'You said you wouldn't mind going back home, but why'd you leave LA in the first place?'

His face tenses in a way that tells me I've hit on something. 'I grew up with my mom, stepdad and stepbrother, never knowing much about my biological father. He wasn't ever in the picture and we never talked about him, but then . . .' He cuts a glance in my direction, only to quickly look back to the road. 'I stumbled on my birth certificate and there he was, his name in black and white, and it was a shock really.'

I'm instantly intrigued, getting more information than I anticipated. I didn't know any of this. My overactive imagination crafts all sorts of drama plots. His real dad is his stepdad's brother, or a neighbour he's known all his life, or is secret service and pretends to be a furniture salesman. It has to be twisted, or else – 'Why the shock?'

'Turns out he's a musician. Pretty well known, actually.'

Oh, this is even better! 'Who? Would I know him?'

'Unless you live under a rock, yeah.' He taps the wheel again. 'But he's never been in the picture, and after I confronted my mom about it, I learned he wants it that way.'

His words hang in the air a moment, their meaning in question. 'Did he know about you?'

'Yeah, but me popping up as his kid wasn't going to go over well in the media for his family or for my mom. They had an agreement.' He changes lanes and turns into my complex. 'Anyway, in exchange for my mom keeping a low profile, he paid for my college and then some.'

Things click into place: his expensive apartment, and how he's able to live off what I pay him. I let my head lean against the seat. 'Wait, that doesn't explain why you left LA.'

'Yeah, well. I was angry at my mom. I mean, I get his silence, but not hers.' He parks, but pauses, hands still on the wheel. 'I wasted a lot of time wondering about him and why he wasn't around when I was a kid.'

'Huh.' I stare at him for a second, taking in his features: the dirty blonde hair, the curled lip. He suddenly seems . . . fuller. It's still Jasper, but a more rounded-out version. 'So are you going to tell me who he is?'

Squaring his shoulders, he faces me directly. 'Are you going to tell me about Ollie? What really happened between you guys? Why you broke up?'

My heart jumps. This is what normal people do. They share

their stories. But I don't have a story – I have a nightmare, and we already discussed that.

Jasper's tone softens. 'When's the last time you saw him?'

'It's been forever.' My chest already aches. I've had enough today.

He's careful with his words, and really, he has good cause to be. 'Tell me why you like the guy. I mean, if you're still hung up on him, he must be, like, I don't know, perfect.'

'Far from it.' I glance up. 'But he's – I don't know. He's Ollie.' I half-smile.

'And that means what? You gotta give me something . . .'

'You really want to know . . . ?' When he nods, I lean back to think. 'OK, ah, when we were young, he'd say my freckles were a map to the constellations, and that I was lucky because I would never lose my way. Then he'd point them out on my cheeks.' I smile wider, remembering. I hadn't thought of that in forever. 'I always hated them, and he somehow made it . . . Well, he's *always* had a way of making me feel at home in my own skin. Does that make sense?' I laugh and roll my eyes. 'Probably not. It's all goofy, melodramatic teen stuff.'

'But it's your goofy and melodramatic teen stuff, so I like it.' Jasper leans over, and I watch his eyes searching for imaginary lines along my dotted face. 'I also like your freckles.'

My smile fades. This is somewhat intimate all of a sudden, and I'm not sure what to do. Stay or go? If I stay there will be trouble, so . . . there's only one reasonable action, and I don't need the Magic 8 Ball to tell me what it is.

'See ya.' I pop the latch, and bolt.

CHAPTER 17
Devil Inside
INXS, 1987

Speak of the devil

Dr P. called first thing this morning to make sure I planned on coming in. He was worried because I left abruptly yesterday, visibly shaken.

So I'm here, back in his office. I don't want to be, but I gave my word. I didn't promise to stick around, however. My nerves are frazzled, and bickering with Dora via text isn't helping. She wants details on my date with Jasper, still not accepting it was a work thing.

DORA: OK, well then, when is your date with the Basket Case?
LIBBY: Never.
DORA: You're killing me, Libbs.
LIBBY: They've all been disasters. Has pregnancy affected your memory?
DORA: No, just my feet. I swear they're two sizes bigger.

She can't even see them any more, so what does it matter? The door opens, and Dr P. waves me in.

'Hi,' I say, and gather my stuff, quickly flipping the volume tab to off and putting the phone away.

'How are you today?'

I plop into my seat, not sure how to answer. How do you explain everything's closing in, even the walls of his office? Does he have more books? The stacks have multiplied. For someone trying to push me forward, he's kinda stuck in the past. He could eliminate some of this clutter, and the dust it collects, by reading on a tablet. Actually, so could I.

'So . . .' He takes his seat.

'So,' I repeat, and fiddle with my assorted jelly bracelets. My wrists are covered in them today.

'Who's Frankie?' Dr P. motions to my T-shirt. 'I get the *relax* part, but what doesn't he want you to do?'

'Oh, ah, he doesn't want you to ask,' I say, glancing down to the bold black text, definitely not wanting to explain the meaning.

After a beat he forgets, setting up the small table and metronome in front of me. He locks eyes with mine as if inquiring whether I'm ready. I'm not, but I know I need to keep going. Like Dr P. said, if you're going through hell, don't stop. I can't stop.

Not here. Not *again*.

But how do you escape if the devil's inside?

'You remember what I told you about EMDR, eye movement desensitization and reprocessing? How it allows memories to flow freely?'

My lips twitch with a one-sided shoulder-shrug to mean *sure*.

'Good; then we can start right where we left off, OK?'

'Where we left off was me leaving.'

Dr P. ignores my comment, leans over and taps the pendulum so it swings. The *tick, tick, tick* fills the room. My heart beats twice as fast, filling the spaces in between like the connecting minor scale. The combination is sharp and out of tune.

'Please.' He motions to encourage me. 'Follow with your eyes. And just as before, concentrate on the sound and imagine a well. The bucket is at the top and every click lowers it deeper inside.'

I drop my gaze and follow the movement. Left then right, left then right, left then right.

Tick, tick, tick.

Dr P. doesn't say anything.

I follow it back and forth, back and forth. Seeing the well. The open field of tall grass. No butterfly today. Instead there are menacing crows circling against an inky black sky.

Tick, tick, tick.

My shoulders start to relax a tiny bit as I focus on the scene.

'We were talking about your accident. You pictured yourself in the car, reaching for the radio or changing a cassette tape, and the car in front of you had suddenly stopped.'

At once I'm there, but again, the image is glitchy. I can almost feel the motion as I turn the wheel frantically in the opposite direction, trying to regain control. 'Like I said, I swerved and spun on the gravel.' The sound of kicking dirt and pebbles replays.

'Right. And you said it forced you into oncoming traffic. A delivery truck. You last spoke about the impact, remember?'

How could I forget? My heart swells. His words hang between us.

Tick, tick, tick.

'What else can you recall?'

'The man. He sat up high in the truck and . . .' It's not really his face, more his expression that's stayed with me. With wide eyes, his mouth opened in a scream I couldn't hear. It was deafening all the same. I've seen this a thousand times in my dreams.

'Libby?'

'Yeah. The impact was quick, more a severe jolt than anything.' The pain came after. Often healing hurts more than the originating incident. No one tells you that. They should.

'I hit my head on the glass and when I woke up, my car was in the ditch on the other side of the road.'

'What about the truck?'

'He, um . . . hit another car.' My mind's eye sees the steering wheel, my hands still locked in place. A woman's voice asking if I'm OK. 'I don't remember that part, though. I didn't see it. They told me after.'

'At the hospital?'

'Yeah, or maybe in the ambulance.' The siren's loud. There are blurs of faces around me, all talking nonsense. I blink and can't move. My neck's restrained. A man says something to me, and I black out. I'm AC/DC's 'Back in Black', and like the lyrics, *let loose from the noose that's kept me hanging round*, I wake again to repeat the confusion, told how I barely escaped with my life. After what else they told me, I wish I hadn't.

'Where are you? What do you see?'

I focus again, and this time I see the hospital. 'I'm in the ER.' More faces. So many faces and voices all meshed together, busy. 'I asked what happened and . . .' His face materializes. Dark hair. Handsome. Angry. 'The doctor yelled at me.'

'He yelled at you?'

That's how I remember it.

'Libby, can you hear me?' a man with a leaden voice asks. It bounces from the floor, then from above. *Am I in a tunnel?* I can't tell what direction it comes from. The voice talks to someone else, and then . . . nothing. More black.

'Libby. Libby, can you hear me?'

A light shone in my eyes, then everything went dotty. Everywhere I looked dancing blips blocked my view. 'He said I had to stay awake. That I'd woken several times in a panic, and I needed to stay calm and stay with him.' The voice was irritated and not kind at all. I don't remember all the details, but *that* detail I remember clearly.

'Keep going. You're doing just fine,' Dr P. says, then adds something else, but it doesn't register, as I'm now fully engrossed in memory.

The light blinded my eyes again. I heard muffled syllables not fitting together in full words, ricocheting from wall to wall. The light disappeared and restored the bouncing spots. There was a beeping noise. I listened to its steady rhythm. Shapes with movement formed all around me. I tried to speak, but it came out gurgled and dry.

'Here, just to wet your lips. Go slow,' said a kinder, softer voice. Ice tumbled to my lips from a plastic cup. Someone else helped me to sit, but I became dizzy. I put my head back down.

'Get a straw,' the woman said. 'Let's take this slow, OK?' A pillow under my head propped me up. Someone bent the straw to my lips, so I tried to drink. The icy water felt like tiny shards of broken glass.

'What . . .' I cleared my throat to get the sounds out right. 'What happened?'

'You were in an accident,' the first voice said. I looked round the room. I was in a hospital.

'Welcome back,' the sharper voice said. 'Wake her every two hours and keep me updated.' Then he left.

'I want you to remember three words for me, can you do that?' The kinder voice belonged to a woman, a nurse with short dark hair and full round cheeks. I blinked.

'Pen, house, ice cream.' She waited for me to repeat.

'Pen, house, ice cream,' I said. I'm in the hospital. I was in an accident.

'I'll ask you again in a few minutes, so try really hard to remember them, OK?' She smiled then picked up my chart.

Pen, house . . .

'Libby? Tell me what you see,' Dr P. sounds so far away, maybe because I am.

'A male nurse woke me later. I was hooked up to IVs and groggy from the sedative that they had given me.'

The nurse placed a hand behind my shoulders and shifted the pillow underneath. 'Sorry. I know you're tired, but we need to wake you every couple of hours. Is this OK?'

To be even slightly upright made me queasy.

'Do you know where you are, Libby?' The nurse smiled. Lines

formed on either side of his mouth in deep creases, and tiny crinkles by his eyes showed he smiled a lot. I liked him instantly.

'I'm in the hospital; I had . . .' I cleared my throat. 'I'm in the hospital.' My body ached. 'I'm really sore.' The words gargled and strained. My throat was dry again.

'OK, honey, I can fix that.' He grabbed my IV, read the bag, and proceeded to switch it with a new one.

I had a plastic tube in my arm taped in place. Yellow iodine stains surrounded it. I hadn't noticed that before. The nurse explained it was to keep the vein open for the IV, and brought me a fresh plastic cup of water and ice. He adjusted the straw so I could reach it. 'Here ya go.'

My head was killing me. The round-cheeked nurse from earlier strolled in and the male one smiled, turned and left. It was hard to keep track of anyone.

'I asked you to remember three words; do you remember?' she asked.

I looked down. I didn't remember anything about three words. My thoughts felt fragmented and disjointed.

'That's all right. We'll keep playing this game until you can recall them. After all, you took quite a hit, so it's best to take it slow.'

'Libby?' Dr P.'s voice sounds like it's coming from an intercom.

In my vision I look up, expecting to see one.

'You need to vocalize what you're seeing. Tell me what's happening.'

'A nurse is telling me how I hit my head, that it's called a grade-three head injury.'

She set the cup back on the small side tray. 'That means you were unconscious more than conscious, and you're struggling with a small amount of amnesia.' She paused, allowing the information to sink in.

It didn't.

'Let's try our three words again, OK? Repeat after me, pen . . .'

'Pen,' I said.

'House.'

'Ice cream,' I blurted, because I did remember that.

'Yes, ice cream!' She smiled. 'Progress already.' She used a pen light and asked me to follow it. 'See? And even this says you'll be fine. Both pupils are the same size, and you're tracking the light.' She jotted down more notes on my chart before she left. Light spots followed my line of sight.

'Libby?' It sounds like I've dropped into the imaginary well and Dr. P's speaking to me from above. 'What about the driver of the delivery truck? What happened to him?'

His question tethers me back, the spots giving way to his office, the metronome, the *tick, tick, tick*. My chest hurts. Emotion takes every available space, and my lungs can't expand past them to fill with air. I really can't breathe.

'Keep your eyes moving back and forth. Do you remember them telling you about the other vehicles involved in the crash?'

'Yes.' My heart pounds faster. My shoulders tense. 'The doctor. He sat on the edge of my bed.' I knew, somehow I knew what he was about to say and couldn't look at him, instead I focused on my hands. The cuts that marred them.

'What did the doctor tell you, Libby?'

'That the driver of the truck was going to be fine, that he walked away, treated only for minor injuries.' The doctor had paused then, so I glanced up, and for the briefest of seconds, I saw a hesitation in his expression, confirming my worst nightmare. The one I still live with.

The *tick, tick, tick* rotates the other way now, pulling up contents, memories, things long forgotten. Things better left alone.

I'm drowning. Water swells above my ankles, knees, higher and higher until it's at my chest, filling my lungs.

'Libby, vocalize the words.'

I'm rocking.

'Libby, *say* the words. I need you to say the words.'

I don't want to do this. Not again. 'No.'

'Say the words.' Dr P.'s tone is stern, loud.

'No!' Now *I'm* speaking loudly, almost shouting.

The scene repeats in fragments. Everything's in slow motion.

My hands.

The doctor.

His words.

'Libb—'

'He *died*, OK!? I hit the truck, and the driver lived, but . . . there was a passenger, and he didn't. He died. I killed him . . .'

I see the pendulum again. I'm only now aware of the tears that cascade one after the other down my cheeks. 'It was my fault.' I whisper the words. 'Completely my fault,' I say again softly. My shoulders shake violently, but I'm holding my breath. Only when I can't any longer, do I gasp for air.

♫

I've been sitting alone in Dr P.'s office for almost an hour, decompressing. He's allowing me some space. I'm numb, emotionally spent, and tracing the chair's intricate jacquard pattern with my finger. At least I'm not crying.

A soft tap at the door and it opens. 'Can I come in?'

I nod.

Dr P. is wearing that face. That face that says *I understand, but I don't know what to say.* I've seen so many people wear it: the teachers at school when I returned two weeks later; my friends before they started avoiding me to return to the regularity of the everyday; people I didn't even know. What happened made people uncomfortable. It was too heavy, too much, especially for my friends. I mean, we were kids. Someone died because of me. I get it, but I don't like that face.

Dr P. quietly sits with me and actually, if I don't look at him, it's nice. Maybe nothing needs to be said. Maybe you just need someone beside you. I take a deep breath and refocus. I'm not sure what to do now. I didn't know what to do then.

Dr P. leans close, his tone is soft, reassuring. 'It's very important we follow this through. You must be here tomorrow first thing. Say, 10 a.m.? We're not quite done, Libby.'

He doesn't know the half of it.

I'm at home, not sure what I feel. I'm not crying; I'm not anything. I'm numb. It's not like I didn't know what happened. I mean, of course I *knew*, but I had forgotten little details like the roundness of the nurse's cheeks, the doctor's tone and the hospital smell. I despise that smell.

It's as if the details somehow disappeared, and I chose not to dwell on the fragments that didn't. I mean, what's the point? There is none. I can't change anything.

Pulling my comforter up over my shoulders, I rest my head on the sofa arm and fumble with the DVD remote. I've decided to play hooky for the rest of the afternoon and am watching *Ferris Bueller's Day Off*, because, well, I need one. Maybe I really am like Cameron: a neurotic mess, happy living in his own misery. Is that why I can't get past this? Can't forgive myself?

John Hughes based Cameron, and Charlie Sheen's character, Garth Volbeck – the guy at the police station – on a boy he knew growing up. At the start of the movie in the original screenplay, Ferris gives that boy's backstory, saying how he stayed over at this boy's house once and heard him crying in the middle of the night. He explains how there was not one specific thing the boy was upset about. He was conditioned to grief.

That lost monologue speaks directly to me. I'm conditioned to grief.

I inhale deeply to force everything down, and closing my eyes, I rub above them, needing the noise in my head to mute and the swell in my chest to ease. For the first time I crave the nothingness of going underwater, but I can't even cry. I don't have a single tear to drown in.

I get that life should have a certain amount of struggle. But shouldn't there be a hard limit for the amount? An expiration date for the duration?

There's a soft knock on the door. I blink.

'Libby?' More knocking.

'Hang on,' I say, pushing myself upright and shoving back the comforter. *Why is anyone here?* I find my feet and stumble from the couch towards the door, almost tripping over my shoes. Rubbing at my eyes, I force them open with splayed fingers and concentrate on the deadbolt –and *there*, the door swings free.

Jasper's standing on the other side. His head's thrown back. He looks confused. *I'm* confused. 'Why aren't you at the store?' I sound froggy, so I cough to clear my throat.

'It's after five. You never showed and didn't answer any of my calls, so I got worried. You OK?' His eyes travel down.

I follow his gaze. Cross-stitched seams line my arms and run along my sides. My shirt's inside out. Was it like this earlier with Dr P.?

Jasper leans on the door frame with his shoulder. 'I wanted to run some things by you, but you're in no condition to . . .' He eyeballs me. 'Anything.' He steps closer and places a cool hand to my forehead, causing my hair to stand straight up.

The sensation's nice. I haven't had anyone check my forehead since I was little. I'm tempted to throw out a fake Ferris cough, but never get past the thought.

'You don't seem to have a fever,' he says, pulling away his hand only to return it to flatten the hair that stayed upright. 'Have you eaten anything?'

Have I? I had a coffee before my appointment, and I do remember making toast, but can't recall if I actually ate it. It may still be in the toaster. And when I sat down to watch the movie . . . my mind blanks. I glance up and shrug, 'cause yeah, I don't know.

'Well, you need to eat. Let me make you something, OK?'

He's already through the door before I can protest or answer, so I meander to the couch to reset the movie I started, but my head falls to the sofa arm and I watch Jasper instead. My cat Lucky brushes up against his leg, and Jas reaches down with a return rub hello. Starr doesn't like strangers and is probably lurking nearby.

I can't help but take him in. The tats, earrings, ripped jeans. Even with all that, he's a good-looking man – maybe not in the polished traditional sense, but am I? In a lot of ways, we make sense together. Have I ever really considered him? I know the answer, of course.

Jas turns suddenly, catching my eye.

I'm emotionally spent and can't seem to muster the strength it takes to talk, let alone explain anything.

I wonder what he'd say if I could?

CHAPTER 18

'Weird Science'
Oingo Boingo, 1985

Weirdly comforting

Wrapped in a sweatshirt, with the sleeves pulled down over my fisted hands, I follow the sidewalk round my apartment complex. I normally don't take walks. Usually I just watch my neighbours push baby strollers, jog, or drag fussy toddlers in a wagon from my window as I do the dishes. But this morning I need the movement, the fresh, crisp air, the open space. God, I just need to breathe.

It's like I'm carrying this oversized box. I have both arms tightly wrapped round it, can barely see over the top, and can hardly manage due to its weight. Both Dr P. and my friends are pestering me to let go and be open to others, but that's what they don't understand: my hands are full, and I can't put it down. It's my burden. If I don't carry it, who will?

My phone chimes to signal yet another text from Dora. Foolishly, and in a moment of weakness, I told her the Basket Case emailed and suggested a date for Saturday. I glance at the phone's screen:

> **DORA: You said yes, right? So now you officially have a date for your party!**

I text back:

> **I said NO. I'm already a basket case. Don't need a nutty buddy.**

Actually, nutty buddy bars sound good. I may have to pick up a pack on my way to Dr P.'s. There's something comforting in pulling apart the wafers and eating each piece separately.

> **DORA: You'll like this one. Trust me.**
> **LIBBY: Trust you? Forget it. Project Libby is Alan Parsons Project over.**

Ignoring the next chime, I kick at a rogue piece of chalk left on the pavement where children have drawn hopscotch squares. I'm surprised anyone even remembers this; it's not hi-tech gadgetry, just a simple, honest game. It also develops neural pathways that become conduits in the brain later in life. Maybe that's the problem with this generation: kids are raised without movement. Of course, my parents blamed MTV, and *their* parents said the world's downfall was due to rock 'n' roll.

I jump-hop through once, then turn and do it again with even more bounce in the opposite direction. My mottled brain could use some new sparks of activity. It's time I figured everything out, and maybe I should reconsider Saturday's date. I don't know. I'm at least going to see Dr P. again, which is a huge step. I just need to one hundred per cent commit. Or be committed, because I'm not sure I can do this, even if I want to.

In order to consider a major move from New York to LA and move forward with my relationships . . . I may need someone to rip the box from my hands.

The cab ride to Dr Papadopoulos's office seemed abnormally quick. Instead of the typical morning traffic and delay, every light was made and we zipped right over. It was as if the universe was making sure I arrived on time. Which I did – but now I'm late because I'm outside, leaning against the building, ignoring my ringing phone and talking to myself. 'I'm coming, OK?' I say, looking at the screen as if Dr P. can hear me. I've been out here for at least twenty minutes.

The moment it stops, it starts again. Each beat of the Men at Work 'Who Can It Be Now?' ringtone plays on my nerves because there's no question it's him. 'Fine!' I yell, causing the man walking by to look at me questionably. 'I'm fine,' I repeat with a glib wave to move him along.

I *can* do this. I *am* doing this. Look at me go. Like the determined and foolish Little Red Riding Hood, I march over the river (in this case a puddle), push through the doors, and into Dr P.'s office I go.

The minute I walk into the waiting room, he swings open his door. 'So you finally decided to come in. Good.' When I give him a confused look he motions to his window and adds, 'I've been watching you stalk around out front.'

'What big eyes you have.' He doesn't ask and I don't explain.

Dr P. starts chatting immediately about anything and everything as I peel out of my jean jacket. This one's my favourite, with embellished fringe hanging from the front and back seams. Over time, half of the strands have been braided, and the ones that have come free hang crimped from the position. I get situated in the large wingback chair, still holding my jacket, and immediately start weaving the fabric strands.

Dr P.'s still making small talk. Maybe he's trying to make sure I'm comfortable. I'm anything but. I'm beyond heavy; I'm spent. My muscles ache with bone-weary exhaustion, one I've never quite experienced. He doesn't bother to ask if I've slept; it's apparent I haven't, from my lack of effort to hide it. If I was a zombie from Michael Jackson's 'Thriller' video before, now I'm like Peter Gabriel in 'Sledgehammer', with the crazy stop-motion rollercoaster hair that spikes out in different directions.

'So tomorrow's your birthday,' Dr P. says, as if I needed the reminder. He intertwines his fingers and rests them across his middle as usual while waiting for my acknowledgement.

'Yup.' That's all he gets. I'm less than thrilled, so he's lucky to have gotten that.

'And tomorrow's also when your store is to be vacated, correct?'

'The timing's poetic, don't you think?' I shake my head. 'I'm not going over the hill – I'm being launched by cannon.'

He smiles, slightly. 'So what are you going to do, Libby?'

I blink. 'I don't know. Guess I'll just pull from my inner Power Station and "Bang a Gong" and get on with it. What else can I do?

I'm screwed either way.' Lifting my chin, I put everything out there. 'If I don't sell, they'll just replicate the store and call it something else. It's a clean slice across my jugular. The bleed-out's slow, but death is absolute.'

Dr P. leans back thoughtfully, ignoring my morbid state. The chair squeaks in protest. 'So why not sell? Walk away with a nice payoff? That seems the most logical choice.'

Jasper's idea runs through my mind, but to sell Pretty in Pink? 'So they own my store, and I lose the one thing that makes sense in my life? Then what? If I'm not Libby who owns Pretty in Pink, then—'

'Who are you?' His eyebrows rise and his lips pull wide, exposing his teeth. It's the kind of smile that spreads slowly, waiting for its meaning to resonate.

My God, he is the wolf, and a clever one at that. My head falls to rest on the chair back.

The stupid essay.

The truth is, I don't know who I am, and it's harrowing to discover this so late in the game.

His brows pull down in thought. 'You realize the accident was just that, right? An accident?'

'Sure, but that doesn't change anything. I'm still responsible.' I readjust my leg, shifting my position in the chair.

'You mean it doesn't change your guilt.' Dr P. takes in a full breath and releases it slowly. 'You were sixteen, almost seventeen when the accident happened, correct?'

'Yeah, it, um . . .' Pulling in my lips, I bite against them momentarily, then in one quick moment of bravery force out the words. 'It actually happened *on* my birthday.'

Dr P.'s eyes soften as the pieces fall into place. I shrug, not knowing what else to say. I mean, it's obvious why I hate the day now.

He leans forward. 'Your friends, they know this, of course?'

'Yeah, of course.' I nod. 'Every year they try different ways to . . .' I lift my hand, not sure how to explain.

'They're trying to remind you *your* life, the one you were fortunate to still have after such a tragic accident, is worth celebrating.' He nods in understanding. 'I'd say they're good friends, indeed.'

I know. They are. But he still doesn't quite understand. How do you celebrate the worst day of your life? A day that changed every day that followed? Tears well up in my eyes.

'This confirms what I've suspected all along. After the accident, guilt prevented you from moving on, because someone else couldn't. It's probably what keeps you trapped in the Eighties.'

Jolted, I sniff, wipe at my eyes and protest. 'My store is Eighties vintage. I *profit* from the Eighties.' My God, I can't believe I'm explaining this again. It's the Eighties intervention thing all over. 'It's my work, what I do for a living.'

'It's where you *live*.'

I don't look at him. Instead I focus back on my jacket's tassels and start unbraiding the newly created ones.

Dr P. gives an exaggerated exhale. 'And Oliver – maybe he's the last person you allowed yourself to be really open with, because he was *before* the accident, and that's why you hang on?'

I'm ignoring him, focused on the uneven plaits.

'And if you're honest, Libby, you know what I said before is true. You've never given *anyone* a real chance, and I bet . . .' He pauses, causing me to glance up. 'I bet if you'd met Oliver as an adult *after* everything, he wouldn't have gotten one either. It's only because he already occupied space inside your heart that he remained there when it closed.'

The word *closed* sits in my ears, causing chills. My heart's not closed. It's irrevocably broken. I spread my jacket out over my legs, debating whether I should put it on, really wanting to go.

'You're holding onto the past so tightly, Libby, you're not allowing for a future. Any future. With *anyone*.' Dr P. reaches across to his desk and pulls back a manila file folder. 'There are clinical reasons you're reluctant to let go, to move forward.' He opens the folder and glances inside at the contents, which I can't quite see.

My heart's racing and my skin prickles. *Do I want to know?*

'We know you struggle with depression, and now we know where it stems from, where it started.'

'I knew where it started—'

'But you dissociated yourself. I bet you've never told anyone what *really* happened, or talked about how you feel.'

I still haven't. 'I've apologized to the family more than once, and I try and do nice things for them.' The backs of my eyes burn hot with tears.

'And have they forgiven you?'

I nod, then wipe at my eyes. 'Yeah . . . they're good people. The best, that's why it's so unfair. They didn't deserve for this to happen to them.'

'You didn't either.'

My eyes snap to his.

His voice is low, reassuring. 'You're a good person too, Libby.' He shifts so he's perched on the end of his seat and continues,

'You wish you had died instead, don't you? You feel guilty for surviving.'

I don't say anything. I couldn't if I wanted to, because it's true. I swallow hard.

He nods, not needing a response. 'This is common when dealing with this type of situation. It's a coping mechanism, and just like depression, it's a symptom of something broader. Something scientifically documented and labelled.' He wets his lips, eyes still locked to mine. 'Have you ever heard of survivor syndrome?'

I shake my head.

Dr P. sits back and scans the open folder on his lap. 'It's when someone has guilt at surviving a traumatic event when others didn't. Why not you? Why them? Why should you get to keep living when this other person doesn't, right?' He sits upright again. 'You have all the classic symptoms. Lack of sleep, bouts of depression, anxiety about change . . .'

The muscles of my jaw tense even more. 'But I *know* it was an accident.' I clear my throat and continue, bravely and with conviction. 'I just . . . I just looked down at the wrong time. If it hadn't been gravel, I wouldn't have lost control. None of it would've happened. It wasn't on purpose.'

'Logically, yes, I believe you do understand that.' Dr P. sits back, closes the folder and taps it. 'However, knowing it was an accident isn't enough.'

The swell in my chest bloats larger, and I clench my jaw to hold it all in.

'Libby, you won't live because they can't. You haven't forgiven yourself enough to move on. In fact, you punish yourself. You deny yourself real relationships outside of those that were previously established; you fight against change, in fear of what? Forgetting what happened? You won't allow yourself true happiness.'

He rolls his chair even closer and leans in. 'You need to believe you're *not* to blame, you didn't do anything wrong. And that *everything* you feel is justified and allowed. It has a clinical name, and you can heal from it. You can heal from this.' He's nodding with compassionate eyes.

Mine are overflowing with tears, one after another. His words act as a life preserver, but I'm frozen and can't quite reach.

I don't have to.

Dr P. takes both my hands firmly in his. 'You lived . . . you *lived*, Libby. Don't you think it's time you started *living*?'

CHAPTER 19
'St Elmo's Fire'
John Parr, 1985

Full five-alarm

It's late, but I couldn't sleep, and instead of sitting around my apartment haunted by the past, I find myself at Pretty in Pink faced by the future. Mine. The one I need to embrace and finally allow.

I have to sell.

I know this, and yet I'm flooded with regret. It's strangely quiet, as if the store somehow knows that I'm here, and why. I'm also talking with Ollie.

'Sorry to bug you so late,' I say, clicking the ballpoint pen with my thumb again and again. The sound echoes as I walk around carrying a clipboard and paper. I have the guesstimate itemization to use as a reference, but Criminal Seth wasn't anywhere near the correct value of things. But how could he know?

He listed how many wooden display shelving units I have and assigned a dollar amount, but what isn't noted is how the one in front is covered in celebrity signatures. Slowly, I trace the scribbles with my fingertips: Winger, Cinderella, even Gloria Estefan, they all stopped in. Lines of teenagers wrapped through the aisles and out the door just to score an autograph and photo and, before they left, I'd have them sign this.

'You're obviously upset; you OK?' Ollie sounds sleepy.

'Sure . . . no. I don't know.' I stop as sheet lightning illuminates both the sky and the sales floor in silent bursts of shocking brightness. It's not even raining. Autumn's drastic temperature shifts seem to confuse Mother Nature and create the temperamental weather New York is known for.

'It's just, Seth didn't have the itemized list of assets right for the store, and . . .' My mouth forms a tight line. *Don't cry. Don't.* 'If I'm going to accept their offer, it needs to be accurate.' This is frustrating.

'I really can't believe you're selling Pretty in Pink, but I'm proud of you.'

'I haven't told anyone. I only just decided. And really, I could still back out.' I glance over to the photos that hang framed on the back wall. Every in-store event and record signing is documented with a snapshot. I'm in most of them. So are Dora, Finn and a few recent ones with Dean. Ollie's in the ones from when I worked here in high school. It's like my own Libby London yearbook. At least I get to keep these. And *God*, look at me: ratted hair, star dangle earrings, and the clothes . . . OK, so not everything's different.

I wipe at my eyes and keep going. 'It's about time I moved on anyway, right?'

'Isn't that what we've all been saying?'

'Yeah, but it's hard.' I sigh in frustration. 'Seth didn't even list the rare vinyl collections in the display case, or the collection of concert tickets in the front cabinet. I mean, those are worth a small fortune.'

'Well, just make sure you do. If they want Pretty in Pink they have to pay its worth, right?'

'Right.' The lump in my throat lodges impossibly deep. This is the easy part, the things I can assign a dollar amount to, but what about the rest? How do you put a price on your soul?

Looking round, I take it all in, then crumple to the floor so I'm leaned against the checkout counter, the itemized list lying to my side. This is too much. 'God, I don't know if I can do this.'

'It's just *St Elmo's Fire*, Shortcake. That's all this is.'

I smile through my tears because I know exactly what he means. Another movie we spent far too many hours debating over the phone while growing up. I'm Jules, alone in my own melodrama, completely beside myself. Oliver is my Billy. The boy who refuses to grow up, and yet, he's the only one who can get through and help.

'Remember in the movie how Billy holds up a can of aerosol hairspray and with one flick of a lighter, creates a quick burst of flame?' Oliver says, knowing full well I do.

'Yeah.' I give the definition without thought. 'Unlike lightning, which travels forward in a heated streak across the sky, St Elmo's Fire burns blue and spherical and moves nowhere.'

'Right. It's caused by a disruption, and exists only in the gap.' He says it again. 'It's caused by a disruption, Libbs. It exists only in that gap.'

I sniff and wipe at my eyes. 'Like me. My life. Is that what you're saying?' I had such a disruption, and I've moved nowhere. Only existing, only loving, within that gap.

'You have to let go, Libbs. Of everything. The accident was just that. No one blames you, except *you* . . .'

My face folds in with tears. God, what I wouldn't give to curl up in his arms right now. To smell the scent of Polo and feel his lips on my forehead as he cradles me in his embrace. 'I wish I could go back in time and warn myself.' The soft tears have turned to real ones, my voice cracking between the sobs. 'I'd scream "Don't mess with the music, Libbs. Leave it alone, listen to the birthday tape later." Maybe then—'

'Maybe it would've happened anyhow,' Oliver says. 'How do we know what's fated?'

'I always thought *we* were fated.'

Dr P.'s words repeat in my head. 'Have you ever told Oliver how you feel?'

'Libby? You there?'

My heart's pounding heavy. 'I need to tell you something.'

'You know you can tell me anything.'

'OK.' I take a deep breath to steady my nerves. I'm over-whelmed, but determined to force the words, because they're honest and that makes them beautiful. Love is beautiful. And I have loved this man my whole life. 'When we were together, I felt . . . special. My crazy red hair wasn't a mess, it was wild and exotic. My freckles were adorable instead of embarrassing and if I was Jules before, I'm the character Wendy now. Because I'm just like she was with Billy, I'm in love with a man that isn't available.' My head drops into my hand. My shoulders quake from trying to keep it together.

The sky flashes white again, and after a beat, a deep roll of thunder answers its call. I clear my throat, run a hand through my hair and start again. 'It's just that I want you to know . . .' You'd think this wouldn't be as hard. I take another deep breath.

'Hey . . .' His voice carries a familiar reassurance. 'It's OK. Just say it, Libbs.'

I let my head drop back, so it thumps against the wood behind me. My heart swells. I could just wrap myself in the memory of his embrace, forget everything I was about to say and fall right back into our same old pattern, and for the moment I'd feel better. This empty ache would be filled and I could breathe. But then it's the same old life, a life with no future. And I think, finally, I'm ready to have one.

'I wish I would've said this forever ago. God knows I wish you were here, so I could say it to your face. But I had plenty of chances, and I didn't and . . .' A nervous smile plays on my lips. 'I, um . . .' My head rocks. God, this is awful. 'I *still* love you, Oliver . . .' It's almost a whisper. 'I do, and I always have. And I think . . . No, I *know* I always will.' My voice cracks. 'And I'm not sure how to move on. I'm not sure I can, even though I have to.'

The sky surrenders to its downpour. I surrender to my own, and openly weep.

CHAPTER 20

'Holding Out for a Hero'
Bonnie Tyler, 1984

No more waiting around

I'm officially thirty-three years old today. It's not the getting older bit that bothers me so much; it's not. It's the memory that comes along with it.

Worst birthday ever.

And now, on this one, I'm facing a reboot future without Ollie or Pretty in Pink.

It's a literal do or die, because this *can't* go on. I debated my options all night and decided it's time I accepted the truth – I'm the one who's fresh from the fight, so I need to be strong and fast and larger than . . . well, my messed-up life.

At least I have to try.

My first, get-a-grip action item was completed before I showered, dressed and left to take on this day. This *re-birth* day.

I faxed Finn the updated inventory and assets list so he can get it to the Lander Property Group. If they believe the offer to buy

Pretty in Pink is under serious consideration, I won't have to vacate the premises today. This at least buys me some time, and I need just a little bit more.

My second action item is to get Dora to chill. She's been blowing up my phone via text all day. *What are you wearing tonight? Do you need us to do your hair? Do you want a ride?* This has gone on and on and on. And if that wasn't bad enough, Jasper keeps calling me with stupid questions like *Where's the stapler*? I mean, *really?*

But I get it: they're worried, and I've gone MIA again. But this time it's different – instead of running away, I've been busy kicking off a little Eighties intervention of my own. I've decided to tackle this birthday business straight on.

The first place I ventured was the overpriced Park Avenue store Dora's so fond of. I enlisted the help of a saleswoman, who recruited two more, and let them go to town choosing my birthday ensemble.

'That's impeccable,' said the first salesgirl, regarding the pair of slacks they had me try on.

They felt like butter to the touch, smooth and silky under my fingertips. The price reflected the material, but the colour? In the mirror, I turned, eyeing them doubtfully. 'I don't know . . . they're just so beige, basic—'

'Brilliant, yes, they're absolutely brilliant,' the other sales associate assured me. 'Although I'm not sure about the shirt.'

'Right, definitely need a different shirt,' said the third woman. 'And if we change that then . . .'

'Right, the slacks don't match.' They all agreed.

They spent the next few hours swapping this for that in a

strange wardrobe merry-go-round with heated commentary and debate, only to settle on the first outfit I tried on. The sales women called my look 'boho chic'. I think it's boho-boring, but it's smart-casual and shows a new polished, sophisticated . . . *person*.

The fawn belted chinos and blush-pink button-up are perfectly polished – like Claire, Molly Ringwald's character, or Wendy from *St Elmo's Fire* – while the double-looped costume pearls add a bit of dramatic flair like Demi Moore's character, Jules. None of it is really me, but I'm still trying to figure out who that is, remember?

After the shopping was done, I glanced at my hair in the mirror. That, at least, *was* me: it was Basket Case crazy. Then I eyed the time, deciding to make one more stop: Fringe, Dora's fancy-schmancy salon.

Their chosen scent of the day to cover the ammonia stench was sandalwood – still nauseating, but better than the lemongrass of last time. The stylist paled when she saw me in the reception area, and quickly changed direction.

'Wait, wait, wait . . .' I chased after her. 'I come in peace. Promise.' I showed her the photo in the hair magazine that I'd been considering, and after a few tense moments of darting her eyes between my head and the glossy photo, she pushed out a sigh of surrender and accepted the challenge.

'Are you *sure*?' she asked.

'Yes?' Which meant no; I mean, this was my *hair*. Was I really considering such a drastic change? Yes. *Finally*, yes. I nodded again.

'Well, if you're going to do it, you need to do it right.' She took the magazine and thumbed through the pages, stopping every so often to hold a glossy picture up next to my face and compare. 'What do you think, Shauna? With her face shape?'

'I don't know,' Shauna said, with a slight tilt to her head. 'She's more heart than round. What if you did a bias cut?' She took over the magazine, flipping pages intently.

Blah blah blah – this went on for an eternity, or at least thirty minutes. Finally, after confirming with every stylist, nail tech, make-up artist, masseuse and customer, they chose the perfect style. The first one I'd shown them.

Two for two. Maybe I do know myself after all.

Back in the chair, my heart raced as the stylist unclipped the banana clip (this time like a pro), gathered my hair into a pony-tail with one hand and brushed it through with the other. My palms grew moist. What was I doing? Maybe I shouldn't. This was craz—

Too late.

I glanced down. A huge mass of curly red locks lay on the floor beneath me. With one skilled snip, she had sliced straight through my whole identity.

Another hour of shaping, and it was done.

God, what had I done?

My signature long locks were reduced to a mop of loose curls high above my shoulders in a short curly bob. I was Baby from *Dirty Dancing*. There's a character I never once considered. She was dorky, yet confident. She carried a watermelon, but stole Johnny's heart. I could be Baby, yeah, because no one put her in the corner! And I do like watermelon.

But now? Here I sit, blinking at my reflection in the taxi window. My neck's exposed, and it's cold. I never knew it could catch a chill. I also didn't know I had a skinny neck – finally, I can say something on my body is.

I'm like ET when the little girl dressed him up with the wig. Except it's not a wig, and I'm not blonde – and I can't go home, because I've already arrived at my destination. I'm sitting outside the banquet hall entrance where my not-so-surprise birthday party is under way inside.

'Lady, is this the right place?' the cabbie asks for the second or third time.

'Yeah, I, ah . . . I just need another minute.' Tonight is meant to be a new start, but as usual, I can't get started. I'm stalled in the cab.

Peering at my reflection again, I give myself a small mental pep talk. You're a new and improved woman. You *can* do this. I eyeball the springy locks that frame my face. You're also a poodle. *Ugh.* Maybe I need a nudge that everything's going to be fine. Just a small sign would help.

Knock-knock-knock.

'Aah!' I jump, startled by the man with long wild black hair and mirrored sunglasses pressed up against the glass. He's also wearing a top hat.

'Hi! I've been waiting on you!' His voice is distorted through the glass.

'He yer date?' nosy cab man asks, with a smirk.

'Let's hope not,' I say, debating whether I should tell him to hurry up and take off, or roll the window down and ask the guy for an autograph – he's dressed like Slash from Guns N' Roses.

'Libby, it's me.' The man lifts the shades slightly and smiles.

I crack the window a hair, still uncertain, then blink with narrowed eyes. 'Dr Theo?' Oh God, why is he here? Like *that*?

'Hi, Libby!' Another head pops out from behind his shoulder. No wig, but he's wearing a Members Only jacket and has a clip-on earring. 'Dr Weaver, remember?'

Busy hands burst between them, a flurry of activity with neon fingernails. Translation woman's here, too.

I asked for a sign, not someone *who* signs.

'So, ya good?' cabbie man asks.

I sigh, pay, and since they're not leaving, pop the latch and force them back a little with the car door. Stepping out, I fake a smile while I take them in. 'Wow.' That's all I say.

'Wowza is right. You cut your hair,' Dr Weaver says, pointing.

Sign woman translates. Who knew *wowza* could be signed? I'm staring at them, they're staring at me.

'Great costume,' Dr Weaver says. 'I love Molly Ringwald.'

'I'm not in costume.' I glance down at the pinkish shirt and double strand of long pearls. Add those to the short reddish hair and yeah, OK. Whatever. 'So, you're here because?' It's an *almost* question. The kind that begs for explanation, but really maybe I don't want to know.

'"Welcome to the Jungle" – well, welcome to your party,' Dr Theo says, sing-song. 'Dora asked us to escort you inside. And we're happy to, you know, to make sure you don't overdo it—'

'With your *condition* and all,' Dr Weaver adds while looping an arm through mine, leading me forward, making me hesitate even more. 'Are you feeling OK? Any fevers of late?'

'What about the hives?' Dr Theo asks from the other side. 'Any more reactions?'

I laugh. 'I'm having a pretty strong one right now.'

Inside, Dead or Alive's 'You Spin Me Round (Like a Record)' thumps and vibrates, but I'm the one turned round. I've time-warped. The hall is blinged-out Eighties. And I didn't need a souped-up DeLorean that requires a nuclear reaction to generate the 1.21 gigawatts of electricity to get me here. All it took was Dora. A pregnant, hormonally-charged force of nature.

I'm pretty sure they raided my store to decorate. Now I understand why Jasper kept calling me every ten minutes, asking me where things were stored.

'She's here!' Finn yells from somewhere, but I don't see him.

No, wait, there he is. He sees me, then ducks out of sight. *What's that about?* Dr Theo says something about getting everyone a drink. The interpreter interprets and then follows him, leaving me with Dr Weaver. He's snapping his fingers, completely off beat. Maybe he's already had a few?

'Can you excuse me?' I don't wait for a response, and dart into the crowd on a mission to find Dora. There are seriously a *lot* of people crammed in here.

'Whoa, your hair.' It's Robbie, one of the teens who work weekends at Pretty in Pink. He's wearing a 'Save Ferris' T-shirt from the store.

I think 'Save Libby' would be more fitting.

'Are you Molly Ringwald?' His eyebrows arch as he regards my hair. 'Cool, 'cause that so fits with Pretty in Pink and all.'

'Where's Jasper?' I ask, ignoring the question.

He shrugs. 'Dunno. He called asking where you were.'

I keep going on the prowl for Dora, Dean – 'Finn!' He's already gone again. *Why is my dentist here?* 'Hi, Dr Meyers.' I wave, hoping he doesn't remember I was a no-show for my last cleaning. They always scrape too hard, and I swear there's a conspiracy. I only have cavities after a visit.

'Libby!'

I turn, and . . . 'Here Comes the Hammer', or rather, Nigel Harrington, the Athlete. He's shirtless, a huge gold chain draped across his bare muscular chest, wearing black drop pants and gold-rimmed glasses, but that's not the worst of it: he has the parrot. Not the real one that ended up with the Criminal, but the mangled one from mini-golf. It's wearing a neck brace, and is fastened to his suspenders.

'What d'ya think?' He's shuffling back and forth in a weird hobbling motion while pumping his massive arms and singing 'Can't Touch This'.

Don't want to. 'What are you doing here?' And *why* would he have that blasted parrot?

'Finn invited us, and since you sent the card, I thought we were cool, so . . .'

'Oh, right, definitely.' I smile, remembering Finn's glowing testimony of him: Strong Man champion in Vegas, gym owner, helps troubled youth. We can be friends. I have room for new friends. 'I'm really glad you're here, Nigel. Thanks for coming.'

'Too Legit, Too Legit to Quit.' He's dancing again – he needs to quit. He puffs his chest and pulses his pecs, left then right, to match the chorus he's still singing.

I debate whether I should point out that MC Hammer's peak of popularity was really in the early Nineties, but decide against it. 'Nigel, Nigel,' I say, interrupting his me-party. 'Where *is* Finn?'

'Oh, I think he's at the bar. Did you want something?' He stops gyrating and wipes at his forehead, where small beads of sweat have formed.

'Yes, please. Something strong.'

'Cool, and when I get back, we're gonna "Turn This Mother Out". Another left-right pulse of the pecs, and he's gone.

Oh my *God*. Something catches my eye behind a man in purple Prince attire – it's Finn's head popping out from one side of him. He pulls it back and juts it out to the man's other side.

'I see you, Finn!' I shout, my voice breaking in the middle as I make tracks in his direction, cutting around people.

'Happy Birthday, Libby!'

'Wow, your hair. Great costume.'

'Didn't even recognize you!'

'Hi! Hi, thank you,' I smile-nod and keep moving. *Damn*. I've lost him again. They're all up to something, I know it. I turn and scan the dance floor.

'Libby!' A hand's held high, waving frantically.

Oh, come *on* . . .

It's the Princess. So far he's the only one that has the Eighties done right: caked eyeliner, thick white smudges across each cheek, dangly earrings. He's Adam Ant. He sashays in my direction, twirls me round by my hand and kisses it in the most dramatic fashion. 'Look at you. Love the hair. Molly Ringwald, right?'

'Sure,' I say, without inflection. I've given up trying to explain it wasn't intentional. Maybe it was unintentionally intentional? Dr P. would have a field day with this one. 'Where's Finn?'

'Ah . . .' Adrian spins, his index finger pointed like a wand. 'Probably backstage.'

'Backstage? There's a stage?' I look through the crowd, and yup, there is in fact a small platform in the rear of the hall. My stomach turns. Finn's head's up again – well, his hair. It's spiked so high it's like the Jaws fin swimming through the mob. I follow, making a quick and direct line across the dance floor. I plan on making waves, but stop short, because there she is. The indomitable Dora.

I think. She's head-to-toe neon, wearing a blonde bobbed wig and wound in pendants. I eye the jewellery. All mine, so it's definitely Dora. When she turns in my direction, it confirms it. She's Madonna from 'Vogue', although pregnant, so definitely not 'Like A Virgin'. I charge. 'You completely raided my closet and my store!'

Her eyes narrow, then go wide. 'Oh my God. Oh my God! Libby? You're here? You're here!' She squeals with a little bounce skip-step, her hands covering her gaping mouth while staring at my hair. 'Dean, look! Look at Libbs!'

Dean turns, and the whole scene's repeated. '*Whoa* . . . I don't even recognize you.'

I don't recognize Dean. He's in parachute pants with his hair gelled back like Elvis. I'm not sure it's a cohesive Eighties ensemble, but it shows effort. I also think those might be my pants.

He inhales sharply. 'Oh, you're that chick from those movies, right?'

'Sure.' Why fight it?

'It really *is* you.' Finn appears from nowhere, reaches out and touches my hair.

'Don't even act like you didn't see me.' I point, then turn to the others. 'And *what is all this*? It's Eighties? And you invited the Athlete, the Brain, the Princess and—'

'Hi, Libby!'

I squint to be sure. 'My dry cleaner?'

'We invited everyone.' Dora smiles. 'Dean, call Jas and tell him she's here.'

'Call him?'

'Apparently you've been missing.'

'Missing? No . . .' I wave a hand to present myself. 'I've been—'

'Becoming Molly?' Finn's lips pull down.

Mine pull up to mock him.

'Anyone need a drink? 'Cause I do.' Like that, he's gone.

Dora smacks my arm. 'Don't move – we need to get things rolling.'

Oh, God.

CHAPTER 21

'Don't You Forget About Me'
Simple Minds, 1985

Never have, never will

Dora leaves me, only to appear on stage a few minutes later. She has a mic. I'm already afraid and looking for exits.

'Hello?' She taps it a few times and fiddles with the switch. 'OK, yes, it's working . . .' Dora's speaking really loud, so her voice echoes from the small amp and squelches. 'Everyone gather round, because we have a few announcements.'

Bye. I turn. Dean stops me. Or Elvis. I'm really not sure. He actually has sideburns.

Finn jumps on stage and smiles. I shake my head to mean, *you're rotten.* He smiles even wider to say, *I know.*

Dora begins. 'First, let me start by thanking everyone for coming to celebrate Libby London's birthday!' She points to me. Dean nudges me towards her, so I push back. As the room fills with applause, I turn to make my escape.

'Hi.' It's my chiropractor, Dr Hong. He's wearing a red leather jacket. He waves. That's when I notice the sparkly white glove. Nice.

I smile and turn back round. I hate them. My neck's warm, and now without my hair as cover, the splotches are on display for all to see. I plaster on a smile and tug at the pearls round my neck.

Dora continues. 'Our dear Libby London was perpetually lost in the Eighties.'

'So we stepped in to help her find her way,' Finn leans over, claiming the mic and the spotlight. 'As everyone's aware, a few weeks ago we surprised Libby with an Eighties intervention. We started with a modern makeover. But this being an Eighties-themed shindig . . .' He motions to me again. 'Of course she's gone Molly.'

Oh my *God*. 'I'm not Molly Ring . . . I mean, I didn't do it on—' My words are lost in the applause. I scan over their heads for a bar. *Is there even one here?* I really need a drink.

Dora's loving this. She also loves the mic. She swipes it from Finn again. 'To bring our Eighties girl into the twenty-first century, we set her up on a series of blind dates from the movie that defined the decade she's been stuck in: *The Breakfast Club*.'

Giving up on the mic war, Finn just leans over. 'And in case you've been under a rock and haven't been following our now sponsored hashtag, #80sIntervention, on Twitter and Instagram – here's some highlights as we give introductions.'

'Sponsored?' I ask to anyone within earshot.

Dr Hong's wife, standing beside him, nods. 'Oh yeah, they have a salon donating a free makeover experience for the best Eighties photo. It's been a hoot to follow.' Roaring laughter fills the room.

I turn, look up, and oh. Dear. God.

It's me.

All their stupid snap-flash photobombs and selfies plastered for the world to see – actually, that one's kinda cute, *but God*.

'You still won,' Dr Hong's wife says. 'And the salon did a fabulous job.'

'What?' I have to think about whether I paid my stylist today. Did I? Maybe I didn't. I've won best Eighties photo, even now? As pics of each Breakfast Club date appear on the pull-down screen, they wave and take a formal bow. Nigel throws both massive arms into the air and Adrian does a fancy spin. The sign-language woman lifts a drink to say *cheers*. I have no idea where Dr Theo and Dr Weaver are. Probably at the bar. Where I'd rather be.

I throw accusatory glances at Dora and Finn, scared of what this is leading up to. When the presentation starts to loop, the music's dimmed down. Finn has the mic again, and his smile is epic. It reminds me of when we were kids and he and Ollie were up to something. I'm instantly on edge.

'So, yes, we set poor Libby up on five stereotypical dates—'

'Five?' someone shouts. 'I see only three.'

'Right, well, the Criminal turned out to be one – sorry, love.' He nods to me. 'And the Basket Case . . .' His hand splays on his chest, right across his heart. 'Well, this whole thing was designed to give one poor unfortunate soul the chance to shine. And that was—'

'Me,' a voice says from the crowd.

Everyone spins round.

I focus to where heads are turned, and – short styled hair, clean-shaven jaw, fully modern-cut suit – 'Jasper?'

His smile's crooked.

Mine's full. 'What is this?' My heart's beating triple time.

Dora rips the mic from Finn's hands, triumphantly. 'You *did* date the Basket Case, Libbs. You guys hung out a few times. And in fact, he set this whole thing up.'

'Big gesture,' Jas yells, pulling back my attention.

'Really big gesture,' I say, more to myself, completely stunned and still trying to piece it all together. If he wanted to go out with me, why have me date others? Before I can ask or acknowledge him, the screen behind Dora blasts Bowling for Soup's '1985' video and she starts barrelling towards me, mic still in hand.

'Happy birthday to *my* best friend, *our* Eighties girl, and *your* Libby London! She's finally caught up to the rest of us!' Dora wraps me in a one-armed, awkward pregnant squeeze, whispering near my ear. 'I'm so proud of you, Libbs.'

♫

'Aren't you lovely, just like Samantha from that movie.'

'Leave it to Libby London to do the Eighties right.'

'Happy Birthday, Moll – er, Libby.'

Fine. So in trying to de-Eighties, I'm finally seen as my Eighties icon. Makes no sense, but whatever. I smile, nod and thank everyone. I'm still trying to wrap my head around Jasper doing this Eighties intervention when I spot him. I take a sharp breath to open my lungs from the emotional grip, and smile as he approaches.

'Can we talk?' He rests one hand behind my back; the other motions towards the door.

Mine are mindlessly playing with the looped beads around my now-exposed neck. Why am I so nervous? Outside, the music's instantly muffled. The static inside my mind, however, snaps, crackles and pops.

'No one knew where you were all day. But I guess we know now . . .' He steps close, his blue eyes scanning over my head. 'Wow, you *really* cut your hair.'

'Yeah,' I say, finger-combing it, braced for whatever he may say. He likes it, he hates it . . .

'It's . . . You look . . .' He's shaking his head. 'You're a stunner, Libbs.'

My smile betrays me, so do my words. 'You did all this for me?' I shuffle my feet. 'Which means you openly take responsibility for torturing me with this Eighties intervention thing?' My eyes are narrowed, sizing him up, trying to figure this out. 'You do realize those dates were awful, right?'

His smile pulls wide. 'That wasn't intentional, but yeah, I do.' He laughs.

My mouth drops. 'Why? I mean, *God*, Jas.'

'Because I had asked and asked, and you couldn't see past—'

'The stereotype.' I shake my head and laugh again. 'You're clever. I've always said that.' I drop my chin and peek up at him through my lashes. False ones. The make-up artist at the salon put them on. 'And the makeover?'

'Asking them to set up the Breakfast Club dates, yes, guilty, but it never even occurred to me to—'

'So that was all Dora.' I give a sigh. 'But this . . .' I point to my lack of hair, then my smart-casual outfit. 'This was me.'

'You do look pretty in pink. I like it; 'course, I liked it before.' His smile softens, then pulls unevenly. 'Oh, yeah – I broke your window, so don't freak out when you get home.'

My eyes pop. 'What? *Why*?'

He rubs a hand over his clean-shaven jaw, no trace of the warm smile from before. 'You didn't answer. You weren't picking up your phone either, so—'

'So you broke my window? Wait, why were you there?'

'Told you I'd pick you up at seven-thirty, remember? That's why I was late.'

'Oh, God, that's right. You're the Basket Case.' I laugh, remembering his email. 'You dork, I told you no.'

He smiles and steps closer. 'I'd say it worked out all right.'

'Doesn't explain the window.'

'Yeah, well, you've had me worried, Libbs. Your Top Five. I got it. I figured it out. Message received loud and clear.'

My stomach drops. I actually forgot about that. 'First rule of Top Five: once solved, *you don't discuss Top Five*,' I say softly, and look away.

'Yeah, and the second rule is the same, I got it. But this isn't a game.' His voice has dropped to a low whisper and he's leaned in close. 'It's your life. And you can't end it before it's even begun.'

'What? No, well, yes, but . . .' I'd be lying if I said I'd never thought about it, last night being no exception, but this was more a mix-tape connection with one sad thing in common. Maybe I just needed to talk about it. 'It's not exactly what you're thinking.'

'Then what was I supposed to think?' Jas looks confused. He's still leaning in close. 'Nirvana, INXS, Milli Vanilli, Boston and Crowded House. Each group had a member that took their own life. So I thought—'

'I meant more that each group lost a member before their time.' It's obvious to me now that I've been working up to sharing my story with Jas all along. 'And it does mean something. Something personal, but maybe I can tell you another time? Is that OK?' I half-smile, hoping he understands, then change the subject before he can let me know if he does. I have to. 'So . . . this is pretty big, this gesture of yours.'

'Yeah.' There's a pause, as if he isn't sure of the new direction, but then . . . 'I've heard that's how they're supposed to go. It has to be something so huge, so out of character . . .' Jasper closes all distance between us, and lifts my chin with a finger so I'm forced to look at him. 'So the other person knows it's sincerely from the heart.'

Surprising flutters form in mine. I'm flattered, even intrigued, but I'm also still in love with Ollie, and that doesn't just go away. And it never will, unless . . .

I may have realized before what had to be done, but only now do I believe I can do it. 'What if I had one in return? A big gesture of my own?'

His eyes widen with curiosity.

I take a deep breath. 'We both know I have to sell Pretty in Pink.' I shrug, then offer a hopeful smile. 'So . . . maybe we *should* move to LA and start things up again with Starcades.' The words are coming just as they're thought. 'Because I can't stay here, not with someone else owning my shop. I mean, if I want to finally *start* my life, then, yeah, I need a real start somewhere else, *with* someone else.' I nervously glance at Jas. 'What do ya think?'

His smile pulls wide and his eyes shine, reflecting the excitement I'm starting to feel. 'I think that's some gesture, Libby London.'

My stomach drops. 'But Jas, this . . . all of this, the Eighties intervention thing and you, well, it's huge and new and I'm—'

'You're not over Oliver, I know. But maybe away from here, in time, you'll finally admit what I've known all along.'

'And what's that?'

His denim-coloured eyes peek out from behind shards of wispy blonde hair and narrow a fraction. 'That you're secretly in love with your manager, soon-to-be-business-partner.'

The static from before now zaps straight through to settle in my heart. Again, I'm overwhelmed, but this time it's with something else.

Hope.

♫

The party's a huge success. My new and improved Libby look is a big hit, even if everyone thinks I intentionally modelled it after Molly Ringwald. And everyone is having fun on the dance floor, except Theo, the Brain. He threw out his back while Princess Adrian was trying to teach him some new-fangled hip-hop move. *Oh*, I should introduce him to Dr Hong, my chiropractor.

From my table, I watch Dora and Dean dance. Well, Dean's dancing. Dora's kind of bobbing like a buoy in the water. Her head's the only thing really moving. I'm truly happy they found each other, and they're going to make great parents. I'm not looking forward to telling her I'm moving to LA, but I'll fly back for the wedding, and of course the baby.

Finn's flirting with the DJ. I can tell because of the way he's standing, balanced on one foot and kicking the other one this way and that as he talks. He takes everything in his stride. Not much fazes him. I told him that once, and he said he had his challenges early on with his dad, so he figures he's due a lifetime of easy street – although he loves to make mine as difficult as possible. I kinda love him for that.

The interpreter is dancing with Nigel the Athlete. It's comical to watch. She's stopped signing because she can't keep her busy little hands off him, much to his delight. Dr Weaver's jamming air guitar. I don't think he cares. He's had a few too many and is definitely dancing to his own beat.

Jasper's beside me. The suit coat's gone, the sleeves are rolled and his hair is back to a dishevelled mess, only shorter. 'Did you want something to drink?'

'Only if you can manage to find your way back,' I say in all seriousness. Apparently the bar is the Bermuda Triangle. Every person who's ventured off has yet to return with a drink.

Jasper eyes my cheeks, and the freckles that cover them. 'Yeah, I think I can find my way.' He smiles crookedly, with a chin-nod. 'Just like you, Libby London, just like you.'

I watch him disappear into the crowd; the smile on my face can't be helped. At thirty-three I'm at a crossroads, the middle mark of my life, and it's a real-life *Pretty in Pink* – only I'm the one who's choosing the ending, or rather choosing to finally begin. It's a good feeling.

My eyes cast down with the thought. When I raise them, I see Ollie leaning in the doorway. Long, towering legs, a shoulder pressed to the frame, a hand hanging casually from his pocket. My heart stutters when he looks in my direction. He smiles, and my God, he's still a rock star. He hasn't changed a bit. But then, why would he?

He's forever eighteen.

I've held him there, trying to stop time, trying to make amends, trying to hold on, when really all that's left is to finally let go. Let go and live.

Even if he didn't.

I don't remember where we were going; only that he had made me a birthday mix tape, and I was desperate to hear his words through the chosen songs. I can't tell you how many times I've wondered, what if he hadn't been in the passenger seat? What if we'd left just five minutes earlier or later? What if I hadn't looked down to mess with the cassette? What if . . .

I remember the Ferris Bueller debate, and how much I wanted to prove him wrong. But I've come to realize Ollie was right after all. Ollie said, 'He's real, Libby, just not in the context of Cameron's depressed fantasy. He created Ferris, or at least that version of him, because he had to. He needed a hero.'

I have, too.

I've needed Ollie.

Life moves pretty fast, but my life stopped when his did. I wouldn't allow it, didn't deserve it and hadn't wanted it to move on. But now?

Ollie lowers his chin with questioning eyes. I know what he's asking. Will I be OK? Am I all right? Am I sure?

My heart sits in my throat, the dull and constant ache sharp and overwhelming because I know that I have to be. I blink back tears, smile through them and nod. He mouths, *Love you, Short-cake*, then lifts a hand to his lips, presses a kiss and sends it my way.

I smile. There's nothing left to say, there's only this, only us, and a lifetime of loving followed by an inevitable goodbye.

This is really goodbye.

I take in a deep breath, and slowly let it go.

Finally let *him* go.

'Libbs? Hey, you OK?' Jasper approaches with drinks in hand.

Wiping at my cheeks, I turn towards him and smile. 'Yeah . . . for the first time in forever, I think I'm gonna be just fine.' I stifle a laugh. *God*, these two horrible weeks have been treacherous – and yet they've been the best of my life, because they've forced me to claim one.

Claim *mine*.

So it turns out my birthday wasn't a noose hanging over my head after all.

It was a lifeline.

I've been holding out for a hero for over sixteen years . . .

And today of all days, *I've* finally arrived.

Epilogue

'Are you cold?' Jasper asks, and adjusts the moving van's heat. It doesn't work well, and although the setting sun's still bright, early winter's bite is stronger.

'I'm OK.' I flip the collar of my oversized jean jacket, the one covered in concert badges, and wrap my arms round myself. I'm back to my Eighties wardrobe vibe: it's who I am. I didn't need to be Claire after all. Being Libby's just as cool. Not everything needs to change. Leaning on the door, I stare out the window.

The further west we travel, the more the season winds back. We started with barren maples and dormant grass, and are now passing fields of green. It's still chilly at night, however. I lean heavily against the door and let my eyes close a minute. It's been a long couple of days of travel – well, a long three months.

It's amazing how much has happened. Dora's baby bump has ballooned to epic proportions. If Dora was a Weeble before, now she's simply round. But since this is her last go at pregnancy, she's determined to enjoy every uncomfortable minute. It's a fantastic attitude.

My attitude on my previous birthdays has been nothing short of dismal. But since this is my first go at really living, I'm determined to embrace them moving forward.

We all met at Shermer's on East Broadway before I left. One last get-together for our original Breakfast Club: Dora, Dean, Finn and myself. Jas, although invited, opted to meet us afterwards with the van, saying he had a last-minute errand. And just like normal, our once-a-weeks, fuelled by New York's finest short-stacks, involved news, and not just any random bits of gossip, but something fantastical and life-changing.

That day was no exception.

'I can't believe you're going to LA, Libbs,' Dora said, pouting and twirling her fork in the pool of syrup on the half-empty plate of waffles. She had already taken mine.

Finn patted her arm. 'But we can visit. Think of it: all of us meeting in the city of angels, taking Hollywood by storm. Wouldn't *that* be divine?'

'I'll be back in no time for the wedding, Dora, and as soon as you call with baby news, I'm on a plane. I promise.' My own words sounded foreign to me. I was leaving. I was *really* going.

'Oh, we could get tickets to *Ellen*,' Finn said, already planning their trip. 'And we could take those tours, you know, the ones that drive through the Hollywood Hills and point out where the stars live?'

'And to think, Libby, this all started because of Jasper's Eighties intervention,' Dean said before finishing off his orange juice.

Dora scoffed. 'Jasper's idea, sure, but *we* made it ...' She looked up, as if searching for the right word.

'Brilliant?'

'Magical.'

'Cuckoo like Cocoa Puffs,' I said, smiling.

It is crazy. I *really* said goodbye to everyone. But at least it's not a permanent farewell, right? Even my nightly sob sessions have taken a sabbatical. In fact, I'm doing great. I'm optimistic and excited for a new start at life. But I know how this works: like I said before, when you struggle with any level of depression, you have periods of coping, not the other way around.

This time, however, I'm prepared. Since I'm currently above water, I placed a call before we left to safeguard for the next time when I'm not.

I called Dr Papadopoulos's office and asked for a referral in LA.

'Hello?' I said when I heard the *click*. I'd been on hold for a few minutes, subjected to easy listening, and when the song switched, it tripped me up. After a few bars, I recognized the *I Dream of Jeannie* theme song, set the phone to speaker and maybe danced a bit while I did a last-time sweep through my apartment.

That's when I noticed the converted 45 record clock still hanging on the wall, the one that featured 'That Joke Isn't Funny Anymore'. And, still frozen at four, it wasn't. Not that it was ever a joke – that's the time my accident occurred. It served as a reminder so I'd never forget; not that I ever could.

After a minute, I dug through a box where I'd stashed needed junk-drawer items: corkscrew, lighter and *yes*, batteries. Lifting the plastic clock, I flipped it round, swivelled the dial to the correct time and placed the two double-As inside.

And just like that, the past moved forward.

And wow, am I moving forward – from the hustle and eclectic energy of New York City to the cooler vibe of Los Angeles. I promised Dora I'd call when we stopped for the night and I'm sure she's worried, but Jasper's not ready to call it a day. He has a schedule, and although my frequent rest-area stops are messing with it, he's determined.

So was Dora.

'You'll call as soon as you stop somewhere?' she'd asked, but it was more a reminder. 'And then again tomorrow night, and when you get there, right?' Dora was in Dora mode, all worked up, hormonal, and wearing belly-banded bossy-pants.

But I knew it was just a cover. This was new territory for her, because she was always the one running ahead: first to college, then marriage, having a child, even her divorce. But now? I was the one leaving to embrace a life of my own. Finally. And strangely, saying goodbye when you're the one leaving is easier than being the one left behind. Who knew?

'I'll call, don't worry,' I said, trying to keep things light, but knowing I'd fail. We hugged, and just like before at the dress shop, a moment passed between us. An understanding among friends. Sisters, really. Nothing else needed to be said. She knows and I know, and it's enough. More than enough. Real friendships are like that. They breathe. The link exists even in the pauses, and the connection lasts a lifetime.

'And you give me your word you'll be back for the wedding?' Dora asked, dabbing at her eyes as we finally broke apart.

'God, of course.' I sniffed. 'And do you give me your word you'll talk to your mom about that hideous fish-gut dress?'

Dora laughed, full and loud. 'No promises.'

I reached over and included Dean in our squeeze. 'Take care of my bestie.' But I already knew he would. He always does. Dean's a stand-up guy.

Finn leaned over, pecked my cheek, and gave me specific instructions 'Make sure you find a two-bedroom place, because I, for sure, will be coming for visits and I don't do couch-camps, got it?'

'Got it,' I said, and smiled. Finn had teased me as a child, sat beside me at Ollie's funeral and loved me like a sister as an adult. It was only fitting that he'd helped me bid farewell to Pretty in Pink.

Along with another colleague who specialized in commercial law (not the Criminal), Finn oversaw the store's sale to the Lander Property Group. I thought the formality of signing the documents would take maybe thirty minutes. That's all it took the first time. The business simply changed hands when the lease had been signed over.

Not this time. Not at this level. Too many attorneys and too much money required pre-negotiations and renegotiations. After I reviewed the final paperwork several days prior to the day of sale, I thought, what could be left? A million more signatures, as it turned out. My hand actually cramped. When the last required 'sign here' tab was pulled, I froze with the pen mid-air.

Finn leaned in close, with brows furrowed but reassuring eyes. I peered at him anxiously, not saying a word. My mouth had gone dry. There wasn't enough air, and the room shrank. I mean, this was it. I'd scribble one more *Libby London,* and it was gone.

Pretty in Pink was gone.

Everything I've known and worked for. Everything I was. One autograph, and it was signed away. Would they love her as I had? Would they take care of her? Would they appreciate the building's strange quirks, know what to do when it stormed and the power tripped? Or that the back room would sometimes flood from the storm drain? Or how to fix the neon sign when the 'k' in Pink flickered?

How much remodel were they considering? They mentioned new carpet, a paint job and replacing the front door that sticks when the temperature shifts. Would she still be the same underneath the new shine?

Am I?

Finn offered a soft smile and gave a nod of encouragement. With it, I placed the pen to paper, and told myself I wasn't leaving her behind, I wasn't abandoning her, I was *setting her free*.

I was setting us *all* free.

'Hi, pretty lady.'

And I'm seriously tempted to set Bluebeard free at the next rest stop. Finn kidnapped him from Seth's office, and Jas swung by and picked him up. That was his errand, the sneak. Worst going-away gift ever. Which means it's the best, because it's typical Finn.

Thinking of gifts, before I left, I called in another yearly subscription for Mrs C. This one's for wine, and I sent another baby swing so they wouldn't fight over where it should be stored. I think Ollie would approve.

I also sent a small present to Dr P. as a thank you. It's just a new retro sweater to replace one of his worn-out ones, and it's not enough, but really, nothing could be. I fought him the entire way, but he never quit on me, not once. He patiently listened, prodded, explained, and in the end, he freed me. Not from the pain, but from the guilt of *feeling* it, and that's more than huge.

That's life-changing.

I think about the *who am I* essay. The one I finally finished. The one I included in Dr P's present. And I think I got it right.

Dear Dr Papadopoulos,

I've accepted your challenge to write an essay on who I think I am. In the simplest terms, and in the most convenient definitions, this is what I've found:

I am a Brain: someone who runs her own business and, without a college education, has attained success.

An Athlete: conditioned to grief, but able to fight through and survive.

A Basket Case: to quote Ferris Bueller, 'Sooner or later, everyone goes to the zoo.'

A Princess: a woman deserving to be treated like one.

And a Criminal: someone quite capable and worthy of stealing another's heart.

And although I believed labels to be limiting, I'm now grateful to learn they clinically exist and do in fact apply to

me. Instead of defining my identity, they defend it. Who am I? At thirty-three, I'm finally ready to find out. I hope this answers your question.

Sincerely yours,

Libby x

'You're smiling,' Jas says, with a sideways glance.

My brows furrow. 'What? No, I'm not.'

He rests his arm high on the oversized moving van's steering wheel and glances from the road to me. 'What are ya thinkin' about?'

'Um . . .' I'm half-tempted to ask if I'll meet his family when we get to LA, or if he'll ever share who his famous rock-star dad is. Maybe he can come to our new shop and do a signing? 'I was thinking of our new store. We still need a name.' I straighten in the seat, still looking at Jas: ripped jeans, crap concert shirt and dirty blonde hair. The setting sun casts an iridescent gleam to his faded-denim eyes.

He reaches out and turns down the radio. 'Well?'

'Well, Pretty in Pink is clearly Eighties, but *High Fidelity* was released in 2000, and they had a vintage store called Championship Vinyl—'

He pulls a face that means he doesn't care for it.

'Yeah, I'm not crazy about the name either, but . . .' My brows lift. 'Top Five? It's the main character's record label, and he makes musical lists for everything, which is where I got the top five game from.' I shrug, knowing we have a long trip to play around with names.

Jas smiles crooked. 'In the movie, does he get the girl? 'Cause in *Pretty in Pink*, he didn't.'

My face screws up. 'What does that have to do with anything?'

'Just answer the question: in *High Fidelity*, does he get the girl?'

'Yes . . .' My mouth contorts as I hold back my smile. 'But only after a while.'

'OK then,' he says softly, his smile pulling wide. 'I say high five to Top Five.' When I reach over to oblige the customary slap, he takes my hand instead and holds it.

After a beat, he glances sideways again. 'You do realize we're riding off into the sunset?'

With a full smile, I give his hand a little squeeze. I always said he was clever.

THE END

'Wait. You're still here? The story's over – close the book. I'm gonna be just fine. This end is a brand-new beginning, I promise . . .' #LibbyLondonLives

'Hi, pretty lady.' #BluebeardMightNot

A note from Victoria . . .

Dear lovely reader,

Thank you for reading Libby's story of forever friendship and her bumpy road through life and love. Knowing what she's been through, what she struggles with, I've become quite protective of her and hope you have too. To empathize with Libby's journey is to be *surprised* by its development, so I need to ask the most important of favours . . .

Please *do* leave your insightful thoughts and reviews (so appreciated!), but *avoid* any spoilers which would take away another reader's experience of discovery. Now that you understand and love Libby too, I *know* I can trust you with her secret. xo

As a thank-you for your candour, please accept this invitation to a private Facebook group – Libby London Lives (https://www.facebook.com/groups/LibbyLondonLives) where Libby's journey can be openly discussed, and I share behind-the-scenes bonus material on *Holding Out for a Hero*.

I also wanted to briefly touch on the very serious and real struggle with depression that affects so many. Libby describes depression as being under water, a slow drowning, and while under, asking for help is almost impossible. She explains, however, that there are also moments of coping. I want to urge anyone who personally battles depression to reach out in these moments of in-between, so the next time the water rises you've secured that needed lifeline. Your life, just like Libby's, is worth celebrating.

With much love and many, many thanks,

Victoria xo

Love like the Movies

**When it comes to finding her leading man,
will it be *Love, Actually* or a *Runaway Bride*?**

Kenzi Shaw has her life scripted-out down to the last line – the career she's building as an up-and-coming marketing exec, the gorgeous fiancé (Bradley) she'll marry in a fairytale wedding, the children they'll raise in her dream home. But when heart-breaking ex, Shane, comes back onto the scene, life starts going off the script . . .

Shane tries to win Kenzi over by re-enacting all the rom-com movies they used to watch together – *Sleepless in Seattle*, *Bridget Jones' Diary*, *Pretty Woman* and *Dirty Dancing* to name a few. He's just a guy, standing in front of a girl, asking her to trust him again. But has he really changed? Not only is her head in a spin over Shane, but now her job is on the line. And with her perfect sister-in-law showing up every tiny thing Kenzi does wrong, she feels like she's permanently in the corner.

Should she risk her sensible life for the chance of a Happy Ever After? One thing's for sure, when Shane meets Kenzi (again), she's suddenly not so sure just who her leading man is . . .